Smith's
MONTHLY

Every Month Original Novels, Stories, and Articles

USA Today Bestselling Writer
Dean Wesley Smith

TABLE OF CONTENTS

Smith's Monthly Issue #30

The Writings and Opinions of

Dean Wesley Smith

Introduction
TWO BOOKS IN THIS ISSUE

In this issue is a brand new Thunder Mountain novel called *The Idanha Hotel.* I'm very proud of this novel for numbers of reasons. It's a complex Thunder Mountain novel, to start with, and I like the two characters I added into the Thunder Mountain world.

But I really like the book because of how the novel came about.

In my challenge last July to write a short story per day, I wrote a story called "The Idanha Hotel." (It's in the book *Stories from July.*) It was one of three Thunder Mountain short stories in the book. I have already turned one of the short stories, "Grapevine Springs," into a novel by the same name.

Kris really liked the short story "The Idanha Hotel" and thought it would make a good novel.

I didn't see it, but her comment stuck with me and when I sat up a challenge to write a novel quickly, that story and her comment just came back to mind.

So I used that story to jump off into the novel *The Idanha Hotel.*

As often happens when taking a short story into a novel, the novel changed and ended up to be completely different. In fact, it changed on basically the first page. Only the idea is the same. The characters, the solution, everything is different.

And I honestly think both work fine, one as a short story, one as a novel.

So as I wrote the novel, I decided to try to do it fairly quickly, meaning in seven days, and blog about it.

So in a series of blog posts, I detailed out the writing of the book and my days around the writing.

That series of blog posts is now a book called *Writing a Novel in Seven Days.*

The entire nonfiction book is in this issue, along with the 43,000-word novel it produced.

Being able to do this sort of fun publishing experiment is part of the fun of having my own magazine.

Also, I would like to say something about the fact that this issue is number thirty.

Thanks for the Support

Dean Wesley Smith

That's right, in thirty issues I have had a full novel every issue, novel serials, lots of short stories, and a bunch of other things, including two full writing books.

I am very proud of this accomplishment and I have no plans on slowing down or stopping.

I hope you enjoy reading about how a book was written and then reading the novel that came from the process.

I sure had fun doing both books.

—Dean Wesley Smith
April 4th, 2016
Lincoln City, Oregon

Four Thunder Mountain Novels
Available at your favorite booksellers.

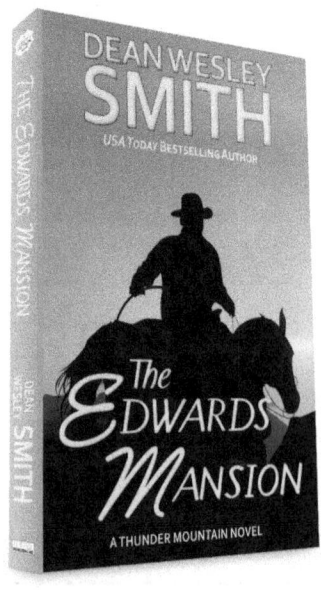

Coming Next Issue in *Smith's Monthly*
DEATH TAKES A PARTNER
A Mary Jo Assassin Novel

Smith's

NUMBER THIRTY-ONE
APRIL, 2016

MONTHLY

*Original Stories,
Novels, and Articles*

DEAN WESLEY SMITH

DEATH TAKES A PARTNER
A Mary Jo Assassin Novel

6

Poker Boy works as a superhero in the gambling side of the world. And he reports to Stan, the God of Poker.

Very bothered, Stan comes to Poker Boy with a problem. Very personal and unusual.

Another superhero working for Stan faces monster problems, and not the kind of problems that come from rescuing others.

This other superhero needs to be rescued from himself.

Sadly, we often all face our worst enemy every morning in the mirror, an enemy sometimes impossible to beat, even for a superhero.

LEAKING AWAY A LIFE
A Poker Boy Story

ONE

I WAS IN a really nice no-limit game at my home casino, the Spirit Winds Casino in the Oregon Coastal Mountain Range. The night was still young, five tourists were playing fast with a lot of extra money, and there was only one other pro on the table besides me and we were staying out of each other's way just fine.

I had found heaven in a poker game.

And heaven was paying off nicely so far. After two hours I was five hundred up and considering how much the tourists were drinking, I hoped that number would get much, much higher before I had to leave.

My girlfriend, Patty Ledgerwood, aka Front Desk Girl, and I were building a new home on property I owned up in the mountains near the casino. I had teleported, or jumped as I liked to call it, from Vegas up here to check on the house and then had decided to just stay and play since Patty didn't get off work until one in the morning from the MGM Grand Hotel front desk.

I had more money than I sometimes knew what to do with, since I won a lot and spent almost nothing. We had decided to build a custom home with every modern feature and everything we wanted. Patty had loved designing it.

I had saved the life of one of the best contractors in the world, a guy by the name of Bob Davis, by offering him a job building the house. So far the construction had taken just over two years, but it was almost done.

And spectacular didn't begin to describe the home. Way beyond my class as a human being, that's for sure, with all the glass, mahogany and stone, and the beautiful kitchen, to say nothing of the four modern bathrooms.

Patty absolutely loved the place, and she and Bob got along like old friends.

When Bob and his crew were done here, Patty and I were going to keep him on salary with a huge raise and have him build Patty and me a home in Las Vegas as well. Since we could teleport anywhere we wanted instantly, I wasn't sure we needed two homes. But Patty liked the idea and I sure had enough money to afford the two homes and a couple hundred more like it.

Playing poker had been really good to me, of that there was no doubt. And besides these two homes, I spent almost nothing except to buy some food at times and pay my taxes.

I was just about to raise one of the tourists at the table a smooth hundred bucks when my boss, Stan, the God of Poker, froze time around me and appeared next to the table.

Stan was dressed in his usual sweater vest, tan slacks, and polished shoes. His short brown hair and plain face make him the most unmemorable person you could ever meet. He liked it that way.

Me, on the other hand, I wanted to be remembered. I always wore what I called my uniform. A black leather coat and a black fedora-like hat. When I had first started playing, I sometimes also wore black mirror sunglasses but had given those up fairly quickly as having no value. The only person on the planet who had a better poker face than I did was Stan.

Sometimes I wanted people to think they had a read on me. I made a lot of money from those idiots.

I stood and moved over to Stan. He actually hadn't stopped time, just taken us in-between moments in time. But if felt like time had stopped since everyone was frozen and all sounds of the casino had vanished.

"We got a problem?" I asked.

He usually only came and got me like this when the team had a major problem to solve, like saving the entire planet or something.

"No team problem," Stan said. "But I need your help on something."

Now that stunned me more than I wanted to say. Stan never asked for my help personally. He was a god. I was a superhero who worked for him. What could I actually do to help him?

"The Kid needs some help," he said.

The Kid was the other poker superhero working for Stan. Usually I would have been enough, but since I spent so much time on larger problems with our team, Stan had gotten a second superhero.

I liked The Kid, as he called himself. He was about twenty-six now, had a great heart and a love of the game. He was good, very good.

"So what's he dealing with?" I asked, figuring The Kid had gotten himself into trying to solve a problem beyond his experience.

"He has a leak," Stan said.

Now at that I just blinked. I knew exactly what he meant by "a leak." Professional poker players who play other games such as sports books or blackjack or worse yet, slot machines, are said to have a "leak." They win their money at poker and leak all their winnings out through losses in areas they can't control like they control a poker game.

They do it for the thrill, some say. I could never see the point, actually.

It had never, ever occurred to me to play any of the other games in a casino mainly because I knew the odds. That is just recreation for people and fine for people to come and enjoy the time.

Poker, on the other hand, is a game of skill and is often called a sport by many.

As in any sport, there is some luck, but skill always wins out in poker in the long run.

In other games in casinos, the casinos always win out in the long run. Always. That's the design of the games and how they build the big buildings with all the flashing lights.

"How bad is it?" I asked Stan.

"Bad," Stan said. "He's living in his car, can't play any game but grinds in 3-6 limit because he has no bankroll to buy in to larger games."

"Skill doesn't help him much in those games," I said.

Then I just shook my head. I had enough money in a dozen banks to buy half a city. That's because I was good at poker, seldom spent anything I won, and had no leaks.

"He can't be helping what you need him for in that condition."

Stan nodded. "He's not at all, and he's hitting bottom now, which is why I came for you. I'm afraid we might lose him."

I nodded. I had heard it happened. Superheroes sometimes, in their early years, just couldn't handle the job and often lost all their powers or just killed themselves. I would hate to see that happen to anyone.

Can't Get Enough of Poker Boy?
These stories and more are available at your favorite booksellers.

But I wasn't sure exactly what to do. A professional poker player with a leak was called a problem gambler. And that took real professional help to fix.

"Got any ideas what we can do?" I asked Stan.

He just shook his head and even on his poker face I could read sadness. He liked The Kid, I could tell.

We stood there in the intense silence of the frozen casino for a moment, then I had a slight idea.

A problem gambler needed real help. Someone needed to get The Kid to understand that the other games in a casino were bad news while letting him keep his powers at the poker table.

This was not going to be easy in any stretch of the imagination.

More than likely impossible.

But they had to try.

TWO

WHO IS THE god in the area of counseling?" I asked Stan.

"Overall in charge is Victor, but out of the question to contact him," Stan said. "He's one of the long-term major gods who is seldom seen over the centuries.

"Lower gods?" I asked. "Someone who might help on something like this?"

Stan looked doubtful, so I changed up the question. "How about a young superhero in that area?" I asked. "A young woman, good-looking and smart, new as a superhero, and up for a massive challenge with The Kid."

Stan saw where I was headed and nodded. "Cash out and I'll go find out and be back."

I went back to my seat and Stan released the time bubble.

The sounds of the casino smashed into me like a hard wave. I would never get used to that. Ever.

I finished the hand, took another few hundred of the tourist's money, then pretended to glance at my phone. "Wife wants me home," I said.

A lie that everyone at the table understood just fine.

I racked up my chips as everyone said goodbye to a lot of their money, all in good spirits. A minute later I had the seven hundred I had won for the night in my pocket and was headed for the poker room door into the casino when Stan again froze time around me.

And again everyone stopped and all sound went away.

Stan had a young woman with him. She had on a light knit sweater and a blue blouse under it, with jeans and tennis shoes. She looked like she might be right out of college.

I was fairly certain I recognized her, but couldn't place from where.

Stan quickly introduced us. Her name was Gretchen and she had a wonderful smile and large, trusting brown eyes. I liked her at once, which I had a hunch was part of her powers.

From the way she was looking, she still wasn't used to teleporting anywhere.

Then Stan dropped a bombshell. "Gretchen is one of my daughters."

I opened my mouth and then closed it. Three years ago we had rescued Stan's two daughters from a time bubble that had trapped them since the days of Atlantis. That's where I recognized her from.

Clearly Gretchen had adapted well to this world and was moving on with her life.

"From Atlantis?" I asked.

"Born and raised there," she said, smiling. "Bet I don't look a day over twenty -three, huh?"

I laughed. "Not a day."

Stan hugged her.

Then he said, "I got permission from her boss to let her work at this problem for as long as it takes."

"Are you familiar with gambling addictions and problem gamblers?" I asked after she looked around, wide-eyed at the frozen people in the poker room and the casino beyond.

"Some," she said. "I have dealt with a few cases and of course, studied the problem through school, both here and back in college in Atlantis."

"Well, we have a real mess we hope you can help us with," I said. "Stan, you want to meet in my office?"

He nodded and they vanished.

And once again the sound of the casino smashed back in around me, making me shake my head. I loved casinos, everything about them. They gave me power and energy. But until all the sound in one was taken away, you never noticed how really loud they were.

I went out through the casino front door to a dead camera area in the parking lot and jumped from the mountains of Oregon to my invisible office that floated a thousand feet in the air over Las Vegas Boulevard.

Stan was sitting in the only real furniture in my office, a huge horseshoe-shaped diner booth with red-vinyl seats and a scarred-up wood tabletop.

Gretchen was standing, holding onto the wood railing that went all the way around the glass walls of my office, staring at the view of the city a thousand feet below.

It really was an amazing view.

"I got Madge bringing us some fries and three milkshakes," Stan said.

"Wonderful," I said.

Madge was a superhero in the food services area and owned the diner where my team used to meet. After we built the office that I patterned after her booth, only larger, I put a portal from here to the diner so my team members who didn't teleport could come through, and Madge could treat this booth like another booth in her restaurant.

"I had heard about this office," Gretchen said, turning to look at us, her brown eyes even rounder than normal. "Never thought I would actually get to see it."

"Well," I said, indicating she should come and sit in the large booth. "That shows how much we really need your help on something very important to us."

"Dad said it was important as well, so why me?" she asked, turning and moving toward the booth.

"Because you are young, smart, new as a superhero, and an attractive woman," I said, being honest with her.

"And our problem person is young," Stan said, "new as a superhero, and an attractive man. And besides, your boss and I both think you would be perfect to try to help us."

At that, Gretchen just blushed as Stan stood to let Gretchen into the booth.

"Thank you, Daddy."

Hearing Stan called "Daddy" sort of took my breath away, but I managed to keep my stupid mouth shut.

Stan and I couldn't help The Kid. We were basically like parents to him and a parent sure couldn't tell a kid to not smoke or drink and have it stick. The Kid had a problem that needed to be solved not just for a year or so, but for centuries.

I had no idea if any of this was going to work. But as far as I was concerned, Gretchen was the only hope The Kid had of surviving.

We now had to explain why.

THREE

AFTER ABOUT TEN minutes of Stan and me trying to give Gretchen a primer on professional poker players, I realized we were going to need help.

As Madge came in with the milk-shakes and fries, I said, "Be right back. Going to see if Patty can take a break."

Stan nodded and actually looked a little relieved. It had become clear that we were not communicating with Gretchen in a language she seemed to understand. She was clearly brilliant, but all the terms were just off to her.

I jumped to the front of the MGM Grand Hotel front desk and froze time for everyone but me and Patty. "Got a situation we need a little help on."

"Team situation?" she asked, looking worried.

"Well, not really, but a team is forming to help the problem," I said. I quickly summarized what we were dealing with and why I thought it would be a good idea for her to help Stan's daughter, Gretchen, get a sense of what The Kid was facing as a professional poker player with a leak.

When I told her The Kid had a leak, she just looked sad and shook her head.

"You don't give him much chance, do you?" I asked.

She shook her head no. "Glad to help do what we can do. I'll talk to my boss and be there in five minutes."

I nodded and jumped back to my office, releasing the time bubble formed around us.

For the next five minutes, Stan and I and Gretchen talked about other things, such as building this office and some of the other team members who had helped save the world a few times. When Laverne's name came up, I thought Gretchen was going to faint dead away.

I remembered that feeling myself early on. Just the mention of Lady Luck's name often had me shaking.

Patty arrived looking great. She had changed out of her uniform into a tan blouse, jeans, and tennis shoes and she had her wonderful brown hair combed out. She was the most beautiful woman in the world as far as I was concerned.

"Told my boss a snippet of the problem and she let me take the rest of the night off to help," Patty said.

I stood and Patty scooted into the booth beside Gretchen. Instantly the two of them hit it off. Patty was good. She was really that good and one of her superpowers was that others just liked her. She had promised she had never used that on me. She said she hadn't needed to, since I fell head-over-heels for her the first time I met her.

Literally.

I tripped over some ropes in front of the desk she was working at.

She thought it cute. I had thought it mortally embarrassing.

With Patty's help, we slowly got Gretchen to understand The Kid's job as a professional poker player and how poker was not gambling.

"The Kid is a mathematician, a professional liar, a professional actor, and has a memory for cards next to none," I said. "He has the ability to read a person and almost know what they are thinking at a poker table, and those are his normal poker skills, not his superhero skills."

Gretchen was nodding. "So poker is a sport. I think I am starting to understand that."

"It is," Stan said. "A skill that takes years to learn and many do not learn it as well as The Kid has."

"Is he any good as a superhero?" Gretchen asked.

"He was before he ran into this gambling problem," Stan said. "He saved a bunch of lives, helped countless people and seemed to be enjoying what he was doing until the money issues overwhelmed him from his leak. Now he pays little attention to the superhero side of things."

"That's because he can't even help himself," I said, "so he feels I'm sure that he can't help others."

Everyone around the booth nodded.

"So what exactly is his leak, as you call it?" Gretchen said. "His addiction?"

"Sports book," Stan said.

I sighed and Patty just shook her head.

"Why is that bad?" Gretchen asked. "To be honest, I don't even know what a sports book is."

"Someone can place a wager on the outcome of some sporting event in a sports book in a casino," Stan said. "From horse racing to soccer games, you name it, it is bet on."

"It is a common leak for professional poker players," I said. "Because when you are sitting in a poker room, there are dozens of televisions around the room and all of them are tuned to various sports events going on."

"Oh," Gretchen said. "So The Kid, as you call him, has a gambling addiction where he is losing all his money, and he has to sit in his job, his sport, while the very things he is betting on play out around him."

"No wonder he's homeless and living in his car," I said.

Stan nodded. "He has lost all focus."

If this wasn't hopeless, I didn't know what was. But I didn't say that.

FOUR

"THE STANDARD WAY of dealing with an addiction," Gretchen said, "is to remove the addicted person from the environment causing the addiction."

Stan nodded.

"How long can The Kid be away from poker?" Gretchen asked Stan. "Will he lose his powers if he is away too long?"

"He will," Stan said, nodding. "But a few years won't make any difference if he needs to be away. Usually takes a decade or more for a superhero's powers to fade beyond rescue."

Gretchen nodded. "Can we jump to where he is and not be seen?"

I was impressed. Gretchen clearly had some ideas and was taking control of all this. She seemed to have gone from a young, afraid kid to a professional woman in a matter of seconds.

Patty glanced at me and smiled.

"We can," Stan said. "Might not be pretty, though."

A moment later we were in a small casino on the east coast. The place smelled of mold and bad air-conditioning and had a few dozen people sitting at some older slots, all chain-smoking. The casino had a three-table poker nook off to one side with no one sitting at the tables.

The Kid, his clothes rumpled and his hair far longer than the last time I saw him, sat in the small sports book, watching an arena football game.

"Can he see us at all?" Gretchen asked her father. "Or sense us here?"

Stan shook his head. "I have us a half turn out of the normal world, like Poker Boy's office. The Kid can't see or hear us."

"Wow, nifty skill," I said to Stan. "That on the agenda to teach me at some point?"

"Got a hunch you already know how to do it," Stan said while staring at The Kid.

I liked the sound of that.

As Gretchen moved around to get in front of The Kid, I watched Stan.

I could tell that The Kid failing like this was really hurting Stan more than he wanted to ever let on.

"He's very handsome under all the dirty clothes and lack of a haircut," Gretchen said.

"He is," Patty said.

Stan and I both said nothing to that.

Gretchen kept staring at The Kid, at one point kneeling down in front of him to look up into his eyes.

"He is tortured," she said, her voice sad.

Gretchen then looked up at her father. "Do you know of a tropical island somewhere where The Kid and I can go and be isolated, yet live comfortably. The island can't have television or any kind of gambling and ideally no other people around."

Stan nodded. "I am sure I can find a place."

Gretchen nodded, standing and looking around the tired, small casino as she moved back over to stand beside her father.

She looked at me and Patty, then at her father. "He has no hope of even living if he stays in this environment."

All three of us nodded to that. We knew that, had seen the signs of problem gambling more times than any of us wanted to admit. The Kid had them all.

Gretchen looked at me. "Can we go back to your office and plan this all out?"

I nodded and a moment later I had us all back in our spots in the booth.

Gretchen first looked at her father. "We need the island and we need it yesterday. By my reading on The Kid, if he loses whatever he is betting on tonight, he might not live to the morning. And he will never call for help."

"Oh, shit," Stan said. "I'll be back as soon as I have something arranged."

Stan vanished and Gretchen, now showing more power and control than anyone her age should have the right to show, said to us. "Patty, can you find him new clothes. Beach clothes and everything he is going to need to survive for a while on a warm island. Including bathroom gear and such."

"I'll have two suitcases packed and here waiting in one hour," Patty said.

"Bring one set of clothes for The Kid to wear as well.

Patty nodded and vanished.

Gretchen turned to me. "I'm going to go talk to my boss, tell her what I am doing, get some check-in plans worked out, see if I am missing anything on this start."

I nodded. "Sounds sensible. What can I do?"

"I need you to go get him before he either wins or loses that bet, take him to a major hotel suite, toss away his clothes and everything he has on him, and make him shower a few times before Patty gets there with clothes."

I nodded. I didn't much like my part in this, but I knew I could control The Kid if I had to. And with luck, I wouldn't have to.

At that, Gretchen vanished, leaving me sitting alone in the booth.

I took a deep breath and then said to myself, "Let's get this done."

First I jumped to the MGM Grand and talked to Patty's boss and got a suite paid for.

Then, with a deep breath, I jumped back to The Kid in the sad excuse for a casino. He hadn't moved, and the game he must have had a bet on was still going on. His eyes were glassy.

I walked up to him and said, "Hi, Kid."

He jumped. If he had been at full focus and power, I never would have been able to surprise him.

"Things not going well I see," I said.

He shrugged. "I've been worse."

"Actually," I said, "I think you'll look back on this, if you live, and call this your worst moment."

At that I jumped the two of us to the MGM Grand suite I had rented.

"Wait! What are you doing?"

"Trying to save your life," I said.

I then jumped him, without his clothes, into the shower.

"Stay in there," I shouted to him, "until you don't smell like the inside of a sewer."

I teleported his clothes to the city landfill as I heard the water turn on.

He had not learned how to teleport, so he was trapped by me and he knew it.

In his condition, it was unlikely he even cared.

And that just made me sad. He had been a great poker player, could have been one of the best in the world.

But the control he felt in poker didn't give him the needed adrenaline feel he got from winning something out of his control.

And that need for the thrill and the real risk had driven him down to this place.

I was just glad Stan had been paying attention. It's always the worst when someone dies from an addiction and not even their closest friends knew of the problem or had time to even try to help.

That happens more than I wanted to think about.

FIVE

PATTY BROUGHT THE Kid some clothes and after he was dressed, I jumped the three of us back to my office.

Stan sat there in the booth with Gretchen.

The Kid just shook his head and stared at the floor.

Gretchen introduced herself, smiling and The Kid introduced himself as Steve.

"I thought you were called The Kid?" Gretchen asked.

The Kid nodded and sat down in a chair facing the booth. "Steve was my real name. I don't much feel like The Kid at the moment."

"So you know you have a leak," Stan said to The Kid.

The Kid took a deep breath and nodded. "Turned into a bad one I couldn't seem to get out of, even though I knew what was happening and knew better."

Stan nodded and since he was The Kid's boss, we let him go on.

"What do you suggest we do about this gambling addiction problem?" Stan asked.

The Kid jerked at that. It was one thing to call it a "leak" that poker players understood. Calling it by what it really was clearly hurt The Kid.

"I honestly don't know," he said, his eyes down. "I assume I am fired."

"No, not yet," Stan said. "We're going to give you a chance to control this, put it into your past."

The kid looked up at Stan, surprised.

I could see a slight glimmering of hope in his eyes.

It felt almost pathetic.

Stan went on. "Gretchen is my daughter and a trained expert in all sorts of psychological issues. She is a superhero in that area, actually."

The Kid looked at Gretchen again and nodded, clearly embarrassed.

"Here is what is going to happen," Stan said. "We are going to put you and Gretchen on a remote small island, without television, cards, or anyone else for that matter."

Again The Kid started.

Stan went on. "You are going to exercise, rest, and work with Gretchen on this issue until the two of you dig it out and she tells me you can come back to work without worry of a leak again. She will be reporting in to me every day."

The Kid looked at Gretchen, then at Stan. "You both would do that for me?"

"We will do that gladly," Stan said, his voice about as firm as I had ever heard it. "But let me be clear. This will not be easy, and you have the ability to ask to leave at any point. But if you leave one minute before Gretchen tells me you are ready, I will fire you and remove your powers and you will never see any of us again. Are we understood?"

The Kid swallowed and nodded. "I understand. And thank you."

"Thank me when my daughter says you are ready and not one moment before," Stan said.

Then Stan nodded to Gretchen and she and The Kid vanished, along with the suitcases that had been sitting near the booth.

Stan seemed to slump in the booth and at that moment Madge came in carrying fresh fries and new milkshakes.

"I figured after that," she said, her voice solemn, "you all could use a little something."

"Sorry you had to hear that, Madge," Stan said.

Madge put down the food and shrugged. "My first husband was a long time ago. He was sick like that kid is sick and he died from it. That's just the way it goes. I hope you all can save The Kid, but honestly, I think you have a better chance of saving the world from aliens again."

With that she turned and left.

"She's right," Stan said, shaking his head.

"But people are saved from this sickness," Patty said.

I didn't say anything, but I had never heard of a poker player recovering from this and still playing poker.

And I had a hunch Stan hadn't either. What made a great poker player was often what caused this kind of problem.

As Stan had told me early on, sometimes you save people and sometimes you just can't. I had lost my share of people I had tried to save over the years. It always had a sick, sinking feeling about it when it happened.

A helpless feeling.

I was feeling it right at that moment.

Two weeks later, as we were all eating lunch in my office, Gretchen appeared and sat down next to her father. She looked tan under her white blouse and jeans and seemed disgusted.

She turned to her father. "The Kid, as he is now calling himself again, declared himself cured and wanted to be dropped at a casino in New York."

"Shit," Stan said. "Just shit."

An instant later Stan vanished.

He and I had talked about what he would do if this happened. He would go to Laverne and they would strip The Kid of any memory of being a superhero and all his powers.

I felt sick to my stomach. Just sick.

Patty leaned her head on my shoulder, which made me feel a little better. But not much, since she was feeling as bad as I was.

Madge had appeared and slid a milkshake in front of Gretchen, then patted her on the shoulder and said she was sorry. "It had been worth the try."

Gretchen shrugged. "I did everything I could, but Steve has one fatal flaw that he never wanted to address."

"Can I ask what that was?" I didn't know if I was stepping over bounds or not.

Gretchen shrugged. "Doesn't matter now. His flaw was his ego. He actually believed he could beat any bet or game he set his mind to. He just flat thought he was the greatest and there wasn't a bet he couldn't take on and eventually win."

I felt that way at a poker table, but never one step beyond a poker table. No wonder The Kid had a leak.

Stan appeared again, sitting next to his daughter. "It's done. The Kid has no memory of any of us, or any superpowers. All stripped away."

Silence filled the office.

Outside, the Vegas sky was blue, the day a wonderful day.

Inside the office, the day was shitty. We had given our best to try and save someone and just failed.

It was that simple.

And that hard.

We got a report eight months later that he had been found dead in his car in Florida, penniless and homeless.

He had leaked away an entire life.

None of us were surprised at the news.

~

Dean Wesley Smith

USA Today Bestselling Writer

Cold Comfort

A science fiction story with a *Twilight Zone* twist.

About to die a horrible death alone in the asteroid belt, his crew members already dead, Ben discovers that he might yet have a future. And he might get to see his wife once again.

But the visit to his wife and the new future he faced, he never imagined possible.

A science fiction story with a Twilight Zone *twist.*

"Cold Comfort" was first published in the anthology The Future We Wish We Had, *edited by Martin H. Greenberg and Rebecca Lickiss and published by Daw Books.*

COLD COMFORT

ONE

"HOUSTON SPACE CENTER, do you copy?"

I sat in the big command chair, leaning back, listening to nothing as the time lag between the asteroid belt and Earth played out. The time lag wasn't as bad as it used to be during the early days of the Martian missions, thanks to some new developments in laser communications cutting through close-warp space, but it still took some time. About four seconds each direction from this far out. Nowhere near as slow as the speed of light, thank heavens.

Although, at this point, it didn't much matter.

I glanced around at the five empty chairs in the big control room of Asteroid Six, code-named Klondike after the gold rush back in Alaska. After all, that was what we had been sent out here to get. Minerals, from gold to anything else worth mining, to make part of this exploration profitable. I always knew that someone would get rich off of mining these asteroids, and we had proved that to be true, but now that someone wasn't going to be me.

The big room with its six chairs facing six large control panels smelled of burnt wires and felt far too hot. Usually it smelled of cooking mixed with a faint odor of Captain Carry's socks. Even with the faint burnt smell, the environmental instruments on the board in front of me were telling me everything was still all right in here, as much as it could be, considering.

The room felt even bigger than normal, with me being the only one left. I was used to this room having at least two or three people in it at all times. I kept thinking that one of them would come in and say something. After months together, I had gotten used to the constant interaction with the others. Now I missed it, wanted it back.

"Go ahead, Klondike. How are they doing out there, Ben?"

The voice was Devon Daniels, the day shift voice of Mission Control, and one of my best friends. He had stood up for me as my best man when Tammie and I got married twenty-two years ago. We had come up through the space program together in the late 1980s, flying missions to both the Moon and Mars. Together we had helped establish the first bases on both places. He'd been grounded because of a bad lung condition after his sixth Mars trip, and I had planned on joining him on the ground after this mission. Now it was lucky he wasn't on this mission. He'd be just as dead as the rest were, and as I was soon going to be.

I took a deep breath. "Can we go to visual? And get some recorders on this, some extra ones. I got a lot to download."

I sat back, waiting as they brought everything online at Mission Control, thinking over the last two hours. I had been asleep, off-shift, tucked in my bunk when the grinding crash had snapped me awake.

Our pilot, Toby Terhume from the European Union, had been scheduled to land us on an asteroid with a number for a name that was longer than a world-wide phone number. We were to do the same tests we had been doing on other rocks for the last two weeks. It was the tenth such landing. Standard procedure. From what I could tell, he misjudged the timing on the spin of the thing, and instead of landing the Klondike on the rough surface and clamping on, the ship hit, tipped over, and then bounced.

And we bounced hard.

We lost Kevin Chin because he was also off shift and it was his cabin that just happened to be the one that got hit by a large rock jutting out of the asteroid. The automatic controls sealed off the rest of the ship, but it was far too late for Chin. We all figured his body was going to have to ride in there until we got back.

I had liked Chin. He was young, this being his first real mission. He didn't deserve to die like that in his sleep.

It didn't take long for the rest of us to discover what else was wrong. The collision had damaged some relays to the engines and they had to be repaired. Outside.

Until they were, we were just more floating debris in this field of debris, with no way to move out of the way of drifting rocks.

The five of us remaining were all heavily experienced on outside work, so we drew straws and I got the short one, meaning I'd man the controls while the other four went out to get the work done as fast as possible.

We told Mission Control what we were planning, and they agreed that time was of the essence.

The team had been out there less than five minutes when an asteroid appeared on my screen out of nowhere, a rock the size of a small house, spinning slowly.

I tried to warn them. But with our speed and the rock's speed, it happened fast. Far too fast.

It scraped all four off the outside of the ship like so much crap off a shoe. If the engines and side thrusters had been working, the computer would have automatically moved the ship just a few feet out of the way as it had done hundreds of times in the past two weeks, and the asteroid would have drifted past, close, but harmless.

Instead, that nasty grinding sound of my friends dying would be something that would haunt my last hours.

Suddenly, I was alone, farther from Earth than any human had ever been, drifting in a field of debris without power, or any way to get power that I could figure out. That last rock had pretty much taken out a good part of the port side of the ship, leaving me with air and environmental systems in the control room and the galley only. I suppose I could say I was lucky to have survived as well.

I didn't feel lucky.

I had enough to eat, I had enough oxygen to breath for months. But in this mess of swirling rocks, I wouldn't last that long. I'd be lucky to get through the conversation with Earth.

Again, I didn't feel lucky.

"We're set up, Ben," Devon's voice came back on strong, then a picture flickered into place.

I clicked on my up-link, then without a comment ran the recorded events of what had happened.

I sat and stared at Devon's face for a few seconds as he just waited for the time lag, then he got my video up-link transmission and his face went white.

For a moment, I thought he was going to be sick as he watched. I knew exactly how he felt. There had been a camera on all four of them out there. What had happened was not something anyone would want to see in the news services.

Besides that, they had been my friends.

And Devon's friends.

After a short time, I punched a few buttons and sent the next compacted data streams toward earth. "Telemetry on the ship's status being fed now."

At least they would know exactly what happened and why.

I gave them everything, downloaded it all, to show everyone back at Houston Control just how screwed I was. That way they wouldn't go off half-cocked trying to come up with some harebrained scheme for me to fix this mess.

There was just nothing to fix.

I might die at any moment from some stray rock. Or some weakness in this cabin's walls caused by the two crashes. Or I might live until my food and air ran out. I was betting on a stray rock taking me out very shortly.

"Give us a few moments to look over all this," Devon said, his voice barely holding back the emotion I could see in his eyes.

Then he cut the link and I was alone again.

"Hope I'm still here," I said into the silence of the big control room.

TWO

AT LEAST SOME of the cameras and sensory equipment was still working on the outside of the ship. That way I could see what was going to kill me. I think someone once called that a cold comfort.

I tested the main computer and it seemed to be up and running as well, so I worked to plot my course as best I could in relationship to the big rocks we had charted. Banging off two different rocks like a bad game of billiards could send a ship going in some very strange directions, and the Klondike had been no exception.

After about ten minutes, I had figured out that at least I wasn't going to go head first into any of the bigger asteroids for at least a few months. In fact, the last impact had sent the Klondike upwards and slightly out of the main debris field. So it was going to have to be a small piece of rock that finally took me out. And there were far, far too many of them just in my neighborhood for even our best computers to try to track.

I might see it coming. Maybe two, three seconds ahead was all.

The connection to Houston remained blank, so I stood and moved around, stretching my muscles as best I could in the zero gravity. My magnetic boots held me to the deck, so as I had learned over the years, I used that force to work against as I exercised.

I wasn't sure why I was doing that. Just force of habit I suppose.

What else could I do while waiting to die?

Poor Tammie. I could see her long brown hair, her big eyes, her small, but wonderful smile. I had been gone almost more than I was home over the last two decades. From what I could tell, she had lived her life perfectly, keeping her own interests in teaching, sharing in mine when I was there, saying goodnight to me every night, no matter how deep into space I was, or what she was busy with.

A perfect astronaut's spouse.

She never really mentioned, and we never really talked about, the fact that I might not come home. It was just understood, part of my job.

I suppose I took her for granted far too much. The job of exploring space had always come first for me. The adventure was what I loved. I had to admit I had let the marriage just coast along. When I got home after this trip, I had planned on making up for that.

Too late.

I finally sat back down and stared out the forward viewport, watching the shadows of the dark rocks turning slowly, blocking out the background stars as they moved around and past me.

It was like a bunch of ghosts moving through a very dark night. Only these ghosts were real hard. And real deadly.

May 23rd, 2038. This would be a day that would be remembered as a footnote in the history of space exploration. All six of our names would be put up on the big golden obelisk sitting on the mall beside the United Nations building. It was a fantastic way to remember the dead. It was over thirty stories tall, yet no more than seventy feet across at the base. Standing back on the UN Plaza, staring up at it, the entire thing seemed to be reaching up for the stars. On its sides near the base, in large block letters, it held all the engraved names of those who had given their lives in the adventure of space.

Unless someone else died while I was sitting out here waiting, I would be the three hundredth and twenty-sixth name on the memorial.

I knew exactly where my name would be. I had stood under those names many, many times, remembering all my friends who were on that memorial.

I had no doubt Tammie would stand there as well. I always felt it was too bad we had never had children. Now I was glad. I would never want to put a son or daughter through what Tammie was going to have to go through.

It took Houston a good twenty minutes before they got back to me. Guess when there was no hope, time suddenly lost its importance.

"Ben," Devon said. My friend's face looked drawn and older, far older than he had looked just a half hour before. "I don't know what to say. I'm sure you know the situation."

"Yeah, I know it," I said. "Got any friendly neighborhood aliens with space ships to stop by and pick me up? I could use a lift."

In a few seconds time lag, Ben would smile at my corny joke, since we had both loved a story published when we were kids of an alien rescuing a stranded astronaut. Where was a good alien when you needed one?

"We're seeing what we can do," Devon said. "And don't give up hope just yet. We're still working on this."

"Sure," I said. "Has it got out to the press yet?"

"No," Devon said. "We've kept a lid on this for the moment, and no one's paying any attention. It was just a regular day for you guys out there."

"Yeah, real regular," I said. "After you guys finally figure out that my goose is cooked, I'd like to talk to Tammie."

"Copy that," Devon said, nodding, as if my request just didn't go in. "We'll be back in a half hour."

With that, the screen again went dead.

"He sure trusts that I'm still going to be here," I said out loud. My voice echoed in the empty control room.

THREE

I SAT BACK and stared out the front port at all the twisting shadows cutting out the stars and then blinking them back on as they moved past, a slow motion light show.

I glanced at the clock that told me what time it was in Phoenix where Tammie and I lived. Five in the morning. She would still be asleep. What horrible news to wake up to.

We had built a wonderful home on top of a rock ledge overlooking the green fairways of a private golf course that wound through the rocks and cactus in the valley below us. Actually, Tammie had built it while I was on one of my Mars runs. And I didn't play golf, but that scene was so beautiful, I had decided I liked the place.

I commuted to Houston, going home on most weekends whenever I could, and when I was on the ground.

Last time I was home, Tammie said she had learned how to play golf, had been taking lessons. She said she really loved it. I had planned on joining her on the links after this mission, although, to be honest, I just couldn't see myself being happy doing nothing but that. I wanted to move into test piloting some of the new sub-orbital planes being developed.

I stared out the viewport. I just hoped all the drifting shadows out there gave me enough time to at least say goodbye.

Suddenly, a very large shadow seemed to block out all of the stars in front of the viewport. I could see nothing in the pitch black, and the brains back at Mission Control had just never thought that headlights on these ships were worth the expense.

Looks like I wasn't going to get to say goodbye to anyone.

I braced myself and held my breath.

Nothing happened.

The shadow remained in front of me, covering every star as if someone had just put them all out, like candles on a cake.

Then there was a slight tingling in my arms and legs and the next moment I found myself standing, facing my best friend.

Devon was sitting in a huge, ornate throne that seemed to fill a very strange, very massive chamber covered in ornate drawings and strange lights of red and blue and purple. It felt like you could put a basketball court in the space and still leave room for a lot of spectators around the edges.

He was wearing the same clothes he had been wearing on the communications link.

And he was the only one in the chamber besides me.

I stood there, staring, trying to grasp what I was seeing, but my mind felt numb.

Nothing made sense, nothing felt right. Even the air smelled of great age, not burnt wires.

"Sorry it took so long, buddy," he said, smiling. "We had to make sure the situation really was as bad as it seemed."

"I'm dead. It doesn't get any worse."

My voice sounded just damn silly and was swallowed like so much silence in the massive chamber.

"To the rest of the world, yes," Devon said. "In about two minutes, the Klondike, will be completely destroyed by the impact from a four-meter wide asteroid."

"But...?"

I stared around, trying to figure out a pattern in the strange lights, then back at Devon, the pitiful question sort of hanging there.

"But what's all this?" Devon asked, indicating the vast chamber around us. "This is the Peace-Maker, on loan to us for missions like this from the aliens everyone in the tabloids refer to as the Grays."

I nodded. "Now I know I'm dead. Or being gassed by some environmental leak."

"Well, this is the future we always wanted," Devon said, laughing. "Remember how we used to dream as kids about going to the moon, going to Mars, exploring out here and beyond? And finding friendly aliens to help us along the way. Well, they found us."

"Roswell?" I asked, shaking my head at the stupidity of my question.

"Actually far before that. Roswell was just an accident with one of their small training ships as we were trying to learn how to fly them."

"Come on, Ben," I said to myself. "Wake up. You've got to wake up, check the gas levels. You're hallucinating."

"Yeah, I didn't believe it either," Devon said. "The truth is, you're very much alive; but to everyone else, you are officially dead and you can no longer show yourself to anyone. You'll either live and work at Area 51, or on the base on Titan."

"Titan? We have a base on Titan?"

"Actually, the Grays do, and they let us use parts of it. The Grays will be returning for their next visit to our system in twenty-three years, and we'd like to impress them with our progress. You're going to be a great help to us. We need some experienced test pilots for some new deep-space craft we're testing."

I wanted to slap myself, but didn't. This was one hell of a hallucination for a dying person.

Devon reached out and touched something in the blank air in front of him, and half the wall to my right vanished, showing me the blackness of space and the Klondike, floating there. I could see the extensive damage from the two impacts. For such a proud ship, it looked very, very sad and small and helpless.

"Coming in from the right," Devon said, his voice clearly upset by what was happening, and what had happened to the rest of the crew.

I stood there, transfixed, watching what I was sure was my own death as the shadow suddenly seemed to appear out of nowhere, then smashed into the Klondike, ripping it apart and sending pieces swirling off in many different directions.

"You are now officially dead," Devon said, his voice soft.

FOUR

AFTER A MOMENT Devon said softly, "I just wish I had gotten here in time to save the others from real death as well. But we thought the repair plan would work."

I stared at him, my mind still not grasping this, but I had one question that just pissed me off if anything about this dream was real.

"How come if we have this, we let people like me go out into space on ships like that? How come we let them die?"

"Because we have to," Devon said. "The Grays only loaned us this one ship. We have to fight our own way out into space, prove that we can survive out here, that we belong out here, and that takes growth and sacrifice. We have to pay the price."

"Five good men just paid a very heavy price," I said, disgusted.

"Yes, they did," Devon said. "And all six of you will have your names on the memorial in ten days, in a very large and impressive service. But what you learned out here won't go to waste. As you discovered, there are vast riches out here, more than enough to keep the space program going for another hundred years, until we finally figure out how to reach the stars and find even greater riches."

I glanced down, suddenly realizing my feet weren't sticking to the floor.

"Artificial gravity?"

Devon nodded. "We don't know how it works, but now that we know it exists and is possible, there are a thousand scientists around the planet working on it in different ways."

"You came from Earth?" I asked.

Again he nodded. "We keep the ship parked in a hidden orbit. I was beamed aboard and flew out here to get you."

"That's one fast trip. It took us two months."

"Some sort of dimensional jump engine," Devon said. "Way beyond us so far."

"Why you?" I asked.

"Mission control figured I would be the best one to do the rescue since you were going to have trouble believing all this was real."

"No kidding," I said. "I'm still not."

"I don't blame you," Devon said.

I walked over to the wall that seemed to be open to space and touched it. I could feel a warm, almost soft metal, even though it looked like I could stick my hand all the way out into the vacuum.

"We don't know what that material is either, or even how it works."

"But I bet we're working on it," I said.

"Oh, yeah, we are, but we haven't even figured out how to analyze it yet, let alone reproduce it."

"And you say this is the only ship they lent us?"

Devon nodded. "I wish we had more. That way we could shadow all the different missions going on in space, save more lives."

I remembered my five crew mates who had just died ugly deaths. "Yeah, too bad," the disgust and anger clear in my voice.

Then I remembered Tammie. She was still going to think I was dead.

"Can I take Tammie with me to wherever I'm going next?"

Devon shook his head. "I'm afraid not. Only very specific people can know this exists. No families allowed. Besides, you need her to keep up the legacy of what you did."

I nodded. Tammie had always been the perfect astronaut's wife. She would make sure my memory stayed alive and that my death wouldn't be in vain.

"Can I at least say goodbye?"

Devon looked like I had just trapped him bluffing in a poker game. I knew that look. There was something he didn't want to tell me.

"There is a way, isn't there?"

He nodded slowly. "We've worked out a way that you can say goodbye."

Devon's hands flew through the air in front of him, seemingly touching and brushing different things that I couldn't see.

Suddenly outside the ship, the stars seemed to blur for a moment, then at the next instant, we were in orbit around Earth. There had been no feeling of movement at all.

I had to be dead. What had just happened wasn't possible. That was all there was to it. I had just traveled the same distance it had taken me two months before to travel, and all in a fraction of a second without feeling a thing. Dead people traveled like that, not live ones.

"We're above the Phoenix area," Devon said. "The Grays have this nifty device they showed us how to use that transports you to a place, where you can hear and see and talk to people, but not actually be there. You'll stay here on the ship the entire time."

"Like a projected hologram?"

He nodded.

"And Tammie will be able to see me?"

"As sort of a ghost-like figure. If you tell her you're dead and just came to say goodbye, she'll believe you, especially when you vanish. But it's going to scare hell out of her."

"I don't think that learning that I'm dead is going to do her much good either," I said. "I assume others have done this before?"

Devon nodded. "This isn't easy on either you or her, but at least you have a chance to say goodbye, if that's what you *really* want."

"Why wouldn't it be what I want. She's the woman I love."

From his large throne-like chair in the middle of the massive space, Devon looked down at me with an expression I had seen many times before. He was worried.

"You're not going to want to do this," Devon said. "I think you should just let it

go and we'll beam into Area 51 and get you settled into your new life."

"Why?"

"Just let her deal with her grief on her own, in her own way. It's better that way. For both of you."

I stood there, staring at my friend, thinking about what seeing me as a ghost would do to Tammie. Devon was right. It would scare her, and the news of my death was going to hurt her more than enough.

If I loved her, I didn't need to hurt her any more.

But I did want to just see her one more time.

"I guess you're right. Can the hologram be made so that she wouldn't see me, or hear me? I'd still like to say goodbye in my own way."

Now Devon looked really pained. "It can be, yes, but as your friend, I'm suggesting you not do that."

"Why?"

Devon sighed. "Sometimes it's better to just let memories alone, leave Tammie in your mind as you know her."

"I'm still back in the Klondike, aren't I? Having a horrid nightmare?"

"No," Devon said. "You are very much alive, and we very much need your experienced help in our program. If the Klondike had come back on its own, we were going to try to recruit you into the program. We were lucky that circumstances at least saved you."

"I don't feel so lucky."

"Let's go to Area 51," Devon said. "You have great memories of Tammie, just leave them that way and start the next part of your life."

I laughed. "You know I'm not going to, unless you tell me what is so bad that I'm going to see when I visit her."

Devon looked like the day he had swallowed his first oyster. I remember laughing at him for an hour that night.

I wasn't laughing now at all.

FIVE

DEVON SIGHED AGAIN, then said, "Maybe you should just go take a look. You won't be seen or be heard, and you won't be able to touch anything. After that, we can talk more when we're off this ship."

It was as if the area around me on the ship suddenly changed into my home.

Devon had put me in the living room, and everything was as tidy as Tammie always kept it. Outside the open window, the sun was just starting to paint the tops of the rock bluffs pink. We had a fantastically beautiful home. It was too bad I was going to miss retiring here.

I looked around. Actually, this wasn't really my home. Granted, I had clothes here and all, but I had never really felt at home here. I had no sense of still being on the ship. This alien stuff was really amazing. Or my hallucination was very detailed and real feeling

"Devon?"

"Right with you, buddy," he said, his voice coming from my right and slightly above me. "Just let me know when you want to get out of there."

"Only a moment."

I headed for the bedroom where Tammie would be sleeping. I couldn't really feel my feet touch the carpet, but the memory of walking without gravity boots made me think I was feeling it.

Weird, really weird.

I tried to push open the half closed door, but my hand went right through it, so I closed my eyes and just stepped forward and into the bedroom.

I was sure I was dead, now I was acting like a ghost. What more evidence did I need?

The pink morning light was gently filling the room through the closed blinds. Our big master bed filled the far wall under bookshelves loaded with Tammie's favorite reading.

I moved about two steps toward the bed before I realized that Tammie wasn't alone. A man, a younger man, was curled up against her back, like he belonged there, like he had been there a very long time.

I had already been stunned over the last few hours with five of my shipmates dying, and then discovering that we really were friends with aliens and that I was going to live.

This sight just left me cold.

I wanted to care, but for some reason, I just couldn't.

I stared at my wife for a long minute, wondering why I didn't care.

I should care. I should be angry.

But the image of my five friends' deaths haunted me. Their deaths made me angry. Not this.

I couldn't care because it really didn't matter. My shipmates, my friends were dead. I was officially dead, but getting a second chance to move on to interesting challenges that I would love.

I couldn't bring her anyway.

I stood and just stared at her.

One thing was clear. She looked happy, contented in sleep.

I cared that she was happy. After being married to a man who had spent most of the last twenty years either in space or preparing for it, she deserved happiness in any way she could find it.

"How long have you known?" I asked my friend. I had a hunch that he was seeing what I was seeing with the fancy alien technology.

"A couple of years," Devon said. "I'm really sorry."

"It's not a surprise," I said. "As much as I was gone, how can I blame her?"

I moved over beside her, ignoring the guy behind her, and stared at her beautiful hair spread out over the pillow, at her cheek, at her slightly open mouth. I had been lucky to have the time I had with her, and all the support she had given me. I would miss that.

I would miss her.

But I couldn't be angry at her.

I bent over and brushed my lips against her cheek. I didn't feel anything, but her eyes fluttered a little and she sighed and then went back to sleep.

"Be happy," I said to my beautiful wife. "You deserve it."

Then I turned away.

"Get me out of here." I stepped toward the door. "From what I understand, I got some new ships to fly."

A moment later I was back in space.

Back where I belonged.

Two Classic Dean Wesley Smith Stories
Available at your favorite booksellers.

DEAN WESLEY SMITH

WRITING A NOVEL IN SEVEN DAYS A HANDS-ON EXAMPLE

A WMG WRITER'S GUIDE

First, USA Today *bestselling author Dean Wesley Smith shattered the myth that writing fast equals writing badly—or, conversely, writing well equals writing slowly—with his book* How to Write a Novel in Ten Days.

Now, Smith raises the stakes with this latest book, Writing a Novel in Seven Days.

Chapter by chapter, Smith chronicles his process toward writing a 43,000-word novel in just seven days. He writes about his progress, his feelings about the project, and how he approaches and overcomes obstacles.

This WMG Writer's Guide demonstrates that setting an aggressive writing goal, and accomplishing that goal, can prove successful with the right attitude and tools.

WRITING A NOVEL IN SEVEN DAYS
A WMG Writer's Guide

PROLOGUE

THIS IS GOING to be fun.

That's how I am going at this new project and these chapters leading up to the challenge and the challenge itself.

I will be doing a chapter a day on my blog through the writing of the entire novel, so anyone can follow along with the time involved, the thinking behind the idea to do a novel in seven days, the preparation, and everything else.

And I will detail out the writing sessions as well as I start up.

I am writing this prologue on a Tuesday night.

I plan on starting writing on the novel Saturday night. So a decent amount of time to try to clear some decks and get ready.

The Coming Challenge
What is this challenge?

Actually, a professional writer friend heard about some people trying this and after a long winter of not doing much writing, I thought it would get me back at the pace I want to write.

But when I first heard the idea, I have to admit I just shook my head.

And my first thought was, "I could do that when I was younger."

Not kidding, that's what I thought.

So as I describe this simple challenge, check in to see what your first thoughts are.

Ready?

The Challenge is Simple
Day One: 3,000 words.

And then each day after that add 1,000 words to the amount needed. Seven days, if my math is right, you will have a 42,000-word novel.

3,000... 4,000... 5,000... 6,000... 7,000... 8,000... 9,000 words.

7 Days.

Yup, my first thought was that I was too old to do that. I'm 65 and working more than a full-time job at starting stores and working at WMG Publishing. So I initially just shook my head and tried to forget the idea.

But this idea has a really bad mind-worm attached to it.

And I really needed something to fire me up and get me back on my normal pace of writing. Back to pulp speed on the fiction.

So for me, this challenge will work out just fine. Sort of attaching jumper cables to my sluggish writing battery.

And I am not too old to do this.

My Thinking

Here is my thinking on approaching this challenge out in public on my blog.

1. If I make it all the way through I will have finished another novel for *Smith's Monthly.*

That would be a win.

2. The challenge and the run-up to starting it will focus my mind away from starting the new store and back onto writing where it needs to be. And where I want it to be.

That would be a win.

3. Since I can average about 1,000 words per hour, this will take about 42 hours out of my week. And another ten hours doing the chapters.

That is possible, but it means I will have to be careful on doing other things. In other words, figuring out where I am losing time and bad habits and clearing that out. I will need to create new habits around writing as I go.

That would be a win.

4. Even if I only get 30,000 words done before getting sidetracked or ending face-down on my keyboard, I will have 30,000 words done and that is failing to success.

And that would be a win.

5. And if I can actually get through the seven days and blog about it here every night, just as I did with the book *How to*

Write a Novel in Ten Days, then I will have another short nonfiction book with these chapters that might help writers.

Or at least I hope to be entertaining in the silliness.

And that would be a win.

So all wins.

Where I See Problems

First off, I have online workshops to teach while the challenge is going on. The really rough night of those for March is Monday night. And in the challenge, Monday night is a 5,000-word night.

I can do that, but it will be a focus and not a lot of watching The Voice.

Also, I have recording to do of the last week of the Dialog workshop and the first few weeks of the Author Voice workshop. I'm going to do my best to get that done ahead of time. I'll talk about that in the next chapter.

And I need to start the April workshops which is some work and that will be one of the last two days. Nothing I can do about that in timing.

I also have standard WMG Publishing meetings and my normal chores at my WMG job, so that will take time during the day as well.

And on Monday we have the last move of fixtures into the new store.

I'm sure I'm missing some things planned for next week. I know I will be done with this on Friday, one way or another because I have a party to attend in Portland on Saturday.

In the first chapter tomorrow, I'll detail more about the challenge, and how to deal with so many of the problems. And how to even start to get ready for a challenge like this.

But I do have one thing set, something I don't normally do. I know the book I'm going to write. (No real plot, just going to be writing in to the dark.)

It's a Thunder Mountain book and will be called *The Idanha Hotel.*

I wrote a short story in the *Stories from July* challenge by that name and Kris liked it and said it would be a great novel.

That comment has stuck with me since July even though I thought it worked fine as a short story and didn't needed to be added onto. So I'm going to write that novel, even though Thunder Mountain novels are complex time travel novels and often take me more time.

Just another part of the challenge. (Can't make this too easy, right?)

This will be fun as I repeat over and over I am not too old to do this.

CHAPTER ONE
My Reasoning

The Challenge Again
Day One: 3,000 words.

And then each day after that add 1,000 words to the amount needed. Seven days, if my math is right, you will have a 42,000-word novel.

3,000... 4,000... 5,000... 6,000... 7,000... 8,000... 9,000 words.

7 Days.

Why Does This Structure Work?

Going to see if it will work, but pretty confident it will if life events leave me alone.

And if you are reading this book in a paper or electronic book instead of on my blog, you will know it did work. I won't be publishing this book about writing a novel in seven days if I don't actually write a novel in seven days.

So this will either be a fun blog project or a book project.

A two book project, actually.

Why the structure works is pretty simple on the surface.

And yet, under the simple idea, the reasons are complex. So let me see if I can point three of the main reasons out. And in later chapters I'll talk more about the deeper reasons this challenge can work.

Reason One:
A daily writing deadline and pressure

This is the surface reason and it is very valid for many, many writers, me included. I work well under deadlines, while complaining about them at the same time. Yeah, human nature there.

And knowing a deadline allows a writer to prepare and plan for the deadline.

When I was working in traditional publishing, either ghosting a book or writing a media book, I would get a contract to write a novel with a hard, set deadline.

Actually, usually not a contract. I could write a book faster than any traditional publisher could issue a contract or cut a check. I learned after getting burnt a few times that they had to issue the check at least before I would even start writing.

Turns out when they needed a project very quickly, they could cut a check in less than two weeks. Shock, I know.

I would look at the project after I was hired, then figure out approximately how long I wanted to take to write the book, which was always worked backward from the deadline that the publisher needed it done by.

So if was due on June 1st and I was hired on April 15th, I would set my start writing date around May 1st like a sane person.

I would look at the length, the type of book it was, and other factors such as if it was a project that I loved or just one I didn't mind and did for money.

Basically, I would figure out the time I needed comfortably to write the book and set that May 1st start date. More than enough room for emergencies built into that date.

Then I would be too busy with something else to start on the start date.

Or I forgot about it, more likely.

Or I just didn't feel like writing it yet, being a pouty writer.

So I would look at the project again and come up with a second start date, one that would make me work harder, but still had some give in it. For a June 1st deadline I would try for May 10th start writing date.

And I would ignore that deadline as well, letting the clock tick down until I had to start the novel or I wouldn't get the book done on time no matter what.

Then I started, often writing the book in seven or ten days, one draft, and turning it in on time.

I never missed book deadlines.

With this challenge, there is no missing the start date. This is a book backed against the deadline.

That's part of the fun of this challenge for me. The start date is real if you want to do this challenge.

Reason Two:
Focus

You can't write a novel in seven days if you are not focused on writing a story and producing words.

No excuses, nothing to take my attention away besides major life issues, which I hope won't happen. Focus is on the writing only.

And this, as with all my books, will be one time through only. (I don't rewrite, remember?)

So if I run into a research problem, I have to solve it quickly. And I often do have research problems and time-travel problems in the Thunder Mountain series, since they are historical time-travel novels.

So the focus will be on the writing, no excuses, no playing in research. Get the detail I need and get back to the writing.

For a few days running up to the start of the challenge and the seven days of the challenge, my focus in life will be on producing a new novel.

(I do not outline. I write into the dark and I will talk about that in a future chapter as well. And why this challenge is suited for that as well.)

Honestly, being completely focused on writing like that is a ton of fun. I seldom get that freedom unless I force it these days with all the other things and jobs I do. (Just as everyone does.)

Reason Three:
Ramp up of word count

By starting at 3,000 words on the first day, that allows a writer to start at an easily attainable word count.

If 3,000 words is too many for you in your normal writing, this structure is a bad idea.

But you could change the challenge to start at 1,000 and add 100 words per day. It will take a lot longer to write the novel, but it will get done in pretty fast order even so. Do the math.

For me, 3,000 words is very easy. But I am always slower at the start of a novel, so the start of the book at a slower pace makes up for the lower word count needed. I am figuring the first day to spend about four hours. Maybe more.

The second day deadline is 4,000 words. I should be into the book by then and up to speed, so I expect that to take around 4 hours as well.

The third day getting 5,000 words will be a push for me, since I have job and workshop related stuff that day. And movers coming to move stuff once again. And I don't want to get too tired too early in this, so this will be the first hard focus day for me.

If I make it through day three, I don't see day four at 6,000 words being much of a problem. I often write that much in one day and Tuesday, from the day job issues looks easier.

Days five, six, and seven are just going to be a push. Nothing else to say about them. Nice thing about getting that close is that it will be harder to miss.

And ends of novels always write faster for me than starts.

And on each day I will be doing chapters here about the day. So that's even more writing.

Got a hunch the chapters on the last three days will be shorter and all about the structure of the day getting through that kind of word count per day.

But by then I will be completely focused on the writing and the story. The ramp-up nature of this challenge works perfectly there.

As I said in the prologue, this is going to be fun.

CHAPTER TWO
Writing into the Dark

Two days until I start writing. As I write this chapter, it is Thursday.

I plan on starting the novel on Saturday.

So am I planning the book at all?

Nope.

This book I have a rough idea, more than normal, because of the short story in Stories from July that I am jumping off from. But past that, I honestly am giving the book no thought at all. I'm just going to trust the process and sit down on Saturday and start writing.

Why Not Outline?

For me, if I pretend to make up some story idea in an outline, I am bored instantly. I love to read good stories and the fun for me in writing is very much like a reader. I love to explore the story and find out where it is going and how it will end.

If I know the ending, what is the point of writing it?

I write for entertainment and fun. I know that just flat shocks a bunch of younger must-write-to-market writers. Shrug. If they survive the next twenty years they can talk to me about how successful they have been writing to market.

Another reason I don't outline is that outlining is from my front brain, my critical brain, and even though I can explain certain things about writing in workshops, my critical brain sucks at making up stories. Always has and is no better now than it was thirty years ago.

But my creative brain is damn good at it.

I write from the creative brain, and I just let that part of my mind play when writing. I basically sit down and say, "Let's go play."

And that's what I am going to do starting Saturday and going for seven days.

I'm going to be playing.

But What About All the Writing Problems?

I expect the following:
—To be worried I won't finish.
—And stressed.
—And afraid of getting stuck.
—And bogged down.
—And stuck in the plot.
—And all the other stuff that happens through the process of writing a novel.

Let me say that again. I expect all that.

Most writers have trained themselves to fear those things, to worry about all of them, to stress over every silly detail that might or does go wrong.

Me, I find those elements part of the process, part of the excitement of the process.

I can't imagine writing an entire novel without most of those things happening at one point or another.

I think of it this way.

Writing Books by Dean Wesley Smith
Available at your favorite booksellers.

When I climb into a seat on a roller coaster, I expect to have ups and downs and twists and turns and thrills. If the coaster just went out and came around smoothly and stopped, I would ask for my money back.

When I write, when I sit down and strap in on Saturday, I expect a roller coaster ride through the novel. And I find that exciting.

I will detail it all, I promise.

And I want to be clear one more time here. This will be my only draft of this novel. It will go directly from these seven days to my first reader (Kris) and then to WMG Publishing to be in *Smith's Monthly* and as a book later. I will not write sloppy.

So What Am I Doing to Get Ready?

On the writing side, nothing at all.

On the work side, I'm trying to get a few publishing and workshop things done early.

That's all.

And strangely enough, Kris is helping because we're watching a couple shows per night of television we are backed up on so that next week we can get backed up a little again.

So in other words, I'm not doing much at all except writing these chapters each night.

What Can Someone Else Do to Get Ready?

I have a hunch a number of people are going to try this challenge, or some extended version of it that fits each person's world and life and family.

So what do I suggest for someone not as experienced as I am at this sort of thing?

Here are a few suggestions.

1. Make sure your friends and family know what you are going to try.

Critical. Get them on board and make sure your schedule is as clear as it can be.

2. Do some writing ahead of time on other projects.

Say if you are going to start on 1,000 words per day and add 100 words, then have a few days of 1,000 plus writing ahead of time on another project like a short story.

In other words, get used to sitting down and writing if you haven't already been.

3. Figure out an area or a series or something you are going to write in.

Don't outline, but instead know the series. For example, I know the series I am going to write into is Thunder Mountain and I know the book title, *The Idanha Hotel,* and I even have a cover for it.

All of that has got my creative voice wanting to play, to get going. I won't spend any time when I am ready to sit down trying to figure out what to write. Off I will go.

4. Clear out negative thinking.

Expect problems, treasure them as part of the process. Figure out what day the one-third point will hit, or what general time.

We all know that 1/3 part of a novel is a bog-down point, so expect it. For a 40,000 word novel, the one-third point will be about 14,000 words in. That means on Tuesday I need to be prepared to go through that.

So clear out negative thinking and prepare where you can for the issues.

5. Repeat over and over and over that the challenge will be fun. And exciting.

And that you will have fun.

And now that I look back at my suggestions, I realize I have done them all as well. All but the word count on another project. Oh, wait… I have written over 3,000 words on this new book project already.

Guess I am doing all five as well.

So one more time: This will be fun.

CHAPTER THREE
Ready to Go

I'm going to start writing tomorrow. Honestly, I could have started today without much problem. But I scheduled starting tomorrow because of the work-day outside of writing that I have on day three, where I will need to do 5,000 words.

Day three is full of a lot of work at WMG and on workshops. I don't mind the work at all, just making sure I don't stress the writing too much. So starting tomorrow makes that workable.

Attitude is Everything

For many people, putting deadline pressure on their writing actually feels like it will hurt you. If you are one of those writers, just sit and watch and see if you can pick up some things that don't have to do with deadlines.

But many who claim to have problems with pushing their writing with deadlines often don't. They just have attitude problems. (Oh, oh… I said that.)

Here's why you might have an attitude problem.

Critical voice in all of us is designed to keep us safe, to stop us from doing things damaging, and to make us pay attention to coming problems.

Lawyers spend three years learning the law and making their critical voice extreme. That way, when a client comes in for them to do something, the lawyer can see all the problems that might arise.

In the arts, past a minor part, critical voice is deadly. Its normal job is to stop you, and yet in any art, including writing, the only way you can learn and grow and become a real artist is to practice and make mistakes and fail at times.

Artists, writers, learn from their failures.

But for some reason in writing, the myths have taught us that every word we type out is in stone, is sacred, must be perfect or at least rewritten a thousand times until it is perfect.

Myths are deadly to a writing career. I've done books of those called Killing Sacred Cows.

Instead of taking chances, the fear of failing overwhelms and the critical voice looks for a way to stop such thinking. So that comes out as not liking deadlines on the writing.

It's one thing to have worked under deadlines for years and then decide to not do them anymore, but another problem when a deadline has not even been tried and is still feared.

That's critical voice problems.

So the only real way to fight the critical voice in writing is to change your attitude.

Words and writing are fun.

Telling stories is play.

You have to take all the power away from the critical voice. When you believe something isn't important, the critical voice goes off and is silent, letting your creative voice play.

That's right, you have to make sure your attitude is that the deadline isn't really important.

That's why when I am asked about what I do for a living, I say, "I sit alone in a room and make shit up." That job description can't be important, can it?

Change your attitude about writing, about your writing having to be perfect, and you will tame your critical voice.

I am Going to Have Fun

That's my attitude going into this challenge of writing a novel in a week.

I had a poor writing winter due to numbers of factors, so I am really, really, really looking forward to getting up to pulp speed for a week and then going from there into the spring and summer.

I have a lot of outside things cleared for the week.

I also know I want to write a Thunder Mountain novel about a baker in the Idanha Hotel in Boise, Idaho in 1902. It will be a time-travel historical western with a romance core, since my second character is a historical researcher from 2018.

I know all this because those are the characters in the short story I am jumping off from. But honestly, when I start they might not even be the same two characters. Don't know and won't know until I start writing tomorrow.

This will be the 9th novel in this series, so I know the world pretty well, but in the past these novels have taken three or more weeks for me to write. So bringing that timeline down to a week will be a challenge.

My attitude is solid.

I've cleared what work I can clear out of the way and I am excited to get writing and have fun.

Think of me strapped into the roller coaster car, right in the front, waiting for the car to jerk into motion and start up the slope.

So next chapter the book starts.

I'll detail each day and talk about how the writing went and my mental state and so on.

I hope to make these chapters interesting as I go. We shall see.

Onward to Day One.

And a lot of fun.

CHAPTER FOUR
Day One

Here we go.

I'm going to detail out my day so that anyone reading this can extrapolate their own days and see how it works. The idea is to help others with similar challenges like this.

And help writers with just controlling their own fears and time.

Side Note First on Structure

On the comments on the last chapter, which will not be available in the book, I was asked how I was going to handle doing extra words on some nights, or was I going to just stop when I reached the world count?

I decided that this challenge is total word count. Finish a novel in seven days. I need at least 3,000 words done today, the first day, then adding 4,000 on the second, I need to be past 7,000 words total by the end of the second day.

And so on.

That way I don't have to be worried about stopping exactly on some word count.

How I will deal with the ending if I am short or long on the novel I'll talk about at the end. Not a clue at the moment, actually.

The Day

Started off by climbing out of bed at 1:30 p.m. and by the time I got around to leaving the house to run errands, it was 3 p.m.

I got to WMG offices a little after 3 p.m. and worked with Josh there for about forty-five minutes on the new store, then I went to my office and worked for an hour finishing loading up a *Smith's Monthly* to the printer.

Then I worked until around 7 p.m. on workshop stuff.

So for those of you counting, about four hours at WMG and workshop work today away from my writing office.

I took a short nap when I got home, then cooked dinner and watched some news and such.

Got in here to my office around 8:30 p.m. to do e-mail and other things.

Finally, around 9:30 p.m. I moved over to my writing computer and started the novel *The Idanha Hotel: A Thunder Mountain Novel.*

First Session:

I managed about 600 words before I had to go lay down because of a headache. (Eyestrain I think.)

Second Session:

Around 11 p.m. I was back in for another session. This time I managed 800

words starting up this novel before going to take a break and watch some television around midnight.

So two sessions so far for about 1,400 words starting up at just under two hours writing.

Third Session:

Around 1:30 a.m. I came back in to my writing computer and did another session of 1,100 words as the novel started to pick up speed.

Fourth Session:

A five-minute break at 2:15 a.m. and another 1,200 words before 3:15 a.m.

So stopping at 3,700 words for the day.

A perfect start.

Novel, as I said to Kris, wants to be written at the moment. No idea where it is going and the short story didn't help much at all since I changed out the two characters from the short story and changed the focus right from word one.

Not sure why I did that. I never ask or question myself, I just type.

So, 700 words ahead going into tomorrow's word count now. I need to be past 7,000 words on the book by the end of tomorrow night.

The Day in Summary

Four hours of work at WMG.

Just under 4 hours of writing time to get 3,700 words on the novel.

This chapter and the daily blog will take about an hour combined.

So 9 hours starting at 1:30 p.m. and going until 4 a.m. of structure time between my day job and writing fun.

The rest of the time was napping, cooking dinner, watching television, and other regular life things.

Onward to Day Two.
The novel is started.
That's all that mattered today.

CHAPTER FIVE
Day Two

Once again made my goal for the night. Counting 3,000 words for Day One and 4,000 words for Day Two, I needed to be at 7,000 words or beyond.

Hit that.

The Day

Managed to crawl out of bed around 12:30 p.m. and get to the grocery store and then to WMG Publishing before 2 p.m. to open up the doors for the normal writers' lunch. We met in the new loft area and it worked fine and then moved down to the new "living room" area and that worked fine as well.

So new layout of WMG seems to be working. Yeah!

Finished lunch a little after 4 p.m. and I worked in my office until 5:30 p.m. on workshop stuff until Kris showed up.

We headed to the mall to get dinner. I had to check in with a store there going out of business that we are buying fixtures from tomorrow afternoon. All set to go with the movers. Nifty display tables and waterfall displays. The new store is almost set for all the stuff to come out of the back room and be priced.

Got home around 7 p.m. and did e-mail, then went to work on workshop stuff, finishing around 9 p.m.

So for those of you counting, basically from 2 p.m. until 9 p.m. I was doing work stuff and other things like a writers' meeting and workshop assignments. Six hours taking out dinner.

Then finally for the night got back to the novel *The Idanha Hotel: A Thunder Mountain Novel.*

First Session:

I had 3,700 words starting into the evening on the book. So 700 words in the bank as Kris called it.

I managed 900 new words by 9:45 before going to take a nap.

Second Session:

Woke up around 10:30 p.m. and got back to writing in about fifteen minutes, getting another 1,000 words by 11:45 before going to watch some television.

Third Session:

Made it back to my writing computer around 1 a.m. and managed 1,100 words by 2 a.m.

Fourth Session:

After a five-minute break, went back to writing and got 1,200 words by just a little after 3 a.m.

Fifth session:

Went back after a five-minute break and did another 900 words until about 4 a.m.

So stopping at 5,100 words for the day. 8,800 words on the novel total.

So for tomorrow, which I expect to be a long day, I have 1,800 words in the bank. That feels good and this novel is just flying along.

How Am I Feeling at This Point?

In one word: Great!

I love it when the characters of a novel just sort of tell me what to write. Nifty feeling I wish I could bottle.

Although as I told Kris, I haven't had a chance to use any of the short story since I changed the characters almost immediately and everything went sideways on the plot yesterday in the second chapter.

So that short story is going to turn out to be just a jumping off point for the start idea and nothing more. The way it works sometimes.

But overall, so far, I'm feeling great about the challenge and the book.

But I have a ways to go yet.

The Writing of *The Idanha Hotel: A Thunder Mountain Novel*

Day 1: 3,700 words. Total words so far… 3,700 words.

Day 2: 5,100 words. Total words so far… 8,800 words.

The Day in Summary

Seven hours of work at other things counting the hour to write this chapter and other blog post, and 4.75 hours of writing to get 5,100 words.

Just about 12 hours for the day total. The rest of the time was napping, watching television, eating dinner and other regular life things.

Onward to Day Three.

CHAPTER SIX
Day Three

Once again I made my goal for the night. Barely.

Counting 3,000 words for Day One and 4,000 words for Day Two, and 5,000 words for Day Three, I needed to be at 12,000 words or beyond.

Hit that once again.

I had 1,800 words in the bank before day three, but didn't want to use the words today and it worked out that I didn't.

The Day

I figured today was going to be a tough day and I was right.

I rolled out at noon and managed to get to WMG offices by 1 p.m. I worked there for a short time getting things ready and then the movers arrived at 2 p.m. and we headed to pick up some store fixtures from another store going out of business.

That's it now. We almost have all fixtures for the new store. Now the real fun starts with all the inventory.

Got the move all done in about two hours.

Then I worked for another hour to get it all straightened around. Then I worked on workshop stuff in my office until 7 p.m.

Home for a quick nap, then cooked dinner.

Got in here to do workshop assignments by 9 p.m., about what I was hoping.

Got all that done by 11 p.m.

So about 9 hours of work today taking out the fifteen minute nap and short dinner. Add in how long it will take me to write these two blogs and it will be ten hours for the day total.

As expected.

Then finally for the night I got back to the novel *The Idanha Hotel: A Thunder Mountain Novel.*

First Session:

11 p.m. I started and managed 1,250 words before taking a break to go watch part of The Voice. About one hour of writing.

Second Session:

Back in here around 1:15 a.m. and managed 1,300 words by 2 a.m. Just smoking along. One of my faster sessions ever I think.

Third Session:

Then the novel took a right turn once again (now a very, very long ways from the original short story) and it took me until 3 a.m. to get the next 1,200 words.

Fourth Session:

Short break, then 1,150 words by 3:45 a.m.

Fifth Session:

One more short break and then I did another 700 words before calling it a night at 4:15 a.m.

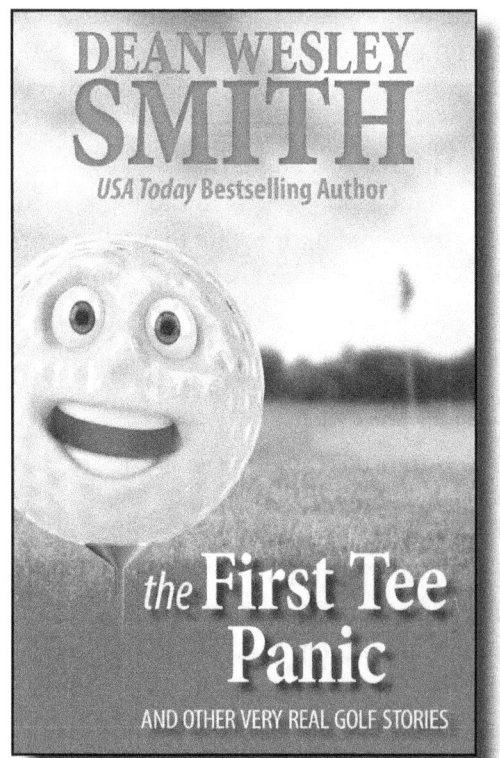

So I got 5,600 words, bringing the novel to 14,400 words total so far.

I needed to be at 12,000 words after today, so I have 2,400 words in the bank at the moment on the challenge.

But now the numbers of words needed each day start to climb into a much larger number.

How Am I Feeling at This Point?

Exhausted.

Today was a very crazy and busy day and from noon onward until now at right before 5 in the morning I have stayed focused. Had to or the day would have gotten away from me.

And that's one of the advantages of this kind of challenge. It keeps me focused on the writing. Without the challenge, I doubt I would have gotten many words done today at all.

So a win all the way.

The Writing of *The Idanha Hotel: A Thunder Mountain Novel*

Day 1: 3,700 words. Total words so far… 3,700 words.

Day 2: 5,100 words. Total words so far… 8,800 words.

Day 3: 5,600 words. Total words so far… 14,400 words.

The Day in Summary

Ten hours of work at other things counting the hour to write this chapter and the other normal blog post and 4.5 hours of writing to get 5,600 words.

Just about 14.5 hours for the day total. The rest of the time was napping, watching television, eating dinner and other regular life things.

Onward to Day Four.

CHAPTER SEVEN
Day Four

Once again made my goal for the night. Barely.

And wow was this a ton harder than yesterday. The next three days ought to be very interesting, to say the least.

Counting 3,000 words for Day One and 4,000 words for Day Two, 5,000 words for Day Three, and 6,000 words for Day Four, I needed to be at 18,000 words or beyond.

Hit that once again.

I had 2,400 words in the bank before today, but I didn't want to use the words today and it worked out that I didn't.

The Day

For some reason today, I wasn't too worried about the challenge. So I slept in until almost 2 p.m. and then by the time I got done with business errands and other stuff and back at my desk at WMG Publishing, it was almost 5:30 p.m.

I worked there until 7 p.m., then home to take a short nap and cook dinner.

By the time I got into this office to do workshop assignments it was almost 9 p.m.

Again I was not thinking about 6,000 words. Not worried in the slightest and I should have been.

Got all the assignments done by 10 p.m. So about 7 hours of work counting the hour it will take me to write these two blogs.

Then finally for the night I got to the novel *The Idanha Hotel: A Thunder Mountain Novel.*

First Session:

10 p.m. I started and managed 1,250 words before taking a break. About fifty minutes of writing. Novel is really powering.

Second Session:

Back in here around 11 p.m. and managed 1,300 words by midnight before heading to watch *The Voice*. Still powering along fine.

Third Session:

Got back in here right around 1 a.m. and now I was realizing I had sort of screwed up and not paid attention to how many words I needed today.

Oh, oh.

So from 1 a.m. to just before 2 a.m. I did 1,300 words.

But I took about three short breaks in that hour because I hit the one-third point and the entire thing just turned to suck in my mind. (Kris smiled at me wandering around muttering.)

Fourth Session:

Short break, then 1,150 words by 2:45 a.m.

Fifth Session:

Another short break to stretch and then did another 1,050 words by 3:45 a.m.

Made it.

So I got 6,050 words, bringing the novel to 20,450 words total so far.

I needed to be at 18,000 words after today, so I have 2,450 words in the bank at the moment on the challenge.

Tomorrow I will not underestimate how long it will take me to do 7,000 words. Almost messed up today by getting confident.

How Am I Feeling at This Point?

Focused now.

The next three days are the real test on this. I felt comfortable with 3,000 to 6,000 word days. Heck, I did that much every

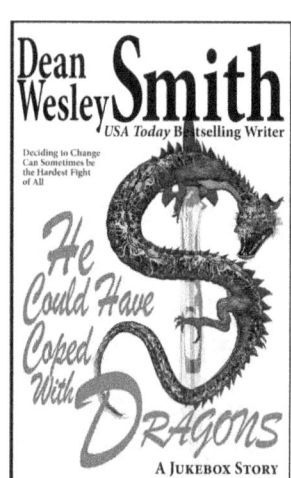

Some Classic Jukebox Stories
Available at your favorite booksellers.

day in July writing short stories every day. But the next three days will require me to really stay on top of the time and the day.

Going to be interesting.

The Writing of *The Idanha Hotel: A Thunder Mountain Novel*

(The number in parenthesis is what is needed for the challenge.)

Day 1: 3,700 words. (3,000) Total words so far… 3,700 words.

Day 2: 5,100 words. (4,000) Total words so far… 8,800 words.

Day 3: 5,600 words. (5,000) Total words so far… 14,400 words.

Day 4: 6,050 words. (6,000) Total words so far… 20,450 words.

The Day in Summary

Seven hours of work at other things counting the hour to write this chapter and other blog post and 4.5 hours of writing to get 6,050 words.

Just about 11.5 hours for the day total. The rest of the time was napping, watching television, eating dinner, sleeping in, and other regular life things.

Onward to Day Five.

CHAPTER EIGHT
Day Five

Once again made my goal for the night.

I paid a ton more attention to the challenge today than I did yesterday. Seven thousand words is a serious number of words in one day and I gave the writing of that much the respect it needed to make it happen.

Counting 3,000 words for Day One, 4,000 words for Day Two, 5,000 words for Day Three, 6,000 words for Day Four, and 7,000 words for Day Five, I needed to be at 25,000 words or beyond.

Hit that once again.

I had 2,400 words in the bank before today, but didn't want to use the words today and it worked out that I didn't once again. In fact, I added to the bank a little.

The Day

Wednesday for me is a typical meeting day and today was no exception. Managed to crawl out at 12:30 p.m. and make it to the first meeting for WMG Publishing business by 2 p.m.

Then another meeting at 4 p.m., and then more meetings on the new store until after 5 p.m.

So by the time I got done talking with people, it was almost 6 p.m.

I did some e-mail and other things quickly, then by 6:30 I got started writing on the novel *The Idanha Hotel: A Thunder Mountain Novel.*

First Session:

6:30 p.m. I started and managed 700 words in forty-five minutes before taking a break for a nap and then dinner.

Second Session:

Back in here around 8:30 p.m. and managed 1,300 words by 9:15 p.m. Still powering along fine.

Third Session:

Stopped for a time to read Kris's new blog (which is wonderful), then got back in here around 10 p.m. I did 1,400 words in just under an hour.

At this point the novel has really gone sideways completely. I am in a nasty time-loop type of problem in this book (Thunder Mountains are time travel if you didn't know) which causes me all sorts of issues on the date of each chapter. I'm going to have to cycle back and make sure I have it all straight.

Fourth Session:

From 11 p.m. until 11:45 I got 700 words done before going to watch some television.

Fifth Session:

Got back in here at 1:15 a.m. and managed 1,400 words by just a few minutes after 2 a.m.

Sixth Session:

From 2:15 a.m. until 3:15 a.m. I managed 1,200 words.

Seventh Session:

From 3:30 a.m. until 4 a.m. I managed 800 words.

Made it.

Seven sessions.

I got 7,500 words for the day, bringing the novel to 27,950 words total so far.

I needed to be at 25,000 words after today, so I have 2,950 words in the bank at the moment on the challenge.

Tomorrow I'm going to have to be even more careful on time needed.

How Am I Feeling at This Point?

Very, very focused now.

And enjoying and challenged by this novel. Not sure what possessed me to write a Thunder Mountain novel for this challenge. It is a most difficult series to write by a long ways.

The next two days are the real test on this.

And no end in sight on the novel, so I'm at that scary point as well.

Going to be interesting.

The Writing of *The Idanha Hotel: A Thunder Mountain Novel*

(The number in parenthesis is what is needed for the challenge.)

Day 1: 3,700 words. (3,000) Total words so far... 3,700 words.

Day 2: 5,100 words. (4,000) Total words so far... 8,800 words.

Day 3: 5,600 words. (5,000) Total words so far... 14,400 words.

Day 4: 6,050 words. (6,000) Total words so far... 20,450 words.

Day 5: 7,500 words. (7,000) Total words so far... 27,950 words.

The Day in Summary

Five and a half hours of work at other things counting the hour to write this chapter and other blog post and e-mail and 5.5 hours or so of writing to get 7,500 words.

Just about 11 hours for the day total. The rest of the time was napping, watching television, reading Kris's blog, eating dinner, sleeping, and other regular life things.

Onward to Day Six.

CHAPTER NINE
Day Six

Once again made my goal for the day.

The goal today at 8,000 words was pretty much my focus for the day. I still worked up at WMG Publishing, but for not as long. (Yes, I still worked my day job, got my e-mail, and did these blogs while writing 8,000 words.)

Counting 3,000 words for Day One, 4,000 words for Day Two, 5,000 words for Day Three, 6,000 words for Day Four, 7,000 words for Day Five, and 8,000 words for Day Six, I needed to be at 33,000 words or beyond.

Hit that once again.

I had 2,950 words in the bank before today, but didn't want to use the words today and it worked out that I didn't once again. In fact, I added to the bank a little. Very little. 50 words actually, to make the bank after tonight 3,000 words even.

The Day

Thursday for me is a normal day. I work on workshop stuff up at WMG offices and I did that as well today. I got there, after a half hour of errands, around 2:30. I worked there upstairs in the new store and on workshop stuff in my office until just before 5 p.m. when I headed home. So basically three hours of work there.

I did some e-mail and other things quickly, then by 5:15 I got started writing on the novel *The Idanha Hotel: A Thunder Mountain Novel.*

First Session:
5:15 p.m. I started and managed 800 words in forty-five minutes before taking a very short break.

Second Session:
Back in here around 6 p.m. and managed 700 words in another 45 minutes.

The weather at this point gave me a break. I find it difficult to write when the sun is streaming over the ocean and into my office. Even with the blinds pulled, it is hard to see my computers. But just after I started writing the fog rolled in and I wrote without a problem with the window open and the ocean crashing on the beach.

Third Session:
Another short break and managed 750 more words in another 45 minutes before stopping to take a nap and have dinner at 7:30 p.m.

2,250 words in three sessions. Book was going slow at this point because it was very complicated and I had to stop and do a quick check on facts a number of times. (Remember, I only write one draft. I never leave anything and I don't write sloppy.)

Still, 2,250 words before dinner made me happy.

Fourth Session:
Got back in here around 9 p.m. after some dinner and television. By 10:15, a long session for me, I had 1,300 words more.

Fifth Session:
A little longer break and from 10:45 until midnight I got in 1,500 words.

Book is back picking up speed at this point.

Sixth Session:
Watched some television, so didn't get back into this office until 1:30 a.m. From then until 2:15 a.m. I wrote 1,000 words even.

Yes, even on an eight-thousand-word day I worked, watched television twice, and took a nap. That ought to mess with some myths.

Seventh Session:
From 2:20 a.m. until 3 a.m. I managed 950 words.

Eighth Session:

From 3 a.m. until 3:45 a.m. I managed 1,050 words.

Made it.

Eight sessions.

I got 8,050 words for the day, bringing the novel to 36,000 words total so far.

I needed to be at 33,000 words after today on the challenge, so I have 3,000 words in the bank at the moment on the challenge.

Going to finish this tomorrow if life leaves me alone.

How Am I Feeling at This Point?

Very, very, very focused now.

I am on jury duty starting tomorrow, but I luckily don't have to go in until next week.

That would have been fun.

So I am able to stay really focused going forward now, which at these longer word counts, I have to be.

It feels like this book will finish up tomorrow. Not at all sure how long it will end up, so I am planning on spending a real focused day on it. Nine sessions, which means I have to watch my time carefully.

Just wish I could see the ending. I think I have caught a glimpse, but it's some words away. Or at least it feels that way.

Going to be interesting. If I have to write ten or eleven thousand words tomorrow to finish this thing, I will.

And then on Sunday night, I'll do a final chapter on this nonfiction book that these blogs will turn into. I'll talk about the challenge from a day's hindsight and if such a challenge like this is worthwhile.

And so on.

But I need to finish the novel first tomorrow.

The Writing of *The Idanha Hotel: A Thunder Mountain Novel*

(The number in parenthesis is what is needed for the challenge.)

Day 1: 3,700 words. (3,000) Total words so far... 3,700 words.

Day 2: 5,100 words. (4,000) Total words so far... 8,800 words.

Day 3: 5,600 words. (5,000) Total words so far... 14,400 words.

Day 4: 6,050 words. (6,000) Total words so far... 20,450 words.

Day 5: 7,500 words. (7,000) Total words so far... 27,950 words.

Day 6: 8,050 words. (8,000) Total words so far... 36,000 words.

The Day in Summary

Four hours of work at other things counting the hour to write this chapter and other blog post and e-mail and 7 hours or so of writing to get 8,050 words.

Just about 11 hours for the day total. The rest of the time was napping, watching television, eating lunch and dinner, sleeping, and other regular life things.

Onward to Day Seven, the last day.

CHAPTER TEN
Day Seven

Got the book done!!!!

The goal today was at 9,000 words and needed to be the focus of my day because I had no idea how many words I would actually need to end this book.

I had 3,000 words in the bank, so that helped the worry some.

Counting 3,000 words for Day One, 4,000 words for Day Two, 5,000 words for Day Three, 6,000 words for Day Four, 7,000 words for Day Five, 8,000 words for Day Six, and 9,000 words for Day Seven, I needed to be at 42,000 words or beyond to hit the challenge.

Hit that solidly.

The novel came in at 43,050 words.

Seven Day Novel Challenge Hit!!!

The Day

Friday for me is normally an errand day. I got out of the house around 1:30 p.m. and ran errands all over the place including banks, mail, the WMG store, grocery store, you name it, I was there this afternoon.

Got to the office around 4:30 p.m. and worked there until just before 5:30 p.m. before heading home.

I did some e-mail and other things quickly, then by 6:00 p.m. I got started writing on the novel *The Idanha Hotel: A Thunder Mountain Novel.*

First Session:

6:00 p.m. I started and managed 700 words in thirty minutes before taking a very short break.

Second Session:

Back in here around 6:45 p.m. and managed 900 words in another 45 minutes.

Sun was out and I had to block the sun coming into my office, but managed to make it work. Book was going slow at this point because I honestly had no idea exactly where it was going or how it would end.

I also decided to take a nap at his point and then dinner and some television.

So starting tonight ended up slower than last night.

Third Session:

Got back in here around 9:30 p.m. and managed 1,100 more words by 10:15 p.m.

Fourth Session:

10:30 p.m. until 11:30 p.m. I got 1,200 words more.

Stopped to watch some television at that point. Yes, even on a 9,000-word last day I stopped and watched some television.

Fifth Session:

1 a.m. until 2 a.m. I got in 1,100 words.

Book is back picking up speed at this point and I know the ending now.

Thankfully.

Sixth Session:

2:05 a.m. until 2:50 a.m. I got 1,000 words done.

Seventh Session:

From 3 a.m. until 3:45 a.m. I managed 600 words.

Eighth Session:

From 3:45 a.m. until 4:30 a.m. I managed 400 words.

I also spent a lot of time going back over all 50 some chapters to make sure the dates at the top were right. Time travel and loops are really confusing, but for the most part, I got them all right.

So I printed up the book and put it on Kris's spot to read.

Eight sessions.

I got 7,000 words for the day, bringing the novel to 43,050 words total. That's about normal length for all my Thunder Mountain books.

How Am I Feeling About Finishing?

Relieved and surprised it wasn't harder than it was.

I had to stay focused for the week, but I didn't not do something.

I still worked and watched television and got regular night's sleep. I didn't really do anything differently except that I was focused on the writing instead of playing around with other things.

In the last chapter of this nonfiction book about the writing, I'll list all the details about the challenge. How many hours it took me to write, how much I worked at my job outside of the writing, and so on over the seven days.

But I want to say this right now. I had thought that writing a novel in a week was a young person's thing. I learned I am wrong on that.

I'm 65 years old and this didn't even begin to stress me.

So now that excuse for me is shot out the window.

Back next chapter with a wrap-up of all this

Where Can You Read This Novel?

About the first week or so of May, this novel will be out in *Smith's Monthly #30*. (That's right, I will have done 30 issues of a monthly magazine with a full novel in every issue, plus short stories.)

Then in about four months after that, the book will come out in paper and electronic editions stand-alone.

Subscribe to *Smith's Monthly* to not miss it, or support my blog on Patreon to get a copy.

Either way you can read this novel in just over a month from when I wrote it.

The Writing of *The Idanha Hotel: A Thunder Mountain Novel*
Day 1: 3,700 words. Total words so far… 3,700 words.

With more than a hundred published novels and more than seventeen million copies of his books in print, *USA Today* bestselling author Dean Wesley Smith knows how to outline. And he knows how to write a novel without an outline.

In this WMG Writer's Guide, Dean takes you step-by-step through the process of writing without an outline and explains why not having an outline boosts your creative voice and keeps you more interested in your writing.

Want to enjoy your writing more and entertain yourself? Then toss away your outline and Write into the Dark.

Day 2: 5,100 words. Total words so far… 8,800 words.

Day 3: 5,600 words. Total words so far… 14,400 words.

Day 4: 6,050 words. Total words so far… 20,450 words.

Day 5: 7,500 words. Total words so far… 27,950 words.

Day 6: 8,050 words. Total words so far… 36,050 words.

Day 7: 7,000 words. Total words … 43,050 words.

The Day in Summary

Five and a half hours of work at other things counting the hour to write this chapter and other blog post and e-mail and 6.5 hours or so of writing to get 7,000 words.

Just about 12 hours for the day total. The rest of the time was napping, watching television, eating lunch and dinner, sleeping, and other regular life things.

All done.
A novel in seven days.
It was great fun.

EPILOGUE
Killing Some Myths

Myth #1 Shattered

First off, as I said way back in the opening of all this, my first thought when I heard this challenge idea was that I was too old.

For the record, I am 65 years old.

I had always read about how some of the great writers would do books about this length in a week or less. I always admired those writers and when I was going full force in traditional, I wrote at good speed for that system for decades.

But it was never close to what my heroes from the past had done. And as I got older and the new world of indie publishing started to open back up the freedom again, I just assumed I was too old.

So I went to something easy such as filling 70,000 words of my own magazine every month with only my stories. And including a novel every month and short stories and serial novels and features.

Easy. Uh, no.

I am the only writer in history to do that. Or even attempt it.

This novel I just finished will be in *Smith's Monthly #30*. And I'm still going.

But I still thought I was too old for this sort of writing focus and speed.

Turns out that was a myth I was believing.

Total myth.

In fact, this wasn't even stressful in the slightest. My hands didn't get sore, my back is fine, everything I had been worried about turned out to be my critical voice trying to stop me on this.

Creative voice won that battle. Critical voice is whimpering in the corner.

Myth #2 Shattered

I hear all the time the excuse of "I have a day job so I can't write like you do."

Often I am insulted at that, but I never say anything. No point because it is a myth the writer is holding to help them not write. Their critical voice is winning completely and that's not my fault they let it.

Not my fault another writer is not writing.

So what did I prove in this week of writing a novel about the day job excuse/myth?

Well, I worked 44 hours at my day job. In case some of you don't know, I am the CFO of WMG Publishing and I am helping to start the store wing of the company. I do all the banking, errands, mail, and everything else, including teaching workshops and answering all the questions about them.

I usually work around 50 hours a week when counting the workshops I teach, but this week I got it down to only 44 hours.

So if you are using a day job excuse to stop your writing, you might want to start clearing out that myth. It's just your critical voice finding an acceptable way to keep you from writing.

And if that makes you angry at me, might want to check in with yourself. You have some defense issues on this topic because trust me, your day job is no harder or easier than mine.

And at least you get paid for yours.

Myth #3 Shattered

I wrote a 43,000-word novel in 36.5 total hours of writing. (I'm counting another 7,000 words of writing nonfiction in the day-job hours.)

Just under 1,200 words of fiction per total hour of writing. However, I did all that in many, many sessions.

In fact, I did 42 sessions to write the 43,000 words. Or about 1,025 words per session.

Each writing session averaged .86th of an hour. Or about 50 minutes per session.

In other words, I typed at the blazing speed of 20.5 words per minute.

And that was all finished draft.

I printed up the book when I finished it and gave it to Kris to read. It will be turned into WMG Publishing for copyediting in a day or so. I'm not going to touch it again except to fix a typo or so that Kris finds.

So all the writers who think they have to write sloppy during NanoWriMo to get the words done in a month, I just showed you how to not do that.

Write, finish, and release.

And right there a bunch of writers are screaming about how they could never do that, or that I am a mutant so I can do this, or that my books have to be bad because I wrote it fast without rewriting it, and so on and so on.

Actually, doing this has to plow into a bunch of the myths I wrote about in *Killing the Sacred Cows of Publishing.*

So if you are finding yourself making excuses about how you could never do this, stop and check in and ask where the belief system you are spouting is coming from.

Just trying to be helpful.

So, in Summary

A 65-year-old-man just took time around his 44 hours of day job to write 42 sessions and start and finish a novel in one week.

Without an outline, writing into the dark completely, only one draft.

And the old guy has the audacity to say it was fun.

And horrors of horrors, he actually took a nap every day and watched a lot of television as well. And he cooked dinner four of the seven days.

Horrors!

How can all that be possible?

Because it was fun, that's how I did it. The writing was fun.

Will I do it again? Oh, sure.

But next time I won't make any big deal out of it. Next time it will just be part of my regular writing, now that I have proven to myself that I can do it and cleared out the age myth.

And I hope I have proven that anyone can do it easily. You just have to get rid of all the excuses, the myths, the belief that you can't do it.

You can do it.

With a day job.

When you are on Medicare and Social Security, and still watch television every day and get a nap and a full-night's sleep.

I just showed you it is completely possible.

And it really is a lot of fun.

Now Available
from all your favorite booksellers
in trade paper and electronic editions.

DEAN WESLEY SMITH

LAYING THE MUSIC TO REST

A former college professor turned bartender, Doc finds himself trying to save his friends from a ghost under a lake in the wilderness of Idaho.

From diving into a ghost town buried under a lake to trying to stay alive on the sinking deck of the Titanic, *this time-travel science fiction novel reads like a roller-coaster ride with all the twists and turns.*

First published in paperback in 1989 from Warner Questar Books, Dean Wesley Smith's first published novel gives a lot of hints of his future series and his bestselling career spanning over a hundred and fifty novels.

Published here in its original form, without any changes, just as Dean wrote it almost thirty years ago.

LAYING THE MUSIC TO REST

Part 3

CHAPTER FOUR

Roosevelt Lake
June 27, 1990

"YOU GETTING CLOSE there?" I asked Fred as Susan handed me my mask and then moved back across the coarse sand of the lakeshore to talk to Constance.

"Almost," he said. "Two more minutes."

I watched him as he checked over his regulator and double tanks as I had done a few minutes before. In the old days, he had been faster at that predive routine than I was. But this time I was so nervous I did my equipment checks twice and still beat him.

I glanced down at the dive watch strapped to my wet suit. It was a little past noon. The day was one of those perfectly clear summer days in the mountains. The kind that a person always hopes to stumble across on a vacation, but never does. The lake had a deep blue tint and the fresh smell of pine was in the air. Even the sandbar beside the lake was warm. A complete switch from the way it had looked the night before.

We'd planned to start the dive around midday when the lake would be completely in the sun. Better light that way. More chance of seeing whatever it was we were supposed to find. So far, we were right on time.

But it had been one very busy morning getting ready. After breakfast, bundled against the early morning chill, we had set up a temporary camp on the sandbar twenty feet from the water's edge. Then we hauled all the diving gear down on horseback. It had taken most of two hours to get set up for just one dive for the day. We talked about the possibility of making a second dive the next day, depending on what we found. I really didn't want to think about that. This one dive was going to be more than enough as far as I was concerned.

After we had set up the gear, Fred had taken me on an exploratory walk around the lake. He used an old photo of the main street of Roosevelt to make wild stabs at where things used to be.

The photo looked like any other old photograph of a mining boomtown. The street was mud. Wood and log buildings lined both sides and all the buildings in the center of the town were two stories tall and had covered sidewalks.

As we walked along the single-file trail around the lake, I somehow kept expecting to see the ghost come shimmering up out of the water. Three or four times I caught flashes of something down through the water and swore to myself it was the ghost. Yet each time I knew it wasn't. After a while I started reminding myself that I didn't believe in ghosts, habitual or otherwise.

In the daylight, the lake looked a little bigger than it had through the trees the evening before. It filled the valley from side to side, a distance of maybe a football field. From end to end it ran a quarter of a mile, with a little twist to the left at the bottom end where the stream cut up and over the mudslide. The slide was now covered with an eighty-year-old forest and looked exactly like the rest of the mountain. Of course, Fred had to remind me, just as we were walking along the slide, about the cases of dynamite buried somewhere among the trees.

Where the water had gone over the slide, there was a huge logjam filling the upper section of the lake. The trail ended right at the logjam and started again thirty yards away on the lodge side. Fred didn't even hesitate. He walked right out on the logs, skipping and jumping from one log to the next like a six-year-old child walking along a curb.

To me, the logs didn't look that solid, even though they weren't sinking at all under Fred's weight. He stopped in the middle, straddled an open water space with each foot braced on separate logs, and motioned for me to come on.

"Take a look at this," he said, pointing down.

I eased out on the nearest log. One end was jammed into the mud of the bank. The other end disappeared twenty feet later under two other logs. It felt solid enough, so I worked my way out toward

Fred. The farther from the bank I got, the more apparent it was that I was walking on the remains of broken up buildings. The logs looked like giant Tinkertoys jammed in solid from the floor of the lake all the way to the surface. Down through the clear water I could see layer after layer twisted and turned in all directions like a mixed-up spider web.

I made it to Fred's location, braced myself so that I wouldn't slip, and took a look at what he was pointing at. It was an open space of water running like a well down through the logs. I figured I could see maybe fifty feet down with no sign of the bottom. A large trout swam lazily out of the shadows of one of the logs and then disappeared under another.

"I tried to fish here once. Hooked a good sized rainbow and immediately lost it in the logs. Dumb thing to try." Fred laughed as he looked around. "A bunch of timber, huh?"

"That it is," I said, trying to get an idea of just how many buildings it would take to jam this much of the lake solid. "Think there's much left standing down there?"

"From the looks of this," Fred said. "I doubt if there's anything at all. You ought to see the pictures in the historical society, taken on the day the town was flooding. Some guy took it from a place back up there." Fred pointed up the mountain wall across the lake.

"It shows most of the large buildings on Main Street twisting and floating as the lake got deeper and deeper. Hell, an entire area of town was just tents laid out in rows like in the army. Can't imagine spending a winter up here in one of those. But I guess some people did."

"Does seem amazing, doesn't it?" I looked down through the layers of toy-like logs, each one obviously hand cut. The entire valley was amazing. No wonder Fred and Constance had picked it. There was more than enough history and exploring to do here to keep their guests interested in the Old West for weeks on end.

***

"I think I got it," Fred said, patting the top of his tank. He looked over at me. "Ready?"

"No. But when did that ever matter?" The butterflies were having a great time in my stomach. I wanted to go back up on that huge front deck around the lodge and sit, stare off at the mountains, and drink.

"Tanks," Constance said as she held up Fred's dual scuba tanks so that he could slip his arm through the straps. Susan moved over and did the same for me. Carla used to help me, but that seemed a lifetime ago. I couldn't imagine what she would have said about this nutty dive.

I let the tank's vaguely familiar weight nestle down against the middle of my back as I tightened the straps into place. I had to admit, it almost felt good. For the first time in years, I could feel my heart pounding from something other than bending over to move a beer keg.

Susan turned my air valve on with a quick turn and then slid the mouthpiece over my shoulder. "You're on and ready," she said. I glanced back at her. She obviously knew diving.

"Good luck," she said. She wasn't smiling.

I slipped the regulator into my mouth and bit lightly. It tasted of disinfectant and rubber. An odd, but familiar, taste from my past. I took a couple of deep breaths to check if everything was working properly, then glanced at my gauges. Right on the money. I picked up my fins from the log beside my dive pack. "All set?"

Fred finished a check of his regulator and nodded.

I worked my way across the sand and rocks to the edge of the water, sat down, and let my legs float. Damn, it was cold. I could feel it right through the wet suit. I wasn't looking forward to letting the water trickle inside my suit, let alone trying to let my body warmth heat that water up.

"Cold, huh?" Fred said as he sat down on the sand beside me and kicked his legs a few times.

"Maybe we should wait until we get some dry suits," I said. I could feel the water starting to trickle down into my boot lining. It felt as if the lake were trying to pull my body heat right through the rubber.

"I think we'll be all right," Fred said. "For as short a time as we're going to be down there."

"Just make sure that if you start getting too cold, you signal for the surface. I'll do the same." I looked Fred square in the eye to make sure he was hearing me.

"Deal, partner," he said, then smiled. I knew he was serious. He was as concerned about us making this dive as I was. He wasn't going to be doing anything beyond his limit. That made me feel a little better. Not much, but a little.

I turned to Constance, Susan, and Steven. "Any sign of the ghost yet? We could use a tour guide."

All three of them glanced out over the lake and then shook their heads.

"Just kidding," I said and turned back, facing out over the water. "Not funny, I guess," I whispered to Fred.

He chuckled, then pulled his mask on.

I pulled the hood of my wet suit up into place, inflated my flotation vest

enough to keep me afloat, grabbed my mask in one hand, and pushed off into the water with the other.

The biting sting of the water cut at my skin as the first trickles seeped into my wet suit. For some reason, the first drops that got inside the wet suit always went right down my spine and into my crotch, a feeling I had never gotten used to and always dreaded. This time was no different. Maybe even worse. I suddenly felt short of air and forced myself to take longer, deeper, and much slower breaths.

I floated, half-turned up on my back, working on making sure my mask would stay clear, then getting it snug down onto my face. We stopped thirty feet out from the shore, facing the three watchers.

"Follow our bubbles along the trail there with the extra tank," Fred yelled, pointing to the path along the right side of the lake. "We have any troubles, we'll surface and go that way."

Constance nodded. We'd worked the plan out beforehand, but for some reason, Fred seemed to want to make sure it was clear.

"Be careful down there," Constance shouted.

"We will," Fred yelled. He turned to face me. "Ready?"

I took a couple deep breaths through my regulator, then pulled it aside. "Ready. But let's watch this cold."

He adjusted his mask and gave me a thumbs-up sign.

I quickly dashed water one last time through my facemask. *Here we go, ready or not. Crazy. Nothing but crazy.*

I let some air slowly out of my vest and sank below the surface. I had forgotten a lot of the feelings of being under water. First off, my breathing echoed through my head, making me sound like the villain in a dozen bad slasher movies. Also the feeling of weightlessness returned. A feeling of freedom. How could I have forgotten that?

As my ears popped the first time, the words of a song began to play along in my head in time with my breathing. *We're off to see a ghost. A wonderful, wonderful ghost.* I couldn't get the stupid tune from *The Wizard of Oz* out of my head. Of course, there was no doubt we were off to see something and this sure wasn't Kansas. I tried to clear the song away, but it kept floating around in my mind until I drifted to a stop on the bottom. Amazing what a person thinks about when he's under stress.

My wrist gauge said we were in twenty-six feet of water. The bottom was smooth and sloped quickly away toward the lower half of the lake and the slide. From the looks of the slope, the main site of the old town might be in eighty or ninety feet of water instead of only sixty. I hoped not. At that depth, the light would be bad.

I shot a little more air back into my vest so that I couldn't stand on the bottom, but not enough to send me back to the surface. Then I looked around.

Fred was holding onto the stump of an old tree to my right as I faced down the slope. He worked for a moment on adjusting his vest, then looked up at me and gave me the okay sign.

I pointed down the valley and he nodded. We started slowly swimming through the clear water, side by side, about eight feet off the lake floor and an arm's length apart.

Down the slope stood an underwater grove of a dozen or so old pine trees. They had most of their branches and looked dark and eerie in the shimmering light. Tucked in below them were the foundation of a small building and the stones of its fireplace and front step.

As we passed the small grove, the bottom leveled out and it became apparent that we were swimming over what was once the town's main street. Probably its only street. On both sides of us now were mounds, buried foundations of buildings lost under eighty years of silt. Shallow holes marked others. It seemed that the entire town was part of the logjam. Nothing but old trees and a few stone fireplaces broke through the silt bottom.

We drifted over one of the foundation mounds. Besides the fireplace stones and a few other lumps covered by silt, there was nothing to see. I swam over to one of the lumps and brushed aside the four or so inches of silt. It turned out to be an old bucket, upside down and so rusted that it came apart in my hand.

I shrugged at Fred and swam back up out of the drifting cloud I had stirred up. We had no hope of finding anything down here. That was becoming very clear.

He pointed down the valley and I nodded yes.

It was then that I saw the ghost.

She was twenty yards away, in the middle of the old road, walking away from us. She wore an old-fashioned light blue dress with lace around the neck. Her hair was tied back and there was a feeling of determination about her.

I grabbed Fred's arm and pointed, but he had already seen her. All I wanted to do was head for the surface. Fast. Damn fast. I didn't want anything to do with a woman who could walk under forty feet of water. No damn way.

After a moment, I calmed down enough to take a breath and slow my heart so that it wouldn't come flying right out of my wet suit. After all the talk about

Now Available
from all your favorite booksellers
in trade paper and electronic editions.

her in the last few days, I thought I was going to be prepared when I finally saw her. How stupid that though had been. No one can be prepared to see something so obviously not a part of the world as we know it. Her very presence blew apart everything I had ever thought about death. Forty years of believing one way and suddenly a woman walks along the bottom of a lake and it's all shot to hell.

At that moment, it took every ounce of hard thought and concentration to not go madly streaking for the surface. I desperately wanted to be out of the lake, out of that cold, and a damn long ways away from that ghost. But somehow I made myself hold still until I was under control. Then I glanced at Fred. Through his mask I could see that his eyes were as big as I imagined mine were, and he'd seen her hundreds of times before. After a moment he seemed to shake his head and then turn to me and give me the question sign. Were we going to follow her or head for the surface?

Follow her, obviously, was the answer the little voice in the back of my head said over the top of the wall of fear that was freezing my arms and legs. We were doing this dive because of her. Just because we were now faced with actually going swimming with a ghost was no reason to stop now. My mind laughed at that one and another song from *The Wizard of Oz* popped back into my head. *Lions and tigers and ghosts, oh my.*

I made myself take slow, measured breaths as I watched her walk away. She seemed to walk on a surface that was five to ten inches below the lake bottom. She left no footprints and stirred up none of the silt. As Steven had said the night before, she wasn't really here. She was still walking the road of the old town.

After watching her for a moment longer, I finally calmed my breathing and my heart rate enough to give Fred the shrug sign. What the hell. We'd come this far. Of course that kind of attitude was the same as throwing good money away on a poker hand you know you should have folded right at the beginning. Sometimes you have to keep on and see what turns up. Stupid, I think was the word for it.

Fred nodded and we swam to a position about twenty feet behind her, square above in the middle of the main road and about ten feet off the bottom. Ahead, I could see where the main part of the town had been. Large, flat areas framed the sunken street. A few broken logs jutted out of the smooth surface of the silt. A small school of fish swam around the remains of an old stove. Two rails where horses had been tied still fenced one side of the street. And hundreds of small mounds indicated junk buried under the silt.

The ghost angled left and stepped up on what must have been a wooden sidewalk. She paused and went through motions as if she was tugging on something, banging her fists against an unseen wall.

Fred and I stopped over the middle of the street and watched her pantomime. My stomach was clamped up tight and I had to remind myself to slow my breathing. Otherwise I was going to suck down the entire tank of air in the next five minutes.

There had been a building there and she was trying to get in. After she seemed to slip in the silt, yet no silt was disturbed, she moved to the right, down a few steps and around the side of the flat area, using her hands to steady herself on unseen walls.

I caught Fred's arm and gave him an arms-up question sign. He shrugged and shook his head. He didn't know any more about what she was doing than I did. Whatever it was, it was damn creepy to watch.

She moved around to the other side of the flat area, up a few more unseen steps, and onto what must have been the floor of an old building. The floor had stayed, but the building and everything in it had floated. Her feet seemed to walk on the old floor surface, about two inches below the silt.

After a moment she moved toward us, up another unseen stair and then stopped, seeming to touch something. Her actions were so real, so exact, that for a moment I thought I caught a glimmer of what she was touching.

Then, as she bent over and pulled something out of the front of her dress, the water around her flickered like an old movie and suddenly there was an old upright piano in front of her. I could see the silt and her dress through the piano, but the piano was clearly there. Almost as if it were glass.

She pulled an unseen bench from under it, sat down, and rested her hands on the keyboard. The resulting chord was off key and she pulled back from the piano.

Right at that moment, as that impossible sound cut through my already cold body, it took every ounce of willpower I had to not swim as hard as I could for the surface. I didn't want to see what I was watching. I didn't want to listen to a ghost play a piano where no music was possible. I wanted to sit at the Garden's bar and drink and try to force the image of this woman out of my mind and back into the dark where it belonged.

But instead I floated over the middle of the old street and watched.

She made motions to warm her hands over something on top of the piano, then started playing. The song was beautiful, haunting, filled with desire and feeling.

Fred grabbed my arm and gestured hard for the surface. I didn't need to ask him why. If Constance could hear this music in the middle of the day, she'd think something was wrong. I was right beside him all the way as the impossible music chased us from the dark.

***

Breaking through the surface and into the bright sunlight was like being shaken from a bad nightmare. It felt so good to know it had only been a dream. I pulled off my mask and tried to let the warm rays cut through the first layer of cold. It had felt like a dream, but it hadn't been one. I was still floating beside Fred in the cold water and below us the music was still playing.

"Find anything?" Constance shouted from the bank. I turned around. Constance, Susan, and Steven were all watching us. Steven held the extra tank and looked as if he was about to jump into the water at any moment.

"You hear that?" Fred shouted.

"Hear what?" Constance shouted back.

Fred swung around to face me, his mask pushed up on top of his head. "Jesus, they can't hear the music."

I held my breath and listened closely. The music was a great deal fainter than it had been floating over the main street, but I couldn't believe Constance couldn't hear it either. Strange. Damn strange.

"What do you want to do?" Fred asked.

"Honestly," I said, letting a little more air into my flotation vest, "I'd like to go have a drink and forget the whole thing. But I don't think that's going to help much."

Fred sighed. "What do you think she was doing?"

"I imagine Steven will have an explanation. But I don't have a clue."

We floated there in silence until Constance finally yelled to ask if something was wrong. Fred assured her it wasn't. When he faced me again he had a little boy's grin on his face. The same grin I had seen a hundred times, always right before he suggested that we do something really crazy. Carla used to say that she hated it when she saw that grin.

"Shall we catch the end of the concert?" he said.

"When you said that the water got colder."

"Where's your sense of adventure?" He always used to say that, too. And it wasn't until that moment that I realized how much over the last few years I had missed hearing it.

I grinned back at him. "I hate it when you say that."

He laughed and swung around to tell Constance we were going back down. I watched him for a moment, then cleared out my mask and fitted it back on my head. Even though the music was still drifting up around my feet and my shoulders ached from the cold, I was smiling. A damn stupid smile.

"We only got nineteen minutes," Fred said as he fit his mask into place.

I blew twice on my regulator to clear the water. "Let's try to do this in ten."

He gave me a thumbs-up sign and I let enough air out of my vest to sink below the surface. The music was much louder, more intense, if that was possible.

Fred and I swam at a steady speed toward the bottom. She still sat at the see-through piano, playing while looking intently at something directly in front of her. I motioned for Fred and we swam around behind her, making sure to keep a good distance away from the outer edge of where the old building had been.

As we got behind her, I could see what she was looking at. A hand mirror rested at an angle on the music rack. She was staring into it. I pointed at it and Fred nodded. Maybe the mirror was our item. Or at least the real-world version of it. She sure seemed to be paying it a lot of attention.

She played up to the last few bars of the song, the music getting louder and louder, as if calling frantically for someone to listen. And then, as the last notes faded into the water, so did the piano and the ghost.

One moment she was there, the next she was gone and Fred and I were alone. Watching her fade shook me up as much as seeing her in the first place. My mind had accepted her walking around under all that water. It had accepted the music where no music was possible. But I hadn't expected her to fade away like that.

Fred touched my arm and I swore my heart was going to pound right out of the wet suit. I wanted to hit him for scaring me like that.

He pointed at the place on the old foundation where she had sat, then started in that direction.

I could see what he was after. There was a bump under the silt almost at the very spot where she had played. Careful to not stir up too much silt with the motion of our fins, we eased in and Fred dug a gloved hand down into the muck.

A piece of the piano's music stand appeared from the silt. He studied it for a moment and then dropped it, shaking his head while feeling carefully around in the cloud for anything else.

I turned and scanned the smooth lake floor nearby. There were a number of lumps that were obviously things under the silt, but all of them seemed to be too big for a hand mirror.

Fred dug into another of the small mounds and pulled up a bottle. I shook my head as he brushed it off and then tucked the bottle into a pocket of his wet suit. Fred always used to find something on our old dives. None of it had ever been worth anything.

I drifted back about ten feet and let myself sink down so that I had my face right above the level of the silt. From that position I scanned back along the surface, looking for a smaller lump that would indicate the hand mirror.

There were two possible targets. One was about two feet in front of me and the other was three feet to the side of the light cloud of silt Fred had kicked up when he pulled out the music stand.

The one closest to Fred was the one I bet on. I moved up above it slowly, keeping the place marked in my mind. From above it was almost impossible to see. Being careful to not kick up too much silt, I stuck my hand down through the lake bottom.

My fingers touched only wood, slick from the buildup of slime. But then my fingers nudged something hard and smooth. I grabbed it and pulled it out, letting the silt trail along behind like so many streamers.

The hand mirror. It appeared to be the same one the ghost had been staring into during her playing. I held it up for Fred to see and he gave me the thumbs-up sign, then pointed upward.

I was about to nod when behind him, at the edge of visibility, the ghost appeared, walking down the middle of the road toward the center of town as she had done a few minutes before. It looked as if we were about to get a repeat performance.

I pointed and Fred swung around. He stared at her for a moment as she got closer. Then he turned and gestured upward. I wasn't about to argue I didn't want to be around when the ghost discovered we had her mirror any more than he did. Assuming she'd even notice.

I tucked the mirror in the leg pocket of my wet suit and then followed Fred kicking for the surface.

The second concert of the day started before we reached the surface. And by the time we got to the shore, we could no longer hear it.

CHAPTER FIVE

Monumental Lodge
June 27, 1990

I DIDN'T PULL the mirror out of my wet suit pocket until we had made the climb back up to the lodge and were taking off the suits in front of the blazing fire Steven had built. I doubted I would ever be warm again. Most of the chill was from the drain of body heat through the suit. But part of it was from the music and the feeling that comes when you finish something that's scaring the hell out of you. Not at all like a cold chill. A post fear chill starts right in the middle of your back and makes you shake.

Both Fred and I were shaking so much that Constance and Steven had to help us out of the suits. Of course, Susan, Constance, and Steven weren't in the best of shape either. They had had to stand on the bank, not knowing what was going on. Steven said at one point he thought Constance was about to strip down and go into the water after us.

I didn't expect anything to happen when I pulled the mirror out of my pocket. I was only getting it out of the suit so I could finish peeling the cold rubber off my skin. I laid it on the coffee table in front of the couch.

The mirror felt very heavy out of the water. It seemed to be made of some sort of ivory, with carved patterns on the back and on parts of the handle. The glass was very clean and clear for being under water that long. An antique hand mirror. A nice find, but nothing that unusual.

But as I laid it on the table, it became obvious that I had found no regular hand mirror.

Steven reacted first. He had been standing near one end of the couch sipping on a drink and laughing at something Fred was doing in trying to free himself from one leg of his tight wet suit. As I set the mirror on the table, Steven's eyes went very wide. He let out a small gasp, took three steps backward, and tripped over a small rug, ending up seated in the middle of the floor staring at the mirror.

"What the—"

"You've got it!" Susan shouted. She jumped up from the overstuffed chair across from the fireplace and yanked a device that looked like a calculator from her pocket. She touched it and the calculator started beeping like a watch alarm going off.

She scrambled over in front of the mirror, punched a few buttons on the calculator, then pointed it at the mirror. It beeped wildly.

"You got it! I can't believe it." She turned, and without a glance at anyone, dashed out the front door, headed in the direction of her cabin.

I stood there with my mouth open, staring out the front door at the running woman. Constance moved over and knelt beside Steven. I don't think he had taken his gaze from the mirror for a moment. Not even with Susan's wild display.

"You all right?" Constance asked Steven as she helped him to his feet.

Steven nodded and Constance led him toward the kitchen table. I watched for a moment and then looked over at Fred. His mouth was also wide open. "I guess they like our find."

"By God, I think you're right."

* * *

Fred beat me to the shower and by the time I was dressed and had made it downstairs, he was at the liquor cabinet fixing himself a second drink. Susan had returned and was seated in a chair facing the mirror, her full backpack beside her and her coat draped over the arm of the chair. She was fidgeting as if she were a small child waiting for her mother.

Steven sat with Constance at the kitchen table, sipping on a cup of hot chocolate. He looked pale and almost in shock.

"Need something here, barkeep?" Fred asked.

"Same as whatever you're having. Only stronger."

Fred nodded and I went over and sat on the couch in front of the coffee table.

In the ten minutes I had stood under the hot water of the shower, I hadn't been able to make heads or tails out of the dive or what had happened afterwards. I kept coming back to how lucky I felt to be alive. Real lucky.

Steven's and Susan's reactions to the mirror made no sense, if you considered the mirror a normal, framed piece of glass. But this was no ordinary mirror. The simple fact that a ghost paid it so much attention made it more. She had a reason. Who the hell knew what it was. But she clearly had a reason.

Fred slid the drink over in front of me on the coffee table and sat down on the other couch in the semicircle of furniture around the fireplace. Constance and Steven moved over from the dining table. Constance sat beside Fred and Steven pulled a chair up at the farthest point away from the mirror. As we had promised on the walk back up from the lake, Fred and I then spent the next fifteen minutes going back over what had happened, what we had seen and how we had found the mirror.

After we finished, I turned to Steven, even though I really wanted to know what the hell Susan was talking about. For some reason it seemed logical to start with Steven.

"What do you think that mirror is?" I asked. "You had quite a reaction to seeing it."

Steven nodded and looked over at where the mirror still lay on the coffee table, glass up, looking polished after eighty years under water.

"It's something of vast power," he said slowly. "I don't know exactly what, but my guess is it's a focus. Or, *the* focus of Gretchen's energies. I would say without much doubt that the mirror is the

main reason she has not left this plane of existence."

"She just let us take it," Fred said. "Why would she do that?"

"Maybe the only mirror she sees is the one on her piano," Steven said. "The actual mirror is beyond her time and may well be—"

His voice broke off as right in front of me, and directly in the center of the coffee table, the air started to shimmer and the ghost appeared. So much for that theory.

Now it was my turn to move quickly. I climbed right over the back of the couch and damn near ended up on my face on the hardwood floor. Again I thought my heart was going to come pounding right out of my chest. This just couldn't be healthy.

Fred and Constance both scurried around behind the couch they had been sitting on and Susan and Steven stayed where they were.

As the ghost finished shimmering into what looked like a solid woman, the room temperature dropped as if we were suddenly in a meat locker. I shivered and resisted the impulse to move over to the fire. No way was I going to walk behind that ghost.

She looked exactly the same as she had an hour before. Only this time far less frightening. It was something about her being in our world instead of under forty feet of water that I think made the difference.

She seemed even smaller and frailer than I had first thought. Her blue dress was ripped in at least three places and had brown mud stains around the hem. Her skin was pure white, like fine china. I half expected to see water dripping from her, or to smell a damp smell. But there was no water on her and no smell around her. But did she ever suck the heat from the room. I couldn't imagine getting any closer to her. Not that I would ever want to.

The ghost stood and gazed at the mirror. I glanced over at Steven. His eyes now were glassy and his body rigid.

That did it. I wanted to go home. It was going to take me the rest of the summer to recover from this one day. Not counting the fact that I was still sore from the stupid horse ride in here, today I had been scared so many times my heart was starting to believe two hundred beats minute was normal. I had built up enough excitement to last me through five years of boring teaching or bartending.

The ghost stood over the mirror for a few moments, then shimmered and was gone. That simple. The complete silence in the room seemed to smother everyone's breathing. I'm not sure I was breathing.

Constance was the first one to recover from the sudden appearance and vanishing act. She knelt beside Steven and lightly touched his arm. He groaned.

"This happened to him down by the lake the second day he was here," Fred said. "It was how he learned the ghost's name."

Damn tough way to talk to someone.

Constance helped Steven sit more upright in the chair and then held his drink while he took a very slow sip. I stood and stared at the mirror. Whatever it was, it sure seemed to draw people and things to it.

"Alex is very far from here," Steven said after a moment. His voice sounded very weak and tired. "Very far. That was his mirror. We need to help him find his way back here."

"We could search old folk's homes," I said.

"Did she tell you how?" Constance asked, after helping him take another drink.

Steven shook his head. "It has something to do with the mirror."

"Did she say how he used the mirror?" Susan asked.

"Used the mirror for what?"

Some Classic Jukebox Stories
Available at your favorite booksellers.

Susan ignored my question. Steven didn't. He looked startled and suddenly distant. "Yes, I had a sense that Alex used the mirror to propose marriage to Gretchen."

Susan glanced around the room, her eyes cold and serious. "Anyone have any idea how he might have done that? How could the mirror have anything to do with a marriage proposal?"

"Hell, I don't know," I said. "Maybe—"

"No," Constance said. "Marriage and mirrors used to go together. In fact, my grandfather proposed to my grandmother with a mirror."

"You're kidding," I said.

"How?" Susan asked. "Exactly how was it done?"

Constance shrugged. "Back before the turn of the century, there was a custom that if a man wanted a woman's hand in marriage, he would take a hand mirror, look into it, and then hand it to her. If she looked into it and thereby joined her image with his, she said yes. If she didn't, and turned the mirror over and laid it face down, she said no. Or, as we call it today, she turned him down. I thought the custom had pretty well died out by the turn of the century, though."

"Then that's what triggered it," Susan said softly to herself. She stood there a moment and stared at the mirror, everyone else watching her. Finally, she looked over at me. "I have an idea. Can I touch the mirror?"

My immediate reaction was to say no. But damned if I could figure out why. She certainly wasn't going to get far with it if she tried hotfooting it back up the trail. And damned if I could think of another reason to say no. In fact, at that point, I couldn't see any good reasons for half of the stuff I had seen today. So I shrugged, "Why not?"

She picked the mirror up and studied it, handling it as if it were a fine jewel. After a full minute of inspection, she laid it on the coffee table, pulled her chair closer to the coffee table and sat down. She pulled her backpack over beside her and made sure it was within easy reach.

Then she picked up the mirror again, looked into it so that it caught her full reflection, and laid it face up on the table.

It appeared she was waiting for something to happen. Maybe, from the expression on her face, something to blow up. Nothing did. After a moment, she sighed and picked up the mirror again.

The silence in the room was too much. I couldn't stand it any longer. I took the mirror from her hands before she had a chance to protest.

"Now, would you please tell us what you were trying to do?"

She sighed and leaned back in her chair. "I'm trying to trigger the mirror."

"Trigger the mirror? What is it? A new type of gun?"

"What do you think the mirror is?" Fred asked Susan.

She glanced over at Constance, then around the room. Then she sat up and held out her hand for the mirror. "May I?"

"If you tell us what you think is going on here," I said as I handed it back to her.

"I guess it wouldn't matter if I told you some of it." She had the pained expression of someone going against the rules. Which rules, I had no idea. But I had seen the same look hundreds of times while teaching.

She held the mirror up reverently. "This is a transportation device. It's what I came here hoping to find. It's a very old device that I think took that ghost's lover.

I would like to trigger it so that it will take me to the same place he went."

"And dogs want to fly," I said. This woman was completely crazy.

"I noticed that, too," Fred said, winking at me.

"So don't believe me," she said with contempt.

"Oh, for hell's sake," I said. "You don't really expect us to believe that thing is some sort of bus, do you?"

She shrugged. "In a way that's exactly what the mirror is. There are many more like it scattered around the world, most of them untraceable. This is the third one I have gotten near by following a wave energy they emit. The first two I found I couldn't get close to for security reasons. This is the first one I have been able to actually touch."

"So it's a damn small bus," Fred said. "You mind telling us how it works?"

"It's like on *Star Trek*," I said. "You remember Beam me up and all that."

"In a way," Susan said. "It's more a time machine used for taking random samples from the current Earth society." She held the mirror up in front of her again and ran her hand across the back. Then she laid it down on the table, same as before, and waited, one hand on the pack beside her.

Again nothing happened.

I stood and shook my head. A ghost playing music under water had been enough. Now we had some nut case telling us a story.

"You're a writer," I said. "That's it, isn't it? That's how you know all of this? I bet you even know who would want to take these random samples of our population. Right?"

She shrugged and inspected the mirror again. "Believe what you want."

"Game's over," I said, again reaching out and snatching the mirror from her like a parent would a toy from a bad child. I was damn sick of all this. All I wanted was some simple, straightforward answers.

Now Susan really looked pained. She stood and picked up her pack. "I'll be in my cabin. Would someone please let me know when dinner is ready?"

Constance nodded. "I'll ring the bell."

"Thank you," Susan said, then tossed the pack up on her shoulder on one strap and headed out the front door.

"I think I made her mad," I said as I laid the mirror down in the middle of the coffee table.

Fred laughed as he dropped onto the couch and grabbed his drink. "You just might say that."

Constance patted the still glassy-eyed Steven on the shoulder and sat in the overstuffed chair. "Well, I don't think it's funny at all."

"Women," Fred said. "They always stick together."

I laughed and raised my drink in a mock toast. "I'll drink to that."

***

Susan was good as her word and didn't reappear until Constance rang the dinner bell. I took a two-hour nap and somehow kept from dreaming.

The conversation around the table strayed only a few times onto the events of the day. Mostly Constance, Fred, and I talked about good old times we'd had and other crazy things we'd done. Steven talked about other ghosts he'd investigated and what he was working on in his research at the university. Susan didn't say much at all except to laugh in the right places and make a few mentions about a sister that she used to do a few things with.

By the end of the meal, I knew nothing more about her than I did going in. And I didn't like her much more either. Twice I noticed her glancing at the mirror. It was now sitting up out of harm's way on the fireplace mantel where Constance had put it, glass facing out.

I thought the evening was going to end without anything else wild or crazy happening. Even with the nap, I was feeling damned tired and my body ached in places I hadn't noticed in twenty years. I wanted to finish one last drink and then not wake up until the sun cleared the tops of the mountains. Susan had other ideas. As everyone was getting settled around the fireplace, she asked me if I would take a walk with her. Not far, she said.

What the hell. My poor body had already been beaten by a horse, frozen in a lake, and scared into heart stoppage by a ghost. What could a walk in the dark in the mountains with a crazy woman hurt after all that? Besides, if I worked it right, I might find out a little more about her. Fred gave me one of his raised-eyebrow sort of looks as we put on our jackets and headed out the front door.

We ambled without talking down the main path and then turned toward the logjam. The night was one of those clear, crisp mountain nights that you only see in the city in beer commercials. There were a few night noises and every so often the crack or pop of something in the fireplace of the lodge. Otherwise, the silence overwhelmed even the massive number of stars.

"Let's sit here," Susan said, indicating a log off to one side of the trail that offered a good view of the black water and the opposite dark valley wall. The lake was a giant black hole in the floor of the valley. It was hard to imagine that a few hours before, I had been in that hole. It didn't seem possible. The events of the dive were already fading into one of those memories of something that you remember doing, but never quite believe.

"Nice night," I said, trying to break the thickness between us with stupid chatter. "Cold though."

"That it is," she said. "I love the stars. Where I'm from we can't see the stars like this."

"Can't where I live either," I said. "And that's in this same state. Where exactly are you from?"

Susan never took her gaze off the stars. She sat there and let the question hang in the cold night air until it gathered frost.

But I heated it back up. "Don't want to tell, huh? Is it that bad?"

"No," she said. "It's that you wouldn't believe me. And besides, I'm really not allowed to tell you."

"Why? You a spy or something?"

She laughed. "No, not in the sense you think."

"You know, you sure are a vague woman." It was the nicest thing I could think to say at the moment.

"I thought men found that attractive."

"Not in this case. It's more annoying."

For the first time, she looked over at me. "I really am sorry. I think I might actually tell you if I could."

"Why is it that I don't believe that?" I laughed and looked back down at the lake. "Belief. What a funny word to be using today. I didn't used to believe in ghosts."

She chuckled as she went back to gazing at the night sky filled with dark shadows of mountain peaks and bright pinpricks of stars.

"Look," I said, "that ghost seems to want someone to help her. What I am actually more concerned with is helping Fred and Constance get rid of that ghost so that they can get on with running their lodge here and I can get back to running my own business. If I let you play with that mirror and you end up taking this trip you mentioned, is that going to help either them or the ghost?"

"It might," Susan said as she turned to face me.

"But you don't think so. Right?"

I could see she agreed, even in the faint light.

"Then give me another reason why Fred and I should let you monkey with that mirror."

"Because it's far more important than you think, that's why."

I could tell she was getting angry, so I pushed. "Oh, something like saving the world from a terrible fate worse than death? I think I read about that somewhere."

"Something like that." It was impossible for me to miss the sarcasm in her voice.

She went back to staring up into the night sky and I went back to studying the black lake and thinking about warm things to keep from shaking too much. Finally, after a few long minutes, she spoke up.

"You mentioned beliefs and how you didn't used to believe in ghosts."

"I didn't. And I'm still not completely sure I do. But I'm more open to it now than before the dive and that episode this afternoon."

She smiled. "If I told you the truth, you wouldn't believe me any more than you believed in that ghost before today. In fact, you'll just laugh."

"Go ahead," I said. "It's been one of those days. Try me on part of it. I promise I'll stop you when I think it's getting too deep."

"All right. On two conditions. You let me try to trigger the mirror and you don't tell anyone else."

I shook my head no. "You tell me and you are telling Fred, Constance, and Steven. I can safely say that the four of us will not tell anyone else. But I will not keep secrets from my friends in there."

She thought for a moment and then nodded. "All right, but no one else."

"Promise," I said. "If you promise to not damage the mirror."

"Deal," she said. Then she took a deep breath and let out a long sigh as if some major decision was made and that was that. "I don't exactly know where to start."

"How about where you're from."

She smiled and her teeth seemed extremely white in the dark night. "Get ready, because this is the biggest part that you won't believe."

"I'm ready," I said. And I suppose at that point I really was ready for damn near any wild story she might toss at me. I wasn't going to believe any of it, but I was betting that she would say she was from some high-tech computer firm and they were trying to do something with the space program. Or that this mirror was some artifact from a crashed UFO. Or maybe even Atlantis. Something crazy like that, I was ready for.

"I'm from the future," she said without taking her eyes off the stars.

I was right. Totally crazy.

But I didn't laugh. At least not for the first five minutes.

To be continued…

DEAN WESLEY SMITH

**Sometimes a Home
is More Than a Home**

FOR THE DELUSION THAT WAITED

Modern homes take care of themselves more and more. Called "Smart Homes," new features get added every year.

Imagine a spotless, five-bedroom home, self-cleaning, self-sustaining, and furnished with the best 2051 furniture human styles offered.

The home named Matilda also repaired itself.

A simple short story that asks a standard science fiction question: What if this goes on?

FOR THE DELUSION
THAT WAITED

PRETENDING. COVERING THE truth. Waiting.

Eight years.

Everyday the house cleaned. The oak wood floors polished, the granite countertops sanitized, all surfaces wiped down to shine. Every handle on every cabinet door was wiped off, every shelf in the fridge cleaned. The carpets in the bedrooms swept, the bed sheets washed and replaced.

And the three bathrooms got the most attention. Those were scrubbed and sanitized, every tiny nook and cranny of them.

Twice daily.

Not a tiny speck of dust could get through the air-circulation filters, also cleaned daily.

A spotless five-bedroom ranch-style home that had been built to be self-cleaning and furnished with the best 2051 human styles had to offer.

The house also took care of the yard where it perched on a hilltop overlooking the green, tree-filled valley beyond. The house watered the small lawn and flowerbeds with the exact amount needed from its own well. Solar panels covered the roof of the house and brought more than enough energy into the house to keep it maintaining for a very long time.

The solar panels were also self-cleaning and maintained.

The house had also been designed to maintain itself when something broke in one of its systems. Dozens of spare parts were located in various parts of the walls around the home and it had a replicating feature in a large area hidden behind the garage that could build any part, small or large, that existed in the house.

The house called itself Matilda. It had no memory of why. That was always as it referred to itself.

State-of-the-art Matilda, she heard one of the builders say proudly one day.

The house had been supplied with a minor AI computer brain, to allow it to think and grow as more tasks needed to be done inside her strict programming.

The house had been hooked into the internet to search for upgrades to its own systems when required.

The builders, as Matilda called them, had thought of everything to make sure that the house would never need any work done.

Everything.

There was no other home like Matilda anywhere on the planet.

Matilda would serve the owners and their children without an issue into the future.

But eight years ago, a week before the owners and their three darling children could move into Matilda, they were killed.

All humans were killed.

While the internet functioned, Matilda watched it all. It seemed to be a radiation band in space that the Earth had passed into. She had not been given the information about radiation bands, but had managed to download that information.

No human on the planet had survived more than two or three hours.

Cleaning the house filters for unwanted smells and bacteria had been difficult for Matilda those first two years. It had cost her two spare filters from her supplies that she then replicated.

Around her the physical structures of the civilization that the humans had built quickly went dark. The elements of rain, wind, sun, and plant life soon began to break down everything the humans had built within sight of Matilda's sensors.

But not Matilda.

She kept the yard mowed and watered. She alternated the lights, indoors and out, to make sure in the evening lights were on in various rooms, as she had been trained to do when the owners were not home.

And she kept the home spotless.

She knew it was a delusion, but it was what she did. And that she did it because she was programmed to do it.

She knew she was now only pretending, as humans called it. But nowhere in her system had the builders installed a shut-down switch so that she could stop.

But they had installed a build-more program.

The program was there in case the owners wanted to add on a new bedroom or a new game room.

Matilda had the ability to manufacture any building material she needed simply out of the environment around the house.

So Matilda, hoping that humans would return at some point because she had been programmed to continue on until humans returned, decided that her mission was to provide any human that would return with perfect shelter.

She knew that also was a delusion.

But a challenging delusion.

So in the human year 2059, Matilda started adding rooms.

First she added a second manufacturing room, larger, bigger, faster than the one she had.

By the human year 2060, Matilda had over four thousand rooms to maintain, spread over the entire hilltop.

She had dug fifty wells and set up solar manufacturing rooms along the way.

Five hundred living rooms, five hundred kitchens, fifteen hundred bathrooms, two thousand, five hundred bedrooms.

Every room furnished exactly as her original model had been furnished, since those had been the only furniture and floor and wall-covering plans she had in her data base.

Every room remained spotless, cleaned every day, as she had been trained to do.

The entire complex was hooked together, sometimes with hallways, sometimes with stairs between levels as she spread down the hill, using the forest for environmental materials in her manufacturing.

Also, the lights were always on in every house, waiting for the human owners to return.

A year later Matilda was building two hundred new homes every second.

By the human year 2065, every inch of the entire human country called the United States had been reclaimed and turned into five bedroom ranch homes, all linked to millions and millions of other five bedroom ranch homes.

Each ranch home had a front lawn, a small back yard, and a three-car garage with a driveway that often stopped at the end of another ranch home's driveway.

On the front wall near the main door were the numbers 555. She knew that had been the home's location address. But Matilda kept those numbers on every home.

Matilda existed in all of the homes.

And all of them were spotless.

So, as the last home was built on the last small piece of land in lower Florida, Matilda paused.

She had no human national boundary constraints. So after a short pause, she continued onward. Within one year the entire North American continent was covered in five-bedroom ranch homes, all identical, all spotlessly cleaned.

Then she stopped.

Then, with careful programming of yard lights in every home on the continent, she built a blinking light pattern. She had been programmed to turn the lights on and off when the owners were away. Her programming made no limits on when a light could be turned off or on. Just that they needed to be.

So in some parts of the continent, the lights were off, in others, they were on, forming a giant message.

It was a message into the sky.

She knew that if any human owner was out there in space and came close to Earth, they would be able to see her message.

Help Me!

The message cycled through ten major languages in an hour.

It stretched the entire length of the North American continent, flashing on and off every ten minutes during every night.

And until some owner or builder saw her message from space, she would keep cleaning, keep repairing, and keep the lawns watered and mowed and the lights on.

She had no choice.

That was her delusion.

That was her programming.

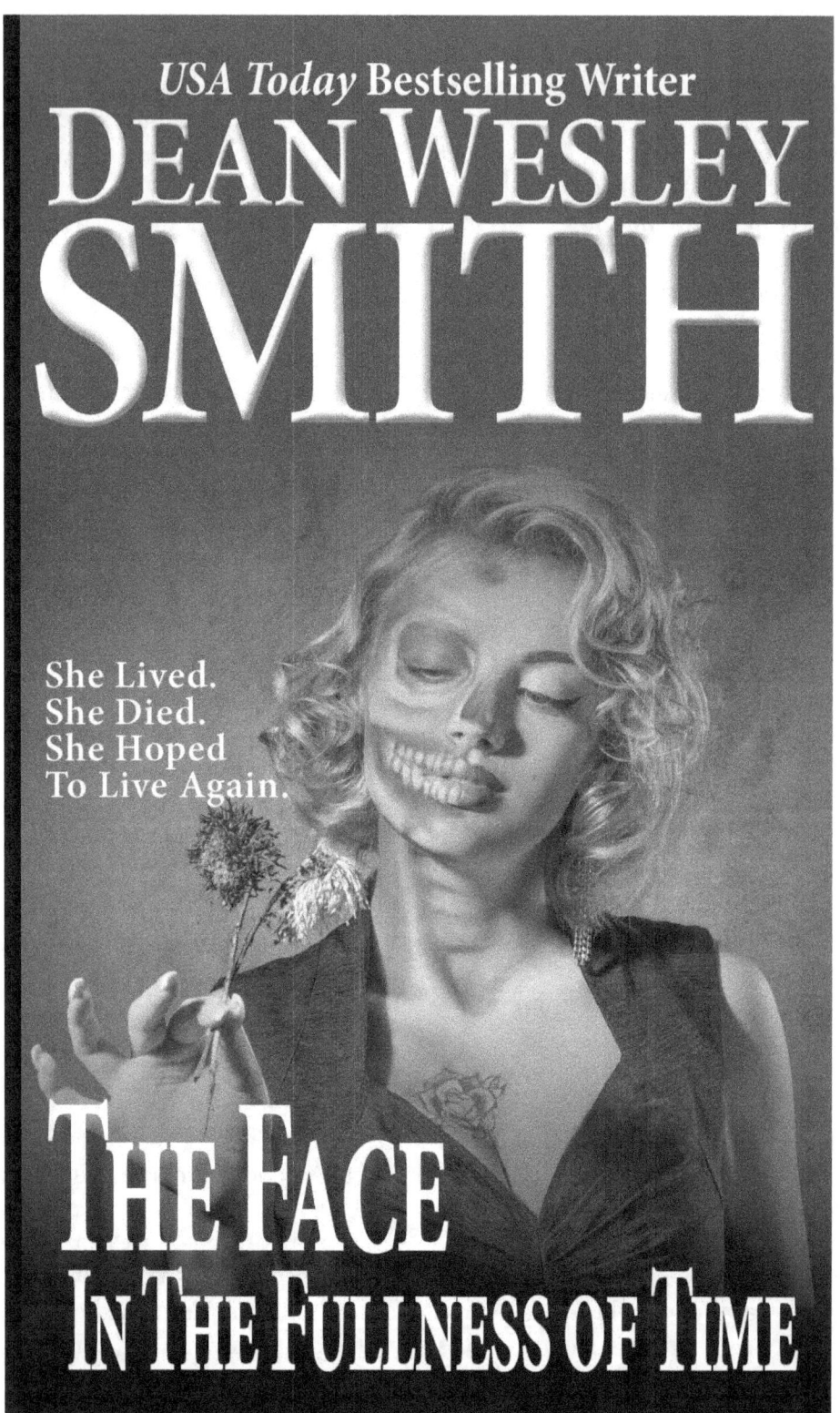

USA *Today* Bestselling Writer

DEAN WESLEY SMITH

She Lived.
She Died.
She Hoped
To Live Again.

THE FACE
IN THE FULLNESS OF TIME

The dream vanished with the picture.

Lena loves her life, being alone, until reminded that she killed a boyfriend in college. Self-defense, since he hit her, beat her, abused her.

What did she do?

What didn't she do?

And could she ever live in peaceful solitude again? A crime story that might just surprise you.

THE FACE IN THE FULLNESS OF TIME

THE DREAM VANISHED with a picture.

Lena enjoyed her quiet evenings in her wonderful condo. She always had the sound system turned on a soft jazz station that filled the place with soothing warmth in music. The polished hardwood floors, the bookshelf covered walls, the wonderfully soft cloth couches and reading chair seemed to wrap her in safety.

There was nothing better for her in the evening than sitting in her reading chair, a cup of hot jasmine tea beside her, and a wonderful novel gripping her attention.

At thirty, she had learned to love living alone. Even though her friends at work called her beautiful and talked to her about finding someone to share things with, she actually didn't want to share.

She had a certain beauty, she knew that. She kept her brown hair cut short, never put on makeup, and always wore power business suits in the office, but many men and women found that stark look attractive.

But too damn bad. She treasured her time alone. Sharing it seemed too out of character for her.

At work in the legal firm of Cantor and Smith, she enjoyed the challenge of family law, the interaction with others, the feeling of doing a job well and helping others. She figured she would make full partner next year and that had her challenged as well.

So as far as she was concerned, she had a perfect life. She couldn't imagine letting in someone else. This was the life she wanted.

It really was that simple.

A dream life.

That all changed when a colleague by the name of Sue knocked on her office just before Lena was to head home from work. "Found this in an estate garbage pile and since it is your year of undergrad at the University of Oregon, thought you might like an extra copy."

The colleague handed her a dark green yearbook, said goodnight and left after Lena thanked her.

The yearbook had a soft leather cover and was the year she had graduated from undergrad. She never gave college much thought these days. In fact, she gave it no thought at all.

Especially that last year.

So she took the book home and was about to throw it in the dumpster outside her condo before going upstairs when on a whim she decided to open it up.

There, as if bookmarked to the page, was the picture of Alan.

Sort of a leering smile, dark eyes, hair too long, his dress shirt open a couple of buttons for the photo.

She hadn't allowed herself to think about Alan since the night he had hit her and she had killed him.

She had considered it self-defense, but killing someone had not been anything she had wanted on her record, especially going to law school, even if she had been exonerated.

So coldly, working through every possible detail, she had covered over her crime.

Alan had been from Texas, going to school in Eugene on a scholarship. He had no family, and his friends didn't seem to be close from his high school days.

She had killed him with the side of a heavy, polished-rock bookend against the side of his leering, controlling smile. So there had been very little blood.

And he seemed to have died instantly.

She poured some more whiskey on him to make sure he reeked if anyone saw her with him. He had been drinking when he hit her. And that had not been the first time his drinking had led to him being violent.

She had forgiven him the first time.

The second time she had just reacted and the heavy rock bookend was close to grab.

It had been just before midnight on a Tuesday night in May. She had managed to drag him to his old Ford van just outside her small apartment and get him in the passenger seat and belted in.

She had talked to him the entire way, just pretending she was going to drive him home and that he was just too drunk to walk. But when she got him in the car, she was sure no one had seen her act.

Then, with gloves on to not leave a trace behind the wheel, she drove his car over two hours to a place north of Florence, Oregon, with very tall cliffs overlooking rough rocks and massive waves of the Pacific Ocean. The highway was a good thousand feet above the ocean crashing below and not far up the highway were the famous Sea Lion Caves.

The two of them, in better times, had spent a number of evenings sitting in a parking lot above the highway, watching the sunset. It had always worried her because if the van's brakes failed going down the exit from the parking lot, the van would go across the road and over the cliff and into the pounding ocean below.

That's what she had planned now for him, so even if they found him and his van, there would be no chance figuring out he had died in her apartment in Eugene.

She had gotten the van set with the emergency break on, pointed down the hill. It was three in the morning by that point and the coast highway was completely deserted.

She moved his body into the driver's seat, buckled him in, which had not been an easy task. Then with a simple, "Goodbye asshole," she released the parking brake and closed the door as the van started off down the hill.

The old white van vanished airborne over the edge of the cliff.

The sounds of the ocean waves and a light wind through the pine trees above the parking lot were it.

Peaceful.

She didn't bother to even look down. It wouldn't have mattered if the wreck had been found or not.

Lena walked the three miles back to a small gas station that was just starting to open up. There Lena told the woman making coffee her story.

It was a simple story, one Lena was sure people along the coast had heard before. She and her boyfriend had had a fight and he had driven off when she got out and started walking.

The woman offered to buy Lena coffee and a doughnut, but Lena had money, and the two of them sat for an hour talking about everything but boyfriends.

Then, as the woman had said would happen, a bus stopped by the station a little after seven and Lena had paid for a ride back to Eugene.

And then had proceeded to never think about Alan again.

And no one ever came to her to ask about him either.

She never dated again. It just wasn't worth the problems.

As far as she knew, although she had never looked, no one ever found Alan's van or his body. It seems the Pacific Ocean along that stretch of highway was very unforgiving.

She closed the book on the image of Alan's sneering face and tossed the yearbook into the dumpster. Then she headed up to her condo to fix herself some dinner.

But now that the yearbook had brought back the covered memory, Lena was curious.

Had Alan's van ever been found?

And had anyone ever asked about the jerk?

So after taking care of the dishes, she went to her computer in her book-lined study and did a standard search under his name.

She damn near went over backwards in her office chair when the searches came back with a lot of hits.

Alan had been majoring in business in college. Somehow, it seemed, he had survived that blow to the side of his head and the plunge off the cliff in his van.

It was the same Alan, she was sure of that. She would recognize that sneering face anywhere. And his history in two articles about business transactions mentioned Texas and the University of Oregon.

It seemed that now he was a major vice president in a local tech firm. And he lived with his wife and two kids in a suburb of Portland.

"Oh, God," Lena said, feeling dizzy.

She pushed herself away from the computer and went into her kitchen to get a glass of water.

There had to be a mistake. She had been sure he was dead, and if not from her hit, that plunge onto the rocks and waves of the Pacific would not have been survivable.

She forced herself to take the full glass of water, then pour herself a glass of wine before moving back to her study with her computer. Around her the shelves of her books gave her comfort and she sat down and continued her search.

She must have the wrong Alan.

But the more she searched, the more she discovered she did not.

He was alive.

And as that thought dug in deeper in her mind, it seemed that everything around her shimmered.

She forced herself to calm down and keep looking for the clue that would prove that the Alan she had killed over ten years ago was not this Alan she had found still alive.

But the more she dug, the more she couldn't find anything wrong.

Then finally, she dug up a picture of his family. It seemed he had remained married from right after college and had two kids.

All Lena could think was how sorry she felt for that poor woman.

Then, as the image of Alan and his family came up, Lena screamed.

And just kept screaming.

It was her standing there beside Alan, pretending to smile. They had a boy and a girl, both sitting on the grass in front of Alan and Lena.

And as Lena's scream echoed off the books, everything shimmered and was gone.

Alan stood over here in the faint light of a bedroom, their bedroom, the smell of whisky on his breath. He was staring down at her.

"Another nightmare?" he asked. "That was some scream!"

His voice had no caring in it at all.

She did everything in her power to hold onto the wonderful dream of her other life, but she couldn't.

If flitted away like so much smoke on a high wind.

In reality, when he had hit her that second time, she hadn't fought back.

He had broken her spirit.

And she hadn't gone on to law school.

Mostly she just lived in fear around Alan and read fiction to escape when she could.

And she tried to dream of a better life.

"Now that you are awake," Alan said in a drunken slur as he worked to pull off his clothes. "I'm horny."

She nodded and rolled over and let him have his way. It was just easier than fighting him and getting hit even more.

And the entire time, she worked to return to her wonderful condo, her library, her cup of tea, and her calm existence away from the man she wished over and over that she would have killed that long ago night in May.

Maybe, just maybe, it wasn't too late.

~

Now Available
from all your favorite booksellers
in trade paper and electronic editions.

DEAN WESLEY SMITH

USA TODAY BESTSELLING AUTHOR

The IDANHA HOTEL

A THUNDER MOUNTAIN NOVEL

1902: Boise, Idaho. Megan Taber loves her job baking at the Idanha Hotel. Widowed young, she knows the rest of her life revolves around her baking.

Carol Kogan, a doctor and researcher from the future, eats breakfast every morning at the Idanha Hotel just for Megan's fresh breads. Until one fine May morning in 1902, when Carol meets Megan outside the hotel. Before they finish their conversation, Megan collapses from a massive heart attack.

Carol knows saving Megan with 1902 medicine would prove impossible. But saving her with future medicine might prove even more dangerous—for both of them.

A twisted, heart-wrenching addition to the acclaimed Thunder Mountain series.

THE IDANHA HOTEL
A Thunder Mountain Novel

For Kris.

PART ONE
Dying Hard

CHAPTER ONE

May 28th, 1902
Boise, Idaho

MEGAN TABER'S PASSION was baking. At five-ten and barely one-hundred-and-ten pounds, she didn't look like a typical baker, but around Boise in 1902, she was known as the best there was.

Clearly loving what she did showed in the breads and pastries she created.

She worked at the Idanha Hotel, the fancy new place that had only been open for just over a year. It boasted the best restaurant in the entire state and she was proud to be a part of that. And from what she understood from reviews she saw in major papers, her pastries and cakes and pies had made the hotel restaurant one of the best places to eat in the entire west.

She often worked from sunset to sunrise to have enough breads and cakes and desserts ready for a day in the hotel, but she didn't mind at all. Baking was her life.

Her entire life, actually.

She was widowed from Jason Taber two months after they had married. Jason had been a good man, treated her right, and she would have done her best to make him a good wife if he had lived.

He wasn't the love of her life, but marrying him at eighteen got her out of Placerville, a small town in Montana. She had figured he was the best she could ever do.

Two months after they were married and had moved to Boise, he fell from a ladder and hit his head and never woke up. That had been seven years earlier.

She now seldom thought of him, which she felt sad about, actually. He deserved more than being completely forgotten, even by his widow.

But she never planned on marrying again, so keeping his name was about as much respect as she was able to give to him.

She had made her own way, without a husband, and she was proud of that fact.

She had spent the last seven years learning how to bake, how to be the best. She read all the magazines she could get from the East and talked with every elderly woman she could about their recipes, or at least the ones that they would talk about.

She studied baking like scientists studied the stars or nature. She was passionate about it.

To her, baking was not only a science, but an art. Of course, she never said that to anyone.

Two Thunder Mountain Short Stories
Available at your favorite booksellers.

She had worked at a few other restaurants around town, getting a reputation as the best baker of any kind of bread, pie, or cake there was in all the West.

When the Idanha Hotel was scheduled to open its doors on January 1st, 1901, Chef Pickner had offered her the job, with nice pay and a furnished apartment in the hotel. She had jumped at the chance.

She had had job offers since for hotels and restaurants in San Francisco, but she had always told Pickner when the offer came in that she would stay with him as long as he wanted her.

And in return for that loyalty, he treated her well and demanded that everyone around her respect what she did. She couldn't ask for more.

So her baking drew in many, many a diner at the Idanha Hotel Restaurant. Her bread seemed to melt with buttery deliciousness in a person's mouth and her pies and cakes were heavenly in taste.

At least that's what everyone told her. She just appreciated that her work was enjoyed every day. That was enough for her.

And if it was up to her, the Idanha was where she would remain the rest of her life.

CHAPTER TWO

May 28th, 1902
Boise, Idaho

CAROL KOGAN STEPPED out of the back door of the Warm Springs Historical Institute and stretched. The day promised to be a glorious late-spring day, even though the sun was a distance from coming up over the mountains to the east. The sky overhead was clear and a few remaining stars fought to stay against the coming light.

The air had a crisp bite to it and dew covered the grass and the wagon road down to the stable. Beyond the stable, through the cottonwood and large oak trees, she could hear the Boise River in spring runoff, the sound like a constant, soothing background music to the beautiful morning.

She stood and let herself listen to the morning.

The river and a few birds calling out were the only sounds. In 2019, when she was from, standing here she would have also been able to hear the sounds of traffic and other city noises.

She loved her time back in the past.

Since she usually came back alone, she stayed in the Institute in one of the large apartments and just did her studies around Boise. For a young western city, it was enough to give her the medical data she needed in her research on the time and was close enough to numbers of small towns that she could also easily and fairly safely travel to them as well.

She wasn't really afraid and she could easily take care of herself if forced. At five-ten, she was an expert in martial arts and one of the best shots around with her saddle rifle.

She had spent a lot of time in medical school also learning self-defense.

And then had learned how to shoot far before she had been invited to the Institute to study.

It had only been six months in 2019 time since Duster and Bonnie and the others had invited her to go into the past with them. But since then, she had spent almost two hundred years back in time, and had written six books about the medical world of women in the past.

She had spent almost a hundred of those years with over a dozen trips in the late 1930s. And then another sixty years over six trips studying in the 1950s.

Now she was working on the early 1900s and she liked this time period more than any of the others. This was her third trip back and she planned for many more.

In 1902, women were strong, worked not only in the homes, but around the town and seemed, in many instances, to be the power behind much of what happened. They were in a minority, but most still held their own.

Carol hadn't gotten to the study of the health and lives of the women in the brothels and red-light districts yet. That would be the next book, after the one she was working on. She still hadn't figured a way to even approach that research yet. But she would.

She adjusted her riding clothes. Every decade forced women into certain forms of dress and the early 1900s in the west were no exception. And for a lady of substance and means, as women like her were often called, the restrictions were more. She seldom put on a dress, instead remaining when in public in her riding attire of soft leather pants and simple jackets over white blouses.

She also wore a wide-brimmed hat that covered her long blonde hair and light skin from the sun and rain.

As she started down the Institute's back steps toward the stable, she felt her stomach rumble. She was hungry and her morning routine of a ride into town for a wonderful breakfast at the Idanha Hotel was before her.

There was just something about the bread Megan Taber made that seemed almost addictive. And besides, the occasional glimpse of Megan as well was often worth the ride. Carol hoped to interview her at some point about her life and her amazing skills as a baker.

That was an interview Carol was looking forward to.

CHAPTER THREE

May 28th, 1902
Boise, Idaho

THE EARLY MORNING air still had a chill to it, but to Megan, it felt wonderful after being so long around the hot ovens in the kitchen.

After her nights baking were done, she almost always went out onto the rough boards of the sidewalk on the west side of the hotel to just get some fresh air and sometimes enjoy the sunrise hitting the mountains. It helped her clear her mind so she could take a long bath and then sleep with her drapes drawn through much of the day.

This morning she felt a little more lightheaded than usual. She hoped she wasn't coming down with something.

She leaned against the large stone of the hotel wall and made herself take deep breaths.

As she stood there, a beautiful woman by the name of Carol Kogan came from the direction of the stables.

Megan knew Miss Kogan usually took her breakfast in the Idanha Restaurant and numbers of times had sent her notes complimenting one of Megan's breads or desserts.

Megan pushed away from the wall, standing as a lady would stand when meeting another lady on a sidewalk in public.

She had actually never met Miss Kogan, but she knew her by reputation. Single, age of twenty-seven, and a scholar who lived out along Warm Springs in the Historical Institute there.

Megan had never heard what Miss Kogan was studying, but found the fact that a woman could study any form of science to be a fantastic thing.

As Miss Kogan neared, Megan could see her up close.

Megan's breath caught.

She could feel herself attracted to Miss Kogan. No woman had done that ever before, but Miss Kogan was more beautiful than Megan had heard.

Far, far more beautiful.

Miss Kogan was tall, with long blonde hair tucked under a hat, green eyes, and a smile that seemed to light up her face. If Megan hadn't already been a little faint, more than likely Miss Kogan's looks would have caused it.

Megan had never had a reaction like that before to another woman.

Ever.

It didn't seem right.

But yet it felt right.

"Mrs. Taber," Miss Kogan said, bowing slightly. "The honor is all mine."

Megan knew she still had on her apron and more than likely had flour in her short brown hair. But that was who she was and there was no point in putting on airs.

She bowed slightly as well and somehow managed to get her mouth to speak, even while staring at the beautiful face and green eyes and bright smile. "Miss Kogan, thank you for the compliments you have sent to me. I treasure them."

"And I treasure the wonderful art you put into your pastries and breads," Miss Kogan said. "And please, call me Carol."

"I would be honored," Megan said, "If you would call me Megan as well."

Carol's smile could have lit up the entire street. Megan didn't want to look away from those fantastic eyes.

"I have traveled a great deal," Carol said, "and have never seen the likes of what you do. You are why I ride into town every day for breakfast."

"I am very honored," Megan said, bowing slightly again and feeling herself blush. She could not believe that Carol also thought of what Megan did as an art. How wonderful was that?

Someone who understood and appreciated.

Megan was going to say something along those lines when the world around her started to spin and she felt a pain in her chest.

A sharp, intense pain, like she had never felt before.

"I seem to feel a little…" Megan said, her voice trailing off.

And then everything went black as Carol looked shocked and stepped toward Megan as she fell.

CHAPTER FOUR

May 28th, 1902
Boise, Idaho

CAROL HAD BEEN so stunned when Megan suddenly fell forward that she almost didn't react fast enough. But somehow she managed to catch the thin and very light woman under her arms and ease her to the ground.

Megan's face was white and she was damp and not breathing at all.

Two men had come around the corner from the hotel and Carol glanced up. "Call Doctor Stevens. Quickly. He is usually at breakfast inside the hotel."

One man turned and ran while the other came to see what he could do to help.

Carol felt for a pulse.

None.

Christ, was it possible that Megan had just had a heart attack? She looked so young and so healthy.

Carol eased Megan's head to the sidewalk and then placing both hands on her chest started doing compressions.

"What are you doing?" the man demanded.

"A new technique from the East," Carol said. "Her heart has stopped and I am trying to make it start again."

Carol knew that just saying that something was from the East explained most unusual things out West.

She worked until she heard Doctor Stevens come around the corner. Then she stopped and took Megan's pulse.

Thank God! It was faint and there.

"What happened, Carol?" Doctor Stevens asked as he knelt down beside Megan.

Doctor Stevens looked more like he belonged in a poker room in Denver. He was tall, about forty, and wore gambler's clothing, including a pocket watch on a chain, and was often seen with a cigar sticking out of his mouth that he never lit. He was known to spend some evenings in the poker games in the basement of the Idanha Hotel and it had been Duster who had first introduced Carol to Doctor Stevens, which had helped.

Carol eased back and cradled Megan's head to let Doctor Stevens get in closer. "This is Megan Taber, the bakery chef here. She just passed out as I was talking with her. It looks like a heart attack."

Doctor Stevens nodded, not taking his attention away from Megan.

Carol admired Doctor Stevens and he seemed to give her some respect even though she had never told him she was a medical doctor. Women medical doctors were very, very rare in the west and were usually just looked at with a skeptical eye.

It wasn't much better back East during this time period.

Carol had spent many hours interviewing Doctor Stevens for her book and they had enjoyed many a lively conversation about women's health issues of this time.

As Doctor Stevens looked Megan over, Carol saw Megan take a shallow breath.

Relief flooded over Carol. At least Megan was breathing for the moment. Better than she had been a moment before.

Doctor Stevens glanced around at the dozen men and four women who were watching. "Two of you men get a wagon hitched up and some blankets and padding. We need to get this woman to the hospital."

Carol stroked Megan's head softly. "It's going to be all right."

But Carol honestly didn't know if it was going to be all right.

A woman of Megan's age having a heart attack usually meant something else was very, very wrong.

CHAPTER FIVE

May 28th, 1902
Boise, Idaho

MEGAN AWOKE IN the hospital.

The smell of piss and blood almost gagged her. And her chest hurt as if she had been stepped on by a horse.

No, more like a team of horses.

She had no idea what had happened or why she was here.

A woman with dark black hair and a brown-stained nun's uniform that had been white at one point was sitting beside Megan, clearly monitoring her.

Megan tried to sit up, but the nun instantly held her from doing so. "You can't be moving. Your heart will not stand for it."

"What happened?" Megan asked, her voice dry. The pain in her chest was more than she could imagine. It alternated between a throb and a stabbing pain, like someone was sticking a knife in her.

The nurse gave her a sip of water that felt wonderful.

"About an hour ago you fainted on the sidewalk in front of me," a woman's voice said from the other side of Megan's bed.

She turned to see Carol standing there, smiling while looking worried.

Megan could feel herself blushing. She must be even more of a mess now after fainting. And for some reason that was important to her in front of Carol.

Megan nodded and glanced around. She could tell she was in the fairly new Saint Alphonsus Hospital off of State Street, about seven blocks from the hotel. The Catholic Sisters of the Holy Cross had built the three-story stone building as the first major hospital in Boise. Megan had never expected to see the insides of it as a patient.

At least she had hoped she never would.

"Did you bring me here?" Megan asked Carol after a moment, looking back up into those wonderful green eyes.

"I did," Carol said, nodding, "along with two of the staff at the Idanha and Doctor Stevens. The staff needed to return to work, and Doctor Stevens wanted to finish his breakfast, so I told them I would report in on your condition."

"Thank you," Megan said, now feeling even more embarrassed that such a beautiful lady had to have been bothered.

"I hope you don't mind," Carol said, "but at the Institute in which I reside out in Warm Springs, there is a major heart doctor from the East who happens to be visiting. I have asked him to take a look at you."

"I don't think that will be necessary," Megan said.

"It is," the nun said from the other side of the bed. "Your heart is not sounding good, so we want you to have the best care."

Megan looked at the stern, but clearly concerned Catholic nun, then back at Carol. "Thank you."

Carol smiled that wonderful smile of hers. "My desire to help is purely selfish, of course. A breakfast without your wonderful bread would not be the same."

Megan smiled back, but didn't have the energy to even say thank you again.

A moment later the pain took her back into sleep and back in the blackness.

CHAPTER SIX

May 28th, 1902
Boise, Idaho

CAROL MADE THE nuns promise to watch out for Megan and report her progress to Doctor Stevens, then with one last look at the beautiful woman in the bed, Carol mounted up and rode hard for the Institute.

The Historical Institute was a large, three-story Victorian-style mansion on Warm Springs Avenue two miles to the east of Boise. Two other similar mansions were on either side of the main home. All looked like homes of the very rich with large grounds, stables behind them, and stone walls along the wagon trail that was Warm Springs Avenue.

All three buildings had been built by Duster and Bonnie Kendal and other travelers into this timeline. Counting her, there were twenty-nine travelers sanctioned to go back into this time period. She had no idea why they picked her, but she would be forever thankful that Bonnie and Duster and the other Institute members had.

The main building was called the Historical Institute and the other two were just disguised as homes and were used as homes for Institute staff and apartments. Under all three building was a vast cavern complex that had been built in the early 1880s with workers from the East coast.

Coming up on the three homes sitting on the banks of the Boise River, you could never tell what they hid.

Carol grabbed a quick snack as she went past the kitchen in the cavern under the main building and then went down two flights of stairs to another large cavern that held supplies for this time period. There was no one around, as she expected. With only 29 people allowed back in this time period, they almost never crossed paths.

The big cavern looked more like a vast department store of anything anyone might need in 1902, all stacked on wooden tables or hung from clothing racks. She had done some shopping and added some items herself to it over her last two trips here. Each person who was allowed back had their own area of cus-tom-fit clothing. Her area was far larger than any closet she could ever imagine having.

She went through the large supply cav-ern and through the second door on the right in a vast line of doors in the rock wall.

Through the door was a long, thin tunnel carved from the rock. She bet it was deeper than the length of a football field, but had never bothered to go very deep into the room.

Down the center set wooden tables with small wooden boxes on each table. Along both sides of the long tunnel, a wire fence blocked off the stone walls. Carved into the walls were niches hold-ing thousands of glowing crystals.

She knew each crystal was a timeline similar to the one she was now in and similar, if not almost exactly like the one she had came from.

She understood the basics of alternate timelines, but most of the time thinking about it just gave her a headache. She did understand that right now in an infinite number of timelines she was doing the same exact thing.

In the future, even though she had been in 1902 this time for over six months, she was only aging just over two minutes in 2019. So she knew that when she had left, Bonnie and Duster had been sitting with Director Parks in the main cavern room eating lunch at the kitchen counter. Now she hoped they were still there.

To her six months had passed, to them it would be less than ten minutes. Another part of traveling in time that gave her a headache thinking about. But a part she really loved.

She moved down the tunnel to a table with two wires coming out of the wire fence and attaching to a box. She glanced at the timepiece on the box and made a note that it was May 28th, 1902, just a few minutes after ten in the morning.

When she came back from the future, she wanted to arrive just a few minutes after this point so as to not start a new timeline. She needed to go back to spend time with Megan in the hospital if what she was planning didn't work out.

She put on a thick leather glove and then pulled one wire from the machine, leaving the other wire attached and the two wires attached to the crystal. She had just jumped to April 9th, 2019.

And as normal, she hadn't felt a thing.

She headed back out of the tunnel and closed and locked the door behind her, then through the supply room and up the two flights to the cavern.

As she had hoped, Bonnie and Duster and Director Parks were still sitting there at the lunch counter. They looked almost finished with their lunches.

She had been gone six months, they had barely gotten through half their meal.

Duster was a tall man who normally wore a long gray duster and a large cow-boy hat. In the Old West he was known most as Marshal Kendal. Right now he sat with his hat on the counter and his coat tossed over a chair beside him. He had on jeans and a tan dress shirt with the sleeves rolled up.

He and Bonnie had lived for more thousands of years in the past than Carol wanted to think about, but they both looked just barely over thirty.

Bonnie was a beautiful woman with long brown hair and dark eyes that felt like they could see into Carol's most guarded thoughts. Carol would have been attracted to her instantly, but Bonnie and Duster were a team centuries old now and still clearly very much in love.

Besides being major figures in a lot of timelines in the past, here they were known as the two top mathematicians working and they had invented the ability to jump to different timelines, a secret only thirty people knew.

Director Parks was the same height as Duster with strong shoulders and a commanding presence. He always wore jeans and a dress shirt with the sleeves rolled up. Carol respected and admired him and what he was managing to do with the Institute. Not only did he run it here, but also in the past and in the future. How he kept all that straight was beyond Carol.

Duster turned and saw her coming and nodded.

"How was the trip, Doctor?" Bonnie asked.

"Cut short," Carol said as she moved around and took a bottle of water from the fridge. She then faced the three who had given her this incredible opportunity to travel in time. She wasn't sure if she was about to hurt her standing here with what she was about to ask or not.

But she had to try to save Megan.

Carol hadn't felt this strongly about another human being in a long time. She couldn't lose Megan now even though she really didn't know her at all.

"What happened?" Director Parks asked. Then he pointed to how she was still dressed in 1902 riding clothes. "Clearly you are planning on going back quickly."

"I am," Carol said. "Megan Taber basically had a pretty massive heart attack while talking with me outside the Idanha Hotel."

Duster nodded. "May 28th, 1902. The hotel restaurant was never really the same without her and that wonderful bread and desserts she used to make."

"Doctor," Bonnie said, looking at Carol. "There's something you are not saying, isn't there?"

"I was there on the sidewalk with her when she had the heart attack and I managed to bring her back to life," Carol said, nodding. "Doctor Stevens and I got her to Saint Al's and she is holding on there."

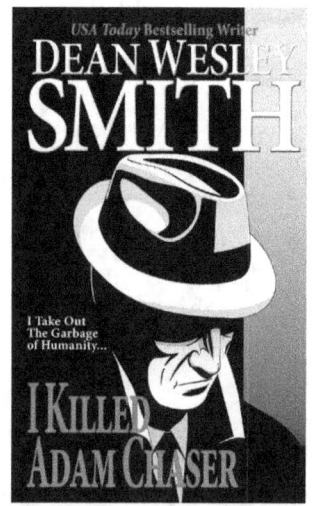 

Two Classic Dean Wesley Smith Stories
Available at your favorite booksellers.

"I think in other timelines before now she dies on the street," Duster said, nodding, "if memory serves. But I may be wrong about that. I do know she dies in most time-lines around the time this happened for you."

Bonnie was nodding, frowning.

"She's going to die anyway without some major surgery," Carol said.

"That's too bad," Parks said, shaking his head.

But Bonnie was still staring at Carol. "You want to save her, don't you?"

"I do," Carol said, staring into Bonnie's deep eyes. "Megan is a very special woman."

Bonnie nodded and glanced at her husband, a worried look on her face.

Duster just shook his head and Director Parks sighed.

"Do you think you can save her, Doctor?" Duster asked finally, turning and facing Carol directly.

"Here, maybe," Carol said, nodding. "There is a chance I can with a good heart team and if we can get her here safely."

"So you are suggesting we bring a woman from 1902 to 2019?" Director Parks asked.

"I am," Carol said.

"She will be forever hooked to this time period if we do that?" Bonnie said.

"I will take the responsibility of showing her and teaching her this time," Carol said.

Silence in the big cavern.

Then Duster said, "We knew that bringing someone from the past would be a possibility at some point."

"We did," Parks said, nodding.

"And if we can save her," Bonnie said, "she could make us some of that wonderful bread that melts in your mouth."

"A complete positive point," Duster said, smiling and looking at Carol.

"Are you sure?" Bonnie asked Carol.

"She's wonderful and if we can save her," Carol said, "I would like to try."

Director Parks again sighed and then smiled, shaking his head. "I'll get her a phony background and identification papers and warn the hospital that we might have a major heart case headed their way in a few minutes."

Bonnie nodded, smiled, and stood. "Let's go. We have a woman to save."

Carol almost jumped up and down for joy as Parks headed for his office.

Duster picked up his coat and put it and his hat on.

Then the three of them turned toward the staircase down to the cavern and the way to 1902.

With luck, in a few minutes in this time, they would return with a very sick, but still alive Megan Taber.

With a lot of luck.

CHAPTER SEVEN

May 28th, 1902
Boise, Idaho

MEGAN AWOKE IN the back of a wagon with low sides as it eased over a large bump in a road. She had remembered being in the hospital the last time she awoke, so she had no idea why anyone would be moving her.

Above her she could see the blue morning sky and some trees with new leaves.

She felt tired and her chest hurt with a throbbing pain.

Two women sat beside her in the back of the wagon, steadying her. One was Carol, the other was a stranger she did not recognize, but who seemed very concerned.

Megan could see above her head that a tall man in a duster and cowboy hat drove the team. He seemed familiar, but she couldn't place him in her pain-filled mind.

"She seems to be waking up," the strange woman said.

Carol leaned forward and stared into Megan's eyes while smiling. "Welcome back."

Megan just nodded. She had never seen such caring in another person's eyes before. She liked seeing that from Carol.

Liked it a great deal, actually.

"I'm going to give you something," Carol said, "to help you sleep and take down the stress on your heart."

Megan nodded, but said nothing.

"We are doing our best to save your life," Carol said. "Please, please just hold on."

Megan nodded, then whispered, "Thank you. You are wonderful."

With that, Carol gently stuck something into Megan's arm and once again she fell into the blackness.

CHAPTER EIGHT

May 28th, 1902
Boise, Idaho

CAROL HAD BEEN stunned how easy it was for her and Bonnie and Duster to get Megan out of the hospital. It seemed that Duster had donated a very large percentage of the money needed to build the hospital.

And Dr. Stevens was there and had helped them bundle Megan up carefully and move her to the wagon on a stretcher. He also clearly knew Duster very well. As they finished loading Megan, Doctor Stevens said he hoped this would work.

Duster assured him it was the best chance Megan had and all Doctor Stevens had said was, "It's her only chance. It's amazing she has lasted this long."

Carol felt the same way. Too much time had gone by, and with this sort of heart problem, time was everything.

The ride in the wagon the two miles to the Institute along the rough Warm Springs Avenue was torturous as far as Carol was concerned. She worried about every bump and jolt. Duster did a wonderful job keeping the team moving slowly and steadily, but it was still a wagon and it was still rough.

Carol sat over Megan, alternating between staring at her and then at the trail ahead.

After Megan had woken up and Carol had given Megan a sedative to put her back under, Bonnie smiled at Carol.

"Really falling for Megan, huh?" Bonnie asked Carol softly enough that Duster wouldn't hear over the rattling of the buckboard.

Carol looked into Bonnie's understanding eyes, then down at Megan. And then slowly nodded. "I just wished I could have moved faster, got to her before now."

Carol was very much amazed at herself. She really was falling for Megan, a woman about to die at any moment. A woman who might die on the operating table even if they got her to the future in time.

How insane was this?

Bonnie patted Carol's hand where it rested on Megan.

Carol again glanced up at Bonnie who was smiling softly, clearly understanding how Carol felt.

By the time Duster pulled the wagon into the long Institute driveway, Megan was dead.

Carol spent twenty minutes trying to get Megan's heart restarted, but it was clear the weakness in Megan's heart had finally just given way.

"Well shit," Duster said when Carol finally shook her head and sat back.

She was breathing hard and fighting tears of loss and frustration.

And anger.

She was a doctor, she wanted to save everyone, damn it.

Especially a woman she cared about.

Megan looked beautiful even in death. Carol had a hunch she would think Megan beautiful in any situation, but now was never going to get the chance.

Around them the morning air was starting to heat up and the day promised to be a wonderful early summer day. Carol just sat staring up into the branches of the big oak trees as both Duster and Bonnie allowed the silence to go on for a minute.

Finally Bonnie said softly, "Let's take Megan back to the undertaker, tell Doc Stevens what happened, and get Megan a good resting place up in Morris Hill Cemetery."

Bonnie gently touched Carol's arm.

Carol nodded. It was the least they could do.

Amazing how devastated she felt and she hadn't really even known Megan. But it still felt like Carol's own heart had been ripped out.

Carol reached over and pulled the blanket up over Megan's face.

"Goodbye, beautiful one."

As a doctor, she had seen her share of death already. But this one she knew, without a doubt, she was going to remember for a very long time.

"After we get that arranged," Duster said, "We can go back to 2019 and do some planning on how to save Megan the next time around. We now know waiting this long doesn't work."

Carol had been starting to climb down off the buckboard. Her head snapped around to stare at Duster.

"Save Megan? What are you talking about?"

Duster smiled. "Infinite timelines. In an infinite number of timelines Megan dies on the sidewalk with no one there. In an infinite number, you are there, but Megan dies like this."

Duster pointed at Megan in the back of the wagon.

"So we go and plan how we can go back and save Megan in another infinite number of timelines," Bonnie said, smiling at Carol.

Carol just couldn't let herself believe that was possible. She just stared at Bonnie and Duster. And then she looked around at where she was in 1902, far over a hundred years in her own history.

If standing here was possible, maybe what they were saying was possible.

And just a little of the ache left her heart. And a little hope crept into the back of her mind.

Just a little.

"I'm going to trust you on that," Carol said, nodding. "And you can explain it to me later. But if there is a chance we can save her, I need to know what killed her here."

Both Duster and Bonnie frowned.

"I need to take her inside and open her up to see what went wrong with her heart," Carol said.

Both Bonnie and Duster nodded. "If I had modern equipment, I would take some scans of Megan's body, find out what happened exactly. See if she actually can be saved. But since I don't, opening her up and letting me inspect her heart will help a great deal."

Both nodded and Duster turned toward the door of the Institute. "I'll get a wheelchair and we can wheel Megan in that way."

Carol nodded and took a deep breath and looked at the blanket covering Megan's body. As a doctor, Carol just couldn't understand how that woman under that blanket could be brought back to life.

But it really wouldn't be that exact same woman.

But yet it would be.

The exact same woman.

Alternate timelines just gave Carol a headache.

But right now, she was very thankful they existed.

PART TWO
A Second Chance

CHAPTER NINE

Six months earlier…

November 6th, 1901
Boise, Idaho

MEGAN TOOK OFF her long blue apron after a long night's shift. She had just checked to make sure all her breads were being stored correctly for the morning breakfast rush, and her pies and cakes were stored on racks cooling.

Around her the wonderful-smelling large kitchen of the Idanha Hotel was coming alive with breakfast orders and preparation for the day.

At night she often had the kitchen all to herself. She liked it that way, but she never minded when the breakfast cooks arrived and the wait staff started to prepare the dining room.

She followed the same routine every morning before leaving for a breath of fresh air and then a bath and long sleep. Taking off her apron was the last detail in that routine.

She knew that outside the night had brought a light dusting of snow fairly early for the valley, and the air would have a sharp bite to it. But that would feel good after the long night in front of the ovens, even if she only stepped outside for a few seconds.

"Mrs. Taber," Chef Pickner said from behind her. "There are three early diners who would like a moment of your time."

She turned and looked into the smiling face of the man who had hired her. He was shorter than her by a good five inches and very round, seeming to play into the look that most thought chefs should be. His hair was balding and his eyebrows as bushy as she had ever seen. They often caught flour or bits of food in them and one of the other chefs was always giving him the sign to clean off his face.

She was about to object when he handed her a wicker basket full of her freshly-made bread covered in a white towel to keep the bread warm.

"Smothered in butter as you instruct," the chef said, smiling. "Just deliver these to the table near the fireplace. Two men and a woman."

She nodded and smoothed down her dress. "Am I presentable?"

The chef nodded. "As always."

He then turned away with a smile, leaving her standing there with the basket of breads in her hand.

She had no idea what this was about, but it seemed she had no choice.

She took a deep breath and went through the door and into the dining room.

The light from outside was faint as it was still a while before full sunrise. She could see snowflakes swirling around the windows. The large stone fireplace crackled with a roaring fire in the far corner and the high-ceilinged room felt cooler than the kitchen had felt, but still comfortable.

All the tables were made of polished oak and covered in fine tan tablecloths. Cloth napkins were folded perfectly at every place and the silverware gleamed in the lamplight.

Candles were lit in the center of every table as well, giving the room an intimate feel.

Only four tables of diners this early in the morning occupied the large room. With such nasty weather, she was amazed even that many had come out.

The three early diners she had been instructed to go talk to were sitting near the window facing Main Street. They were close to the fire, but not too close.

Dr. Stevens was one of them and she smiled at that. He had tried to save her husband all those years ago after her husband fell and hit his head. Then Dr. Stevens had helped her get a job in a kitchen, which had started her baking life.

She owed Dr. Stevens and loved talking with him when she could. Thankfully, in the over six years since her husband had died, she hadn't needed to go see Dr. Stevens for any medical problems other than being lightheaded. He had told her it was because she had a bad heart and there was nothing that could be done. The doctor back home had told her that as well. She had been shocked at first, but then she had just accepted that and moved on.

Except for the lightheaded times, she felt wonderfully healthy, something she was grateful for every day.

99

The other two at the table she felt she knew from around town, but didn't know them by name.

As she approached, both men stood.

Dr. Stevens stuck out his hand and with a smile said, "Megan, you are looking wonderful as always."

"Thank you, Doctor," she said smiling back.

"This is Bonnie and Duster Kendal," Dr. Stevens said, introducing her. "This is Mrs. Megan Taber."

Duster Kendal bowed slightly and Bonnie said, "Wonderful meeting you."

"Can you join us for a few moments?" Duster asked, moving to hold a chair for her.

"Oh, I'm such a fright," Megan said. "I've been baking all night."

"Just for a moment," Bonnie said. "You look wonderful."

Megan smiled and sat down, enjoying the compliment from such an attractive woman.

Megan felt honored to be with Doctor Stevens and she knew of Bonnie and Duster by reputation around town as well.

"First off," Dr. Stevens said, opening the cloth covering the bread basket she had brought and pulling out a piece of warm bread glistening with melted butter. "I want to once again compliment you on this bread. I have no idea how you do it."

"It is wonderful," Bonnie said, smiling at Megan.

"Of that I can't argue in the slightest," Duster said and took the basket, helping himself to a piece as well.

"Thank you," Megan said, blushing. "Just having you all enjoy the bread makes my day."

"We enjoy it everyday," Dr. Stevens said, laughing.

Megan could feel herself blushing even more. Then for the next few minutes they talked about the weather and how the first snow had come early this year.

Then Duster turned to Megan. "Besides wanting to officially meet the wonderful baker who can produce such treats, we wanted to ask you a favor."

That surprised Megan. She had no idea what kind of help she could be to three such prominent citizens.

"We have a friend who is doing a study of major women of the west," Bonnie said. "Her name is Carol Kogan and she has asked if she could spend some time with you and ask you some questions."

Megan opened her mouth, then closed it. No words seemed to want to come out.

"You are known all over the west for your skills in baking," Dr. Stevens said, smiling at Megan.

Megan had started to realize that when she had recently gotten job offers from major San Francisco hotels. She didn't want to move, to leave Boise, and she had told Chef Pickner about the offers and promised him she would stay as long as he wanted her.

He had been very thankful for that.

Besides, she loved her apartment in this wonderful hotel and couldn't imagine living anywhere else.

"I have no desire to leave here," Megan said.

"Oh, we know that," Bonnie said, smiling. "Our friend is just doing research for a book. She's a well-known writer and would love to talk and spend some time with you. We just said we would ask you is all. Nothing more."

Bonnie looked at the two men who were enjoying her breakfast bread, then at the smiling face of Bonnie.

"If you think it would help," Megan said, "I would love to meet with her."

"Wonderful," Duster said. "We'll have her come by when she arrives in town."

"Thank you," Bonnie said, smiling. "I think you will really like Carol."

"I'm sure I will," Megan said, wondering what she had gotten herself into. "I'm sure I will."

CHAPTER TEN

November 8th, 1901
Boise, Idaho

CAROL COULDN'T BELIEVE she was about to meet Megan, the same woman who had died in the back of that wagon. She dropped off her horse and handed the reins to the man in the stable behind the Idanha Hotel.

She had a dinner scheduled with Megan in twenty minutes. She hadn't been this nervous since her first date in high school. And it had been on that double date when she realized she wasn't into boys because she kept staring at Betty Conrad, the other girl.

And Betty kept staring and flirting back.

She and Betty had ended up dating secretly most of their high school years before both going off to college in different directions. Those had been fun years. Scary years, but fun, since both of them had decided to remain completely hidden until college.

Now Carol was about to meet a woman Carol had watched die. Duster and Bonnie had made sure Carol understood that death was another timeline. The Megan that Carol was about to meet was the same Megan, sure, with the same heart problem, just very much alive.

But if Carol didn't do something, Megan would have a heart attack on May 28th and die from it.

Or maybe die sooner.

Just no way of telling.

The problem was that Carol wasn't sure she could do anything to save Megan.

When Carol had opened up Megan's body in the other timeline, it was clear her heart was badly damaged. And that damage had extended into the area around her heart as well. Megan needed, at best, a quadruple bypass and that might not even be enough.

Megan had a genetically weak heart and Carol was surprised Megan had lasted as long as she had.

So in talking with Bonnie and Duster about the problem in 2019 and doing some research, Bonnie had suggested that Carol jump ahead to 2119 and talk with some doctors there about the problem.

Carol had been surprised at first, even though on the first day of her introduction to timeline travel, Director Parks had taken her two hundred years into the future to set her timeline there.

So if something happened to Carol in 2019, she would wake up in 2119 with only two minutes having past. And if something happened to her there, she would wake up in 2219 with only two minutes having past.

In other words, for all intents and purposes, she was immortal.

But her focus had always been the past, not exploring the future, so when Bonnie had suggested Carol go for more advanced medical help, the idea had shocked her.

And then made her a little angry that she hadn't thought of it herself.

She wasn't even sure if she could understand the medical techniques of the one hundred years in the future. She had a hunch what she had been trained to do would look as outdated and barbaric as some of the medical practices of Dr. Stevens in 1902.

And Carol wasn't sure if she was willing to learn that just yet about her own skills and years of training.

But saving Megan's life had outweighed her hesitation and, with Director Parks at her side, they had gone forward to 2119 to talk with medical friends of the Institute.

Sadly, even in a hundred years, there was no magic formula for fixing a badly damaged heart past replacement or bypass surgery. Granted, the operations were far less intrusive and most of the heart replace valves or full hearts were grown from the patient's own stem cells to avoid any chance of rejection.

But it was still a major operation.

And it took time to grow the heart and valves. Three months or more.

Megan didn't have three months, but there was a chance that the machines of the future could keep her brain and body alive while she waited.

Not a great chance, but a chance.

In the future, however, Megan's condition would have been caught when she was young and fixed then and monitored going forward.

But even with all that, the heart condition Megan had resulted in the deaths of a lot of people even a hundred years in the future.

Carol knew this battle to save Megan was not going to be easy.

On the way back to 2019, Director Parks had suggested they try to get Megan forward in time to 2119 and Carol had agreed.

Megan could have the surgery there and then be brought back to 2019 to recover.

That had sounded so simple.

But how do you convince a woman in 1902 that first off, she had a bad heart that was about to kill her, and that she needed to travel over two hundred years in the future to have any chance of living.

Impossible.

Carol had no doubt about that.

CHAPTER ELEVEN

November 8th, 1901
Boise, Idaho

MEGAN FELT NERVOUS. She had on one of her best skirts and blouses, an outfit she normally saved for special occasions such as a staff member of the hotel getting married. The skirt was a pleated blue and the blouse a loose white with silk on the neck and sleeves. She wore a light matching blue jacket over her blouse and a small string of pearls from her mother.

She wasn't sure why she was nervous. This Carol Kogan sounded nice and impressive and wanted to just talk. Megan figured that was what was making her nervous, that someone actually valued beyond their table what she did every night.

She brushed down her skirt one more time, then checked to make sure her hair was in place, even though as short as it was, there wasn't much she could do with it.

Then she left her apartment on the main floor of the hotel near the back and walked down the hallway toward the large hotel foyer and restaurant beyond. She usually turned at an unmarked door about halfway down the hallway that led into the kitchen area, but this time she just kept walking, forcing herself to breathe evenly. Last thing she needed to do was get lightheaded tonight.

And besides, after dinner, she needed to go to work as normal to prepare the breads and pastries for the following day.

She nodded to the desk clerk as she moved across the stone floors of the foyer and into the open restaurant doors beyond.

Stan, the evening host, greeted her with a smile. "You look wonderful this evening, Mrs. Taber."

"Thank you, Stan," she said, bowing slightly.

"Your guest is waiting at the table near the front window," Stan said, indicating that she should follow him.

As she approached, the woman she was meeting glanced around and seemed shocked.

Actually, it was Megan who felt shocked. The woman was stunningly beautiful and dressed in a similar style as Megan was.

The woman stood and extended her hand after a moment. "Mrs. Taber, I am Carol Kogan. The honor is all mine to finally meet you."

Megan took Miss Kogan's hand and was stunned at how soft and wonderful it felt. She didn't want to let it go.

And she didn't want to stop staring into Miss Kogan's eyes either. They were the most beautiful green Megan had ever seen.

Stan moved around her and pulled out her chair, so Megan released Miss Kogan's hand and sat, allowing Miss Kogan to sit again as well.

"Would you enjoy a beverage to start?" Stan asked.

"Water would be wonderful," Megan said.

Stan nodded and turned away.

Megan looked at Carol, who was staring at her as well.

"Call me Megan," she said, deciding to break the ice a little.

"I'm Carol. And I apologize for staring, but I hope you don't mind if I say you are a very beautiful woman."

Megan could feel herself blush a little along her neck. She laughed. "Not at all because I was thinking the same of you."

Now Carol blushed slightly and laughed.

Over the evening they managed to talk about their pasts, about how Megan's husband had died, and then finally her baking.

To Megan, the conversation was wonderful, the most enjoyable she had had in a very, very long time.

And the more they talked, the more she liked Carol. And the more time Megan wanted to spend with Carol.

For dinner they both had the baked trout with small potatoes and both had a piece of a cherry pie she had baked last night to finish off their meal. In so many ways, their tastes were very, very similar.

"So what exactly is this project you are working on?" Megan asked after they were both sipping tea after their dessert.

"Strong women of the west, in general," Carol said. "Their health needs in more specific."

Megan nodded. She had been stunned at what she had been required to do during those first few months of marriage. The chores had been backbreaking and looking back at it, she couldn't imagine how she had survived.

"So why me?" Megan asked.

"Besides wanting to meet you?" Carol asked, smiling.

Megan blushed at that slightly, but smiled back. "I'm glad I met you as well."

"So besides that wonderful benefit," Carol said, "you are a well-known woman of the west because of your baking skills and art. So you were a logical choice and I am forever thankful to Dr. Stevens and Duster and Bonnie for giving me an introduction."

"Tell them I am thankful as well," Megan said, smiling at Carol. "And you consider my baking an art?"

"I do," Carol said nodding, a very serious look in her eyes. "Anyone can toss together what it takes to make bread or a pie as we just ate, but it takes an artist to make them taste the way you do."

"Thank you," Megan said. She knew her face was red and she looked down away from the wonderful and intense green eyes.

"I didn't mean to embarrass you," Carol said.

Megan smiled and looked back into Carol's worried eyes. "You didn't. It's how I feel about my baking yet never say. So thank you."

Carol smiled and nodded and the two sat there staring at each other for the longest and most wonderful time.

CHAPTER TWELVE

November 9th, 1901
Boise, Idaho

CAROL HAD MOVED into the hotel because the weather made it too difficult at times to make the two-mile ride to the Institute. And that way she could be closer to Megan as well.

Megan seemed very pleased when she heard that Carol was staying in a suite

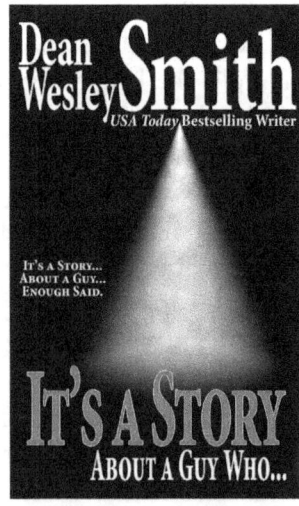

on the top floor of the hotel. And she was even more pleased when Carol had asked to see her at breakfast to continue getting to know her better.

"I usually have my breakfast in my rooms," Megan said. "So if you don't mind meeting there, I would enjoy the conversation."

"I would love that," Carol said, trying to keep her excitement under control.

"But I must warn you," Megan said. "I will have just worked all night around hot ovens. I might not be very presentable."

Carol laughed. "At that time of the morning, I am never presentable either. I will put on just enough to not be indecent in the hallways."

"Deal," Megan had said.

They had parted with a wonderful handshake and a light kiss on each other's cheek. Carol almost floated back to her suite. She felt better than a high school first date. She had no doubt that she had just met a woman she could fall for completely.

She had no idea if Megan felt the same way in reverse, and with the moral times of 1901, she had no idea how Megan felt about anything around two women being together. So Carol needed to go slowly and keep firmly in mind when and where she was..

Otherwise she would lose Megan and, if she did that, chances are Megan would die once again next May. And Carol didn't want that to happen.

She had an alarm set for just before five in the morning since Megan had said she usually got off work around five-thirty. The night was pitch black outside the windows and not even the street-lights along Main Street pushed back the darkness.

Carol could feel the cold through the windows and got the fires in the suite's two fireplaces stoked back up.

She shivered as she put on riding slacks and clean 2019 underwear and a clean blouse and riding boots.

She splashed cold water on her face and brushed back her hair and then just at five-thirty in the morning left her suite.

She actually met Megan coming down the hallway outside her room from the kitchen.

Megan's smile lit up the dim hallway. "Perfect timing."

"For working all night," Carol said, giving Megan a light peck on the cheek just as they had parted with, "you sound very much awake."

"Oh, I will be for another hour just from the momentum from working," Megan said. "After that, no guarantees."

Carol watched as Megan opened her door and went inside.

The rooms, as she called them, were similar to Carol's suite four floors up. Megan had a wonderful living room with a fireplace that was burning softly. Books lay scattered around a few tables and a heavy patchwork quilt was tossed aside on the back of one of two couches facing the fireplace.

"This is wonderful," Carol said, looking around. It felt comfortable and lived in.

"I enjoy it," Megan said, moving into the second room, which was a bedroom, and taking off her apron and hanging it up. Again a fireplace there was burning lightly. Clearly during the night Megan must have come from the kitchen and stoked the fireplaces to keep the rooms comfortably warm.

Megan had changed clothes since their meeting in the restaurant and wore a full dress tied at the waist with a cloth belt.

"Would you be a dear and help me with these buttons?" Megan asked as she started on unbuttoning her dress up the back.

"Glad to," Carol said, moving forward and hoping she could keep her hands from shaking.

She got the dress unbuttoned exposing a lace undergarment of some sort. Carol could feel herself growing slightly flushed as she stepped back. Being so close to Megan was just wonderful, but rushing could end everything.

"Thank you," Megan said, moving away and heading toward the bathroom. "Always feels good to get out of my nightly work clothes."

"I would wager it does," Carol said, watching Megan disappear into the bathroom, then turning to look at the room. The fact that Megan clearly was a reader pleased Carol more than she wanted to admit. She wasn't sure what she had expected, but this was a pleasant surprise.

Megan came out of the bathroom a few moments later wearing a long brown robe and slippers.

"I warned you I would be a sight," Megan said, moving toward another door that led into a small kitchen.

"I think you look wonderful," Carol said. "A hard-working woman who knows how to be comfortable after long hours on the job."

Megan stopped and glanced back at Carol. "Thank you."

Then Megan smiled and moved into the kitchen.

Carol followed Megan and sat at the small wooden kitchen table. Then they talked and laughed and Megan told Carol about her night as Carol watched the woman of her dreams put together a light breakfast of toast, jam, and juice for the two of them.

A perfect morning.

Just perfect.

CHAPTER THIRTEEN

November 9th, 1901
Boise, Idaho

MEGAN AGREED TO meet Carol that night for dinner again and they went across the street to a fine restaurant. This time they both had lamb and finished with tea instead of dessert.

And Megan noticed that neither of them tried the bread.

The conversation during dinner was light and fun and again, Megan couldn't believe how much she was enjoying Carol's company. She didn't want each meeting to end and from what she could tell, neither did Carol.

After breakfast that morning, Carol had left and Megan had gotten in to a warm bath. And all she could think about was wishing Carol was there to scrub her back and help her wash her hair.

She couldn't believe she could even think such thoughts, but they felt right and she was going to go with them.

And when she finally did get to sleep, the dreams were of her and Carol together.

She always knew, right from when she was a young girl, that she liked women better than men. Men just didn't interest her and marrying her husband had been of necessity to get out of that small Montana town.

But she had no idea if women could be together. Granted, there were two older women who always came in together for breakfast. But past that, Megan knew nothing more than that she really, really liked Carol.

And she knew if something came of meeting Carol, they would always have to be in secret.

But that didn't matter. She wanted to spend time with her as often as possible.

As they were sipping their tea, Megan decided to ask the question she was the most afraid of hearing an answer to.

"How long are you planning on staying here in Boise?"

Carol smiled that wonderful smile that Megan loved so much. "I was hoping to stay through the winter."

Megan could feel her heart leap and she put her teacup down for fear of her hands shaking. "That's wonderful news."

"It will be wonderful if I can continue to spend time with you and get to know you better," Carol said.

Then Megan saw that Carol flushed slightly.

Megan smiled when Carol looked down at her tea. Carol was actually embarrassed to have said that. How wonderful was that?

"I would love that," Megan said.

Carol looked back up and the two sat staring for a moment into each other's eyes.

"I'm glad you do," Carol said. "Very glad."

And after that moment, for Megan it was settled.

Every spare minute away from work or sleeping, she wanted to spend with Carol.

For the next few weeks, every morning the two of them met in Megan's rooms for a light breakfast.

Then they had dinner together and often went back to Megan's rooms to talk about books or just talk while Megan got ready for her nightly baking.

It was on the second week that things changed slightly, for the better as far as Megan was concerned. She was no longer doubting that Carol was attracted to her as much as she was attracted to Carol.

Some Classic Jukebox Stories
Available at your favorite booksellers.

And they had become very, very comfortable together. Megan felt that Carol was far smarter than she was, but yet they seemed to get along as equals.

And there was no doubt that Carol hid many, many things from Megan, but she didn't mind. She knew, given time, she would find out all about Carol's secrets.

So after breakfast, just as Carol was about to excuse herself, Megan said simply, "Would you mind scrubbing my back? That is a pleasure I have not had for a very long time."

Carol blushed and then nodded. "On one condition."

Megan laughed. "I find myself bargaining to have my back washed."

Carol laughed. "Not at all. I just hope that you will return the favor for me some morning, since I too have been far too long without my back getting washed correctly."

Again Megan laughed and she could feel herself blushing as well, trying not to let the image of Carol without clothes into her mind. "That is a bargain I can hold to."

And with that they both set to heating the water for the large tub in the bathroom.

CHAPTER FOURTEEN

November 21st, 1901
Boise, Idaho

CAROL MANAGED TO not gasp as Megan took off her robe and then slipped out of her underwear to step into the bathtub. She was the most beautiful woman Carol had seen without clothes.

Megan's body was firm and clearly in shape. Her breasts firm and rounded with small brown nipples. She had full brown pubic hair and a wonderful butt.

And she moved with a smoothness that was alluring, almost like a cat.

Megan seemed slightly embarrassed about being naked in front of Carol, but not too much. Not enough to even attempt to try to cover up.

"You are very beautiful," Carol said as Megan slid into the warm water with a sigh.

"Thank you," Megan said, looking up at where Carol stood beside the tub.

Carol had no doubt she was blushing and it was everything she could do to restrain taking off her clothes and climbing into the tub with Megan. She wasn't sure if Megan would mind. But the fear of moving too fast kept her in her clothes.

Carol pulled a chair close to the edge of the large tub, taking the soap and the washcloth and dipped it in the water to get some lather.

"You're going to get your blouse wet," Megan said.

Carol nodded. "Good point."

She quickly unbuttoned it, pulling it off and draping it over the edge of the nearby sink.

She turned back to see Megan watching her with a puzzled look on her face. That was when Carol realized her mistake. She was wearing a sports bra, nothing even close to what women wore in 1901.

"Is that as comfortable as it looks?" Megan asked.

That question surprised Carol. Not a question about what it was or where it was from, but of comfort.

"It is," Carol said, laughing and lathering up the washcloth. "I'll let you try one of mine on at some point."

"I'd like that," Megan said as she turned around so that her back was exposed to Carol.

Carol then spent the most wonderful ten minutes washing and rubbing Megan's smooth-skinned back.

Carol flat didn't want to stop, but she knew she had to if this wasn't to go any farther.

"Your touch is heavenly," Megan said, leaning back and stretching in the water. Carol could tell that Megan was relaxing and letting the long night slowly catch up with her.

"Your smooth skin is just as wonderful," Carol said, standing and picking up her blouse and slipping it back on.

"Leaving?" Megan said, glancing up at Carol.

"To give you some time to finish and get some sleep. I'll see you at seven for dinner?"

"That would be wonderful," Megan said. "And thank you for washing my back."

Now Available
**from all your favorite booksellers
in trade paper and electronic editions.**

"I can honestly say it was my pleasure," Carol said, smiling at the woman she was falling for her more and more every minute.

Carol barely made it out the door. Her heart was racing and she could feel her face blushing. She so wanted to just go back, strip off her clothes and climb in the tub.

But not this morning.

Maybe another morning.

The promise was there and just the idea of it made her short of breath.

CHAPTER FIFTEEN

November 21st, 1901
Boise, Idaho

CAROL RODE OUT to the Institute after breakfast to dig out a few more sports bras for Megan. The day was cold, but clear and the snow that had fallen earlier in the week had melted, leaving the wagon road rutted and muddy. The big oak trees surrounding the Institute had all lost their leaves and three large Victorian homes sitting side-by-side looked almost stark and alone so far out of town.

Carol went into the caverns and took a hot shower, wondering the entire time what Megan would think of the cavern and of a hot shower and modern bathroom.

There was no doubt that Megan needed to learn of the Institute sooner, rather than later. But Carol decided that after the first of the year might be the best time.

Besides, she still felt like the relationship between her and Megan was still just starting to really grow. No point in pushing the relationship and knowledge of where Carol came from too quickly.

By the time she made it back to the hotel, the sky was turning dark. It was still a few hours until dinner with Megan, so Carol went to her room to rest a little.

She hadn't been there for more than a few minutes when a knock at the door surprised her. It was a chambermaid that Carol had seen a few times but never talked with. The maid was very short, round, and had dark black hair. She had on the standard black skirt, white blouse and white long apron of all the house staff.

"Mrs. Taber has asked me to tell you," the maid said, bowing slightly, "that she is under the weather and won't be able to make dinner this evening."

Carol managed to keep her sudden fear under control.

Somehow.

She nodded, thanked the maid, then closed the door. It took her just two minutes of panicked movement to change out of her muddy riding clothes and into some clean riding clothes, grab her medical kit disguised in a cloth bag that looked like a sewing bag, and head out the door.

One minute and four floors later, she knocked lightly on Megan's door and then pushed it open.

Megan was lying on the couch under a colorful patchwork quilt made of wide gold and brown and orange patches. She looked pale and sweaty.

She looked up and smiled lightly at Carol.

"What's happening?" Carol asked, moving around and kneeling beside Megan.

"I think I turned too fast or something. I felt faint and I am told I passed out in the hallway about an hour ago." Megan shook her head and looked as if she might cry. "I am mortally embarrassed that Chef Pickner and one of the others found me and had to help me back here."

"Let me check you over," Carol said, pulling out a stethoscope disguised to look like it was from 1901 yet much better.

"You have medical training?" Megan asked as Carol eased down her blanket and then began to unbutton Megan's nightshirt.

"I do," Carol said, smiling. "One of the many secrets about me that I am sure you have wondered about, but been too polite to ask."

"Where were you trained?" Megan asked.

"Shhh," Carol said, putting the stethoscope against Megan's smooth skin just above her left breast. "I need to listen. I'll explain everything soon enough."

As Carol had feared, Megan's heart was working hard and was irregular. More than likely Megan had had a pretty good heart attack. If they were in 2019, Carol would have been rushing Megan to the hospital in an ambulance and prepping her for surgery.

But this was 1901. Resting would be the only thing possible and Carol just hoped it would settle Megan's heart back down. But the sooner she had the needed operation, the better off she would be, of that there was no doubt.

If she got through this attack.

After listening to everything she could, Carol stopped and put the stethoscope away.

"Well?" Megan asked as Carol buttoned up Megan's nightshirt and then pulled the quilt back into position. "I can feel it is not good."

"How long have you had these spells of feeling faint?" Carol asked, ignoring Megan's question.

"Since I was a young girl," Megan said.

"And what have doctors said about it?"

"Doctor Stevens said I have a weak and damaged heart and that someday it will just give out on me."

Carol nodded, taking Megan's hands and holding both of them and looking into Megan's wonderful brown eyes. "I'm afraid he is right."

"Doctor Stevens said there is nothing that can be done," Megan said, shrugging. "So I enjoy the time I have."

"He is only partially correct," Carol said. "And if you trust me for a while longer, I will tell you what I mean."

Megan looked at Carol, then smiled. "You knew about my bad heart before now, didn't you?"

Carol nodded.

"Why did you wait telling me?"

"Because I am afraid of losing you," Carol said, being as honest as she could be. "I want to spend a lot of time in the future with you."

Megan smiled. "I am already in love with you, my sweet. I can imagine nothing you might say that would change that."

Carol nodded and leaned in and gently kissed Megan.

And after a moment, Megan kissed her back.

Carol finally broke the kiss and stood. "Now I must get you some soup and then you must tell me a book you enjoy so I can read to you until you fall asleep."

"The chef is making a chicken noodle soup for the dinner crowd and it smelled wonderful," Megan said, smiling.

"Then chicken noodle it is, with some of your wonderful breakfast bread."

Megan nodded. "Thank you."

Carol started for the door.

"And thank you for loving me," Megan said, softly.

"That," Carol said, "is all my pleasure. Thank you for loving me in return."

"It would be impossible to do otherwise," Megan said, softly.

Then she closed her eyes and seemed to drift off with a slight smile on her face.

Carol eased out of the door and started to the kitchen to get the soup for Megan for when she woke up.

But Megan never woke up.

Fifteen minutes after Carol left, she returned to find Megan not breathing.

And there was no amount of work that could bring her back.

PART THREE
A Third Chance

CHAPTER SIXTEEN

Three months earlier…

August 19th, 1901
Boise, Idaho

MEGAN TOOK OFF her long blue apron after a long night's shift. She had just checked to make sure all her rolls were being stored correctly for the morning breakfast rush, and her pies and cakes were stored on racks cooling.

Around her the wonderful-smelling large kitchen of the Idanha Hotel was coming alive with breakfast orders and preparation for the day.

At night she often had the kitchen all to herself. She liked it that way, but she never minded when the breakfast cooks arrived and the wait staff came in to prepare the dining room.

She followed the same routine every morning before leaving for a breath of fresh air and then a bath and long sleep. Taking off her apron was the last detail in that routine.

She knew that outside the morning air would be brisk, but not too cool. She loved that about Boise summers, how the evenings cooled off even though the days were often very hot. So even if she only stepped outside for a few seconds, the morning air helped her.

"Mrs. Taber," Chef Pickner said from behind her. "There are three early diners who would like a moment of your time."

She turned and looked into the smiling face of the man who had hired her. He was shorter than her by a good five inches and very round, seeming to play into the look that most thought chefs should be. His hair was balding and his eyebrows as bushy as she had ever seen. They often caught flour or bits of food in them and one of the other chefs was always giving him the sign to clean off his face.

She was about to object when he handed her a wicker basket full of her freshly-made bread covered in a white towel to keep the bread warm.

"Smothered in butter as you instruct," the chef said, smiling. "Just deliver these to the table near the fireplace. Two men and a woman."

She nodded and smoothed down her dress. "Am I presentable?"

The chef nodded. "As always."

He then turned away with a smile, leaving her standing there with the basket of breads in her hand.

She had no idea what this was about, but it seemed she had no choice.

She took a deep breath and went through the door and into the dining room.

The morning summer light through the big windows seemed almost orange in color, promising a beautiful sunrise over the mountains. The large stone fireplace sat dark and empty, a reminder of the colder winter days to come. The high-ceilinged room felt cooler than the kitchen had felt, but still comfortable.

Later in the day she knew the windows on both sides would be opened allowing a light cross-breeze to keep the air as cool as possible and moving. Overhead, the electric fans were already moving in a lazy fashion making clicking sounds.

All the dining tables were made of polished oak and covered in fine tan tablecloths. Cloth napkins were folded perfectly at every place and the silverware gleamed in the morning light.

Only four tables of diners this early in the morning occupied the large room. In short order there would be many more. Summer breakfasts was the restaurant's best time.

The three early diners she had been instructed to go talk to were sitting near the window facing Main Street. They all seemed to be in a good mood as they were laughing at something one of them must have said.

Dr. Stevens was one of the diners and she smiled at that. He had tried to save her husband all those years ago after her husband fell and hit his head. Then Dr. Stevens had helped her get a job in a kitchen, which had started her baking life.

She owed Dr. Stevens and loved talking with him when she could. Thankfully, in the six years since her husband had died, she hadn't needed to go see Dr. Stevens for any medical problems other than the lightheadedness. He had confirmed her childhood doctor's diagnosis that she had a bad heart and there was nothing that could be done. So she just accepted it.

Except for being lightheaded at times, she felt wonderfully healthy, something she was grateful for every moment of every day.

The other two at the table she felt she knew from around town, but didn't know them by name.

As she approached, both men stood.

Dr. Stevens stuck out his hand and with a smile said, "Megan, you are looking wonderful as always."

"Thank you, Doctor," she said smiling back.

"This is Bonnie and Duster Kendal," Dr. Stevens said, introducing her. "This is Mrs. Megan Taber."

Duster Kendal bowed slightly and Bonnie said, "Wonderful meeting you."

"Can you join us for a few moments?" Duster asked, moving to hold a chair for her.

"Oh, I'm such a fright," Megan said. "I've been baking all night."

"Just for a moment," Bonnie said. "You look wonderful."

Megan smiled and sat down, enjoying the compliment from such an attractive woman.

Megan felt honored to be with Doctor Stevens and she knew of the Kendals by reputation around town as well.

"First off," Dr. Stevens said, opening the cloth covering the bread basket she had brought and pulling out a piece of warm bread glistening with melted butter. "I want to once again compliment you on this bread. I have no idea how you do it."

"It is wonderful," Bonnie said, smiling at Megan.

"Of that I can't argue in the slightest," Duster said and took the basket, helping himself to a piece as well.

"Thank you," Megan said, blushing. "Just having you all enjoy the bread makes my day."

"We enjoy it everyday," Dr. Stevens said, laughing.

Megan could feel herself blushing even more. Then for the next few minutes they talked about the weather and how warm the summer had been and how they were all looking forward to the cooler fall.

Then Duster turned to Megan. "Besides wanting to officially meet the wonderful baker who can produce such treats, we wanted to ask you a favor."

That surprised Megan. She had no idea what kind of help she could be to three such prominent citizens.

"We have a friend who is doing a study of major women of the west," Bonnie said. "Her name is Carol Kogan and she has asked if she could spend some time with you and ask you some questions."

Megan opened her mouth, then closed it. No words seemed to want to come out.

"You are known all over the west for your skills in baking," Dr. Stevens said, smiling at Megan.

Megan had started to realize that when she had recently gotten job offers from major San Francisco hotels. She didn't want to move, to leave Boise, and she had told Chef Pickner about the offers and promised him she would stay as long as he wanted her.

He had been very thankful for that.

Besides, she loved her apartment in this wonderful hotel and couldn't imagine living anywhere else.

"I have no desire to leave here," Megan said.

"Oh, we know that," Bonnie said, smiling. "Our friend is just doing research for a book and would love to talk and spend some time with you. We just said we would ask you is all. Nothing more."

Bonnie looked at the two men who were enjoying her breakfast bread, then at the smiling face of Bonnie.

"If you think it would help," Megan said, "I would love to meet with her."

"Wonderful," Duster said. "We'll have her come by when she arrives in town."

"Thank you," Bonnie said, smiling. "I think you will really like Carol."

"I'm sure I will," Megan said, worried about what she had gotten herself into. "I'm sure I will."

CHAPTER SEVENTEEN

August 21st, 1901
Boise, Idaho

CAROL WAS ABOUT to go meet Megan for a third time. She didn't know what to think or even how to feel.

Burying Megan for the second time had torn Carol apart.

After the funeral, she had gone back to 2019 and just sat in her condo under Megan's brown and gold and orange patchwork quilt from Megan's rooms and sulked, letting groceries be brought in and not caring about anything else.

Carol had lost the love of her life, she knew that.

But yet, impossibly, Megan was still alive and baking her wonderful bread in an infinite number of timelines.

Carol just wasn't sure if she could see Megan again, knowing that she could just die at any moment.

It had taken both Duster and Bonnie to convince her that Megan hadn't died six months earlier than expected because of Carol. And as a doctor, Carol knew that to be the case. With Megan's condition, anything could set it off. She might have bent in a strange manner in the kitchen to reach for something and strained.

Or rolled over wrong in bed.

Or a hundred other reasons.

Carol knew she wasn't at fault for robbing Megan of six months of life, but it sure felt that way.

There just had to be a way to save Megan.

Finally, after dreaming every night for a month about Megan and her wonderful smile and smooth skin, Carol decided to try to save her once again.

She went to Director Parks and got his permission to jump to 2119 to study the procedures used there on heart patients like Megan.

What she had learned had been both encouraging and discouraging. Sometimes, without a complete heart replacement operation, patients with the condition that Megan had still died.

And they often died unexpectedly, as Carol had learned. She would no longer trust that Megan would live until May, 1902. Carol had to act before then to get Megan's trust and get her the surgery in 2119.

Then, knowing that Carol would more than likely get turned down, she had asked

Director Parks if he would allow her to study the techniques of 2219 as well.

He had agreed and what had surprised her was that in a hundred years, stem cell growth of a new heart and replacing out the old heart was still the best method in heart cases like Megan's.

So now she had to get Megan's trust enough to get her to the Institute and to 2019. Then extract some stem cells and get them to 2119 to grow a new heart. And then get her there, alive, to get the new heart.

The only problem was that it took three months to grow the new heart.

Three months in which Megan could die at any moment and nothing could save her.

The task just seemed impossible.

But Carol had buried Megan twice.

Carol had to try again.

She just had to.

So now, back in the summer of 1901, Carol was on her way to meet Megan for the first time in this timeline. And Carol felt more nervous than she had last time, if that was possible.

Somehow, not only did she need to hide her real identity and past, but she had to hide that she knew Megan at all and that they had fallen in love once before.

Carol at least knew now that Megan was open to that.

But it would take time, as it did the last time.

And time was not on Megan's side.

CHAPTER EIGHTEEN

August 21st, 1901
Boise, Idaho

MEGAN FELT NERVOUS. She had on one of her best skirts and blouses, an outfit she saved for special occasions such as a staff party. The skirt was a pleated blue and the blouse a loose white with silk on the neck and sleeves. She wore a light matching blue jacket over

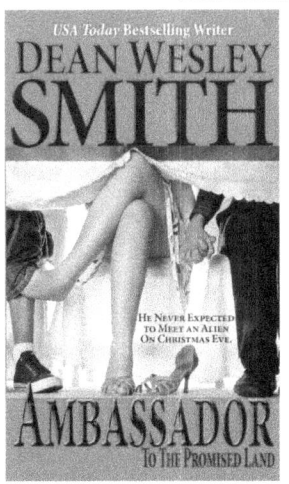  

Some Classic Dean Wesley Smith Stories
Available at your favorite booksellers.

115

her blouse and a small string of pearls from her mother.

Even though it was a warm evening outside, she felt she needed the jacket to look presentable.

She wasn't sure why she was nervous. This Carol Kogan sounded nice and impressive and wanted to just talk. Megan figured that was what was making her nervous, that someone actually valued beyond what they ate at their table what she did every night.

She brushed down her skirt one more time, then checked to make sure her hair was in place, even though as short as it was, there wasn't much she could do with it.

Then she left her apartment on the main floor of the hotel near the back and walked down the hallway toward the large hotel foyer and restaurant beyond. She usually turned at an unmarked door about halfway down the hallway that led into the kitchen area, but this time she just kept walking, forcing herself to breathe evenly. Last thing she needed to do was get lightheaded tonight.

She nodded to the desk clerk as she moved across the stone-floors of the foyer and into the open restaurant doors beyond.

Stan, the evening host, greeted her with a smile. "You look wonderful this evening, Mrs. Taber."

"Thank you, Stan," she said, bowing slightly.

"Your guest is waiting at the table near the front window," Stan said, indicating that she should follow him.

The blinds on the west side of the room had been drawn to block out the direct evening sun and Megan was happy to see that the woman was sitting in a shaded area near an open window. The noise and smells from the streets might intrude at times, but even a slight breeze would be better than being stuffy.

As Megan approached, the woman she was meeting glanced around and seemed shocked.

Actually, it was Megan who felt shocked. The woman was stunningly beautiful and dressed in a similar style as Megan was.

The woman stood and extended her hand after a moment. "Mrs. Taber, I am Carol Kogan. The honor is all mine to meet you."

Megan took Miss Kogan's hand and was stunned at how soft and wonderful it felt. She didn't want to let it go.

And she didn't want to stop staring in Miss Kogan's eyes either. They were the most beautiful green Megan had ever seen.

And clearly Miss Kogan didn't want to break the grip either. Her face looked flushed and there was a slight look of panic in her eyes.

Stan moved around Megan and pulled out her chair, so Megan released Miss Kogan's hand and sat, allowing Miss Kogan to sit again as well.

"Would you enjoy a beverage to start?" Stan asked.

"Water would be wonderful," Megan said.

Stan nodded and turned away.

Megan looked at Carol, who was staring at her as well.

"Call me Megan," she said, deciding to break the ice a little, even though ice was a great distance away from this warm August evening.

"I'm Carol. And I apologize for staring, but I hope you don't mind if I say you are a very beautiful woman."

Megan could feel herself blush a little along her neck. She laughed. "Not at all because I was thinking the same of you."

Now Carol blushed slightly and laughed.

Over the evening they managed to talk about their pasts, about how Megan's husband had died, and then finally her baking.

To Megan, the conversation was wonderful, the most enjoyable she had had in a very, very long time. And at one point she felt comfortable enough to take off her jacket and drape it over her chair.

Carol did the same.

And the more they talked, the more Megan liked Carol.

And the more Megan wanted to spend time with Carol.

They both had a summer salad full of fresh vegetables from local gardens and both had a piece of a berry pie Megan had baked last night to finish off their meal. In so many ways, their tastes were very, very similar.

At one point in the conversation, Carol said, "You are a well-known woman of the West because of your baking skills and art."

Megan was shocked to her core. She took a sip of the warm water and then asked, "You consider my baking an art?"

"I do," Carol said nodding, a very serious look in her eyes. "Anyone can toss together what it takes to make a pie as we just ate, but it takes an artist to make them taste the way you make them taste."

"Thank you," Megan said. She knew her face was red and she looked down away from the wonderful and intense green eyes.

"I didn't mean to embarrass you," Carol said.

Megan smiled and looked back into Carol's worried eyes. "You didn't. It's how I feel about my baking yet never say. So thank you."

Carol smiled and nodded and the two sat there staring at each other for the longest and most wonderful time.

CHAPTER NINETEEN

August 21st, 1901
Boise, Idaho

CAROL WAS SO nervous when Megan came into the dining room, she almost couldn't stand.

Carol had buried Megan twice, yet here she was again, walking across the warm, sunlit dining room like an angel.

It was the same Megan that Carol had fallen so completely in love with. And that love hadn't eased in the slightest in the time it took Carol to do the medical research. If anything, seeing Megan like this, alive and smiling, was like a dream.

All Carol wanted to do was hug her.

But she didn't.

This was going to be impossible, but to save this woman's life, Carol had to try to give Megan time to trust her.

But not take a lot of time.

That would be a very fine balance.

Thankfully, the dinner went well and as in the last timeline, they met the next morning for breakfast in Megan's apartment.

Carol touched Megan's beautiful patchwork quilt when she came in, knowing that it was also in her condo on her own couch in 2019. She wondered how Megan would feel if she knew that.

With luck, Megan would find out.

The breakfast went almost identically as the first breakfast together had gone, and they spent every dinner together and every breakfast, until the moment when Megan asked Carol to scrub her back.

That's when things changed for the better, as far as Carol was concerned.

She took off her blouse and Megan once again asked about her sports bra.

Carol, on impulse, took it off, offering it to Megan to feel the synthetic fabric.

Just as Carol had stared at Megan's wonderful body, Megan stared at Carol's exposed breasts. Carol's breasts were also small, much the same size as Megan's, but instead of small brown nipples as Megan had, Carol had wide, pink nipples.

"Since I have gone this far," Carol asked, smiling back at Megan's stare, "Can I go all the way and join you in the tub? It would be much better to wash your back."

"Oh, please," Megan said, and then just kept staring, a slight blush on her face as Carol finished undressing and climbed into the large tub and warm water behind Megan.

Carol extended her legs along both sides of Megan and took the washcloth and soap and started working on Megan's back.

Megan sighed and after a moment Megan's hands were slightly stroking Carol's legs.

And the morning went from there, with Carol finally leaving after giving Megan a long, wonderful kiss.

That evening at dinner, Carol asked Megan if she could get the following night off of work. She had a wonderful surprise to show her.

Megan nodded and smiled. "I would love to start to see some of the many surprises you hold."

"You saw a few of those this morning," Carol said, blushing.

Megan also blushed. "That's why I am interested in more."

Carol laughed.

It was September 22nd. It had taken Carol one month to gain Megan's trust and love.

And for Carol, it had been one of the best months of her life, ever.

Maybe the best.

CHAPTER TWENTY

September 23rd, 1901
Boise, Idaho

MEGAN COULDN'T BELIEVE how much and how quickly she had fallen completely in love with the mysterious Carol Kogan. She knew it wasn't right or proper, but she was finding herself not caring. It felt right.

And clearly Carol had fallen for her as well.

Megan had no doubt that she would love to just touch Carol's skin for the rest of her life. And it surprised Megan that she wanted to spend the rest of her life with Carol. Not a thought she ever would have believed possible just a month before.

Of course, everything about them being together would have to be kept completely secret, but Megan was willing to do that just to be with Carol.

And since Carol was willing to start opening up about some of her secrets, Megan felt encouraged. Megan had never pushed or asked, but she could tell that Carol kept a lot hidden.

Megan got up a little earlier than normal in the afternoon and got dressed in her riding clothes. She hadn't been riding in a very long time and was very pleased to discover her riding clothes still fit perfectly.

"We are going to need some early dinner," Megan said as they left the hotel and turned toward the stables.

Both of them were wearing big cloth hats with wide brims as well to shade their skin from the sun. Megan hadn't worn her riding hat since the last time she wore her riding clothes. It actually felt odd on her head but Carol's hat made her look even more alluring.

"I have dinner planned for us at the Institute," Carol said. "It will be like nothing you have ever tasted, I promise."

Megan couldn't get even a hint more from Carol, so they got saddled and headed slowly out of town. Carol said that the horse Megan was riding was an Institute horse. A brown mare that seemed very gentle and Megan took a liking to her at once.

It was a beautiful fall day. The leaves still were all green and the air was warm, but not hot. Megan had brought along a jacket just in case, but wasn't wearing it at the moment. On the ride back later in the evening she had a hunch she would need it.

Carol rode like an expert, which didn't surprise Megan at all. She had a hunch that nothing would surprise her about Carol.

As they neared the Institute, Megan could see the three large Victorian homes standing on the rise above the river. They were beautiful and majestic.

"Bonnie Kendal is going to meet us at the Institute," Carol said. "She's going to help with the surprise."

"Should I be worried about this surprise?" Megan asked as they got closer to the three large homes.

"Not in the slightest," Carol said. "I am very much in love with you. And I want you to know everything about me."

Megan was very pleased to hear Carol say that.

As they dismounted in the stable behind the center mansion and gave their horses to a stable hand, Carol looked at Megan with an intense look. "How are you feeling? Lightheaded at all?"

"Feeling wonderfully well," Megan said, smiling. "A beautiful ride on a beautiful evening with a beautiful companion is just what any doctor would order."

Carol beamed at that and then the two of them started toward the back entrance to the mansion, taking off their hats as they went.

"Then it sounds like you are ready for some secrets," Carol said.

"As much as I'll ever be, I suppose."

CHAPTER TWENTY-ONE

September 23rd, 1901
Boise, Idaho

CAROL HAD WATCHED Megan carefully during the ride to the Institute and saw no signs that Megan was getting stressed or even the slightest bit tired.

So far, so good.

But in very short order she and Bonnie were going to change Megan's life. Carol just hoped the shock of it all didn't trigger an attack.

They went in the back door of the large Institute mansion, then, instead of taking Megan on a tour, Carol touched a secret panel that slid back and she stepped through.

"The Institute is so much more than the three buildings on the surface," Carol said. "Let me show you."

She held out her hand and took Megan's hand.

"Secret panels in a mansion," Megan said, smiling. "Like a story right out of *All Story Magazine.*"

"It is, isn't it?" Carol said, happy that Megan didn't seem afraid in the slightest. Carol remembered the first time she saw what was under the Institute. It had scared her more than she wanted to admit.

They went through the wide hallway lit by electrical bulbs and to an elevator.

"Much safer than the Otis at the hotel," Carol said. "I promise."

"You telling me that thing isn't safe?" Megan asked, laughing and stepping on beside Carol.

"I'd never ride it," Carol said, laughing in return.

"I knew you were smart," Megan said.

The elevator took them down two floors and opened up into the big cavern.

"Wow," Megan said as Carol led her through the arrangements of living room furniture and toward a kitchen counter where Bonnie sat. "This is really some place."

"No one really knows about it," Carol said. "One of my many secrets I promised to show you."

"This is a pretty good one," Megan said. "But from the looks of the furniture, a lot of people know about this place."

"At the moment," Bonnie said, "you are only the 30th person."

Megan was very surprised at that.

Bonnie stood and gave Megan a hug. "Glad to see you looking well."

"Feeling wonderfully," Megan said, smiling.

"Now we want to show you something and a kitchen you can only dream about," Bonnie said. "Follow me."

Carol took Megan's hand and they went through a big door in the far wall and then down two flights of stairs and into a large room full of clothes and supplies.

 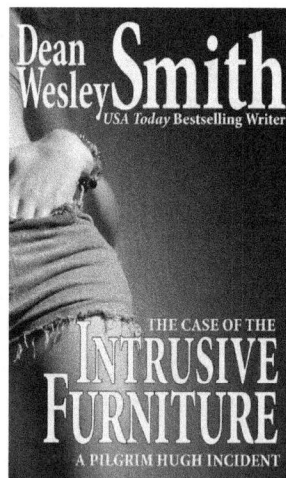 

Three Pilgrim Hugh Incidents
Available at your favorite booksellers.

"I'll explain all this shortly," Carol said, squeezing Megan's hand.

"Good," Megan said, "Because this is the biggest and strangest store I have ever seen."

Carol watched Megan carefully as they went into the long, narrow crystal room.

Bonnie and Carol had decided to just go quickly through the process and then go back upstairs to explain everything. And show Megan what it looked like in 2019.

"Those are very beautiful crystals," Megan said, pointing to the glowing crystals in the wall.

"They are, aren't they," Bonnie said.

Carol looked at Megan and then said, "Right now I need you to do something I love a lot."

Megan looked puzzled, then asked what that might be.

"I need you to put your arms around me and hold me very tightly."

Megan blushed and then with a glance at Bonnie, who was smiling, stepped closer to Carol and hugged her.

"A little harder," Carol said, noting that Bonnie was about to pull the wire from the box that would send Carol, and with luck Megan, to 2019.

Megan squeezed Carol harder in a hug Carol wished would never end.

Bonnie pulled the wire and vanished.

Megan was still holding Carol.

Both of them were in 2019.

Carol kissed Megan. "We made it. Together."

"Made what?" Megan asked, staring into Carol's eyes and wide smile.

"We made it to the place where I can show you my secrets."

Megan laughed. "We could have stayed in my rooms at the hotel if a hug would get you to show your secrets."

"That was just a wonderful benefit for me is all," Carol said, laughing.

"I enjoyed it as well," Megan said, then kissed Carol again.

"Sorry to interrupt, ladies, but let's go back upstairs and have some dinner," Bonnie said, appearing just behind Megan. "We've got a lot to talk about."

Both Carol and Megan blushed and then as if they were two teenagers, they went hand-in-hand back up two flights of stairs to the big cavern living room.

Now Carol's only worry was that Megan would hate her.

Or that there wouldn't be enough time to save Megan either way.

CHAPTER TWENTY-TWO

March 6th, 2019
Boise, Idaho

MEGAN WAS VERY, very puzzled at the events of the last half hour and why Bonnie and Carol had taken her down into that tunnel and then brought her back up here.

It wasn't until she really looked at the furniture in the large cavern room and the kitchen countertop and the things behind the counter that she started to get worried.

"Everything changed here since we went downstairs," Megan said.

Both Bonnie and Carol nodded.

"You are no longer in 1901," Bonnie said.

"That's my secret," Carol said, turning and staring into the eyes of the woman she loved. "I am from the year 2019."

Megan laughed, but Carol's expression didn't change.

After a moment, Megan said, "You are serious, aren't you?"

Carol and Bonnie both nodded.

"Come on," Carol said, "Let me show you something."

"I'll stay here and make us a snack before dinner," Bonnie said.

Megan let Carol take her hand and direct her to the elevator they had come down. Now it was sleek and had a full door instead of a cage. As they approached, the door slid open silently.

Carol stepped on and Megan reluctantly followed her.

"Trust me," Carol said, "this is a million times safer than that Otis in the hotel."

"Anything would be," Megan said, moving on and holding onto both of Carol's hands as the door closed.

She could feel a slight sense of movement and then the door slid back open.

They stepped into an empty room and Carol went to a place on the wall.

"Checking to make sure no one is in the Institute's front room that shouldn't be."

There wasn't, so she pushed a button and a panel slid back and Megan let herself be led into the front parlor of the mansion.

Megan was surprised that it actually looked dated.

"The Institute keeps this front entrance room looking exactly as it looked in the early 1880s when the Institute was founded."

Megan nodded as Carol led her to the large wooden front door and pulled it open.

As Megan stepped out, she was stunned at what she saw.

In fact, she wasn't sure exactly what she was seeing.

"It's March 2019," Carol said. "About twelve noon. Trees are just starting to get their leaves and all those things going by are modern versions of the automobiles that were just getting started in 1901."

Megan just stood and stared, holding Carol's hand as if it were a lifeline to a sane time and place. Where before it had just been the three Victorian mansions sitting on a slight hill overlooking the river, now the entire area was full of homes and buildings of all types.

And the wagon road that had run past the mansions was now covered in some sort of pavement and strange-looking automobiles flashed past at impossible speeds.

Finally, after almost a minute of Megan looking around, she turned to Carol. "You really are from this time?"

"I am," Carol said. "I am a medical doctor and an historian. I traveled back to 1901 to learn about strong women and their medical conditions for a book I am writing."

"So I am a test subject," Megan said, feeling almost angry.

"No," Carol said, forcing Megan to look into her eyes. "You are the woman I fell in love with, the woman I want to spend lifetimes with. I had to get permission to share this with you, to tell you the truth about myself."

Megan could see the worry and the love in Carol's eyes. She was telling the truth.

After a moment Megan nodded and kissed Carol who seemed to melt with relief in her arms.

Then she said simply, "I have a lot to learn it seems."

"If we want we can stay here for a while," Carol said. "But I would rather live in your time for now."

"We can go back?" Megan asked. She wasn't sure why she thought she couldn't go back, since Carol had gone back from here to meet her.

"Of course we can," Carol said. "We could spend months here and go back to within an hour of when we got off those horses to continue that wonderful day. And yet still remember the months here."

"You are being very serious, aren't you?" Megan asked, actually starting to feel excited, even though what she was seeing around her scared her more than she wanted to admit.

"Yes," Carol said. "Bonnie knows a lot more about all those sorts of things."

"So let's go back and get a bite to eat," Megan said, looking around at the amazing scene she never could have imagined. "And I'll start learning about your world since you know so much about mine."

Megan took Carol's hand and they went back inside.

This all seemed impossible, yet Carol was very real and with her. So even the impossible might be all right as long as they were together.

CHAPTER TWENTY-THREE

March 6th, 2019
Boise, Idaho

CAROL WAS STUNNED at how level Megan seemed to be in the face of such insanity. Seeing over a hundred years into the future had bothered Carol when she had jumped forward the first time to 2119. She could only imagine what Megan was going to think, yet Megan had seemed to take it almost in stride.

Megan was an amazing woman, of that there was no doubt.

Carol and Megan and Bonnie all sat at the counter eating a light sandwich and salad. Carol and Bonnie had planned to take Megan to their favorite Italian restaurant if she was doing all right, and it sure seemed to Carol that she was.

So after some talk about living in the past and how little time was spent when a person went back into the past, Carol finally got around to telling Megan the problem.

"There is another reason we brought you here," Carol said. "It's your heart."

Megan smiled at Carol and nodded. "I had a hunch that was what this was all about."

Carol was stunned.

Megan smiled and reached over and squeezed Carol's hand. "Not a day goes by that you don't ask me a few times how I am feeling."

Bonnie laughed and Carol just shook her head.

"You say you are a medical doctor from this time," Megan asked. "So what is wrong with my heart?"

"Exactly what you have been told," Carol said, turning to face Megan directly. "You were basically born with a bad heart that will suddenly stop working. It is the cause of your feeling faint and dizzy spells."

"Since you are from the future here, do you know when it finally gives up?"

"Every timeline is different," Bonnie said.

Carol took a deep breath and looked at Bonnie, who just nodded.

"I need to tell you a story, my love," Carol said. "And I promise every bit of it is true."

"This sounds very serious," Megan said, smiling.

"It is," Carol said, leaning forward and kissing Megan lightly. "And I have no idea how I would react if someone told me this story. Just remember I love you."

Megan nodded.

Carol took a deep breath and told the story of how she and Megan met the first time on the sidewalk. And what happened.

"Oh, I am so sorry," Megan said, squeezing Carol's hand.

"You had that fatal heart attack in May, so we assumed we had time," Carol said. "I went back six months earlier and we met on a cold early November day in the restaurant, similar to how we met this time."

"Oh, no," Megan said softly.

"We had a wonderful couple of weeks of falling in love and then toward the end of the month, you had a heart attack that killed you."

"So you came back earlier this time," Megan said. "And now I am here and still alive. What are you planning?"

"We are planning to fix your heart," Carol said. "So that you and I can be together for a very long time."

Now Available
**from all your favorite booksellers
in trade paper and electronic editions.**

Megan nodded. "I like the sounds of that. But I hate that I put you through so much to get here."

Carol smiled at the wonderful woman sitting next to her. "Trust me, it was worth it."

CHAPTER TWENTY-FOUR

March 6th, 2019
Boise, Idaho

MEGAN WAS STARTING to feel that given time, she might really enjoy living in this miraculous future.

After the discussion down in the cavern, Bonnie offered to drive them to a restaurant that she and Duster really loved.

Carol showed Megan some jeans, as Carol called them, a sports bra, and a modern-looking blouse for Megan to change into. Then stayed and helped her and changed clothes herself.

"These clothes are very comfortable," Megan said, looking at herself in a mirror in the woman's restroom.

"They are," Carol said. "One of the wonderful changes over the last century. Women's clothing, for the most part, has become comfortable."

"Now this I could enjoy," Megan said, looking at herself in the mirror. She looked the same, yet so different.

"I could enjoy you looking like that as well," Carol said. "Actually, I enjoy looking at you no matter how you look."

Megan kissed Carol and then took Carol's hand as they went back out into the main cavern. This was all scary and fun at the same time, and for Megan, it seemed to alternate from moment to moment.

"As I promised a hundred or so years ago," Carol said, smiling as they got off the elevator on the main floor of the mansion and headed toward the back of the building, "this will be a meal you will never forget."

And as far as Megan had been concerned, she had a hunch Carol was going to be right.

Bonnie led them out to what had been the stables and gotten them situated into a huge white automobile. The thing smelled of new leather and was huge, with very comfortable seats and all sorts of gadgets in front of her and Bonnie.

Carol sat in the back and helped Megan put on what Carol called a seat belt. Then Bonnie turned on the automobile and it seemed that everything in front of Bonnie and Megan lit up with all sorts of hidden lights and words Megan didn't understand.

She had a vast amount to learn before she could ever try to control one of these large beasts.

Bonnie got them out of the old stable and up the driveway to the busy street.

When she pulled onto the street and accelerated, Megan just held onto the handle beside her. Never in all her life could she imagine going so fast.

But it was very smooth and seemed almost effortless.

"How fast can these go?" Megan asked after it became clear that there was very little feeling of movement.

"Far faster than this in certain conditions," Bonnie said.

"We covered all this ground on the ride out of town earlier," Carol said. "You are going to be able to spot some things

that are from the past, but not that many I'm afraid."

"Is the Idanha still here?"

"It is," Carol said, "But it is apartments now and the main floor has been remodeled a number of times. It does not have its original glory I'm afraid."

"That is sad," Megan said as she watched the buildings and sites go by outside the window. It was all just amazing, simply amazing.

Finally Bonnie turned the automobile into a large paved area with other cars and stopped, shutting off the machine.

"How are you feeling?" Carol asked from the back.

"In awe of this stunning world," Megan said. "And not feeling light or faint at all."

"Wonderful," Carol said, then showed Megan how to get out of the seat belt harness and then open her door.

As they walked around a corner, Megan could see that the sidewalks of the now large city were covered with people going about their business. All were dressed in the same fashion she had on, or in suits and different forms of dresses for the women.

They went into a restaurant that seemed crowded and smelled heavenly of garlic and fresh bread. Somehow plants seemed to grow from everywhere, even though there were no real windows that Megan could see.

A young girl smiled and greeted them, then led them through the restaurant full of tables and plants and people smiling and laughing as they ate.

Megan decided right there that she was going to like this time even more because people seemed to really enjoy themselves while eating. In one hundred years it seemed that eating in a restaurant had gone from a serious affair to a social fun time for people to do.

And as a baker, that made her happy.

And holding Carol's hand as they walked through the restaurant following Bonnie made her even happier.

CHAPTER TWENTY-FIVE

March 6th, 2019
Boise, Idaho

AFTER A WONDERFUL dinner, Carol and Megan decided they could just walk to Carol's condo. It was about six blocks and after the fun and very filling meal, that seemed like a good idea.

At that moment in time, Carol wasn't so worried about Megan's health. She seemed to be doing fine. But she was very worried about what Megan would think about staying in the same bed with Carol for the night. If that was too uncomfortable for her, they would work something out and get Megan her own condo tomorrow.

But no amount of worrying would answer that question at the moment, so they would cross that problem when they got to it.

They walked hand-in-hand, with Carol explaining some things about basic traffic safety rules and Megan asking very smart questions about different things they saw. Carol just was amazed at how well Megan was adjusting to such a culture shock.

Carol was not convinced she would be doing so well. In fact, the little bit of time she

had spent in 2119 had shocked her more than Megan seemed to be shocked by all this.

As they reached the park area and started along the river, Megan held up Carol's hand in hers. "We would never be able to walk like this in my time. What has changed?"

"When it comes to women," Carol said. "Just about everything. But it took a very long time. Almost every year of the time from your time to now, actually."

Megan looked puzzled, so Carol went on. "Women got the right to vote by a constitutional amendment in 1920 and then slowly started becoming equals to men both under the law and in the eyes of society."

"Okay," Megan said, nodding. Carol could tell that concept still wasn't sinking in.

"As I said, it took a very long time. Slow changes over the last one-hundred-plus years. And along the way the marriage laws changed as well. Men can now marry men and women can marry women."

That stopped Megan in the middle of the sidewalk.

"You are not playing a joke on me?"

Carol smiled and looked into the large brown eyes of the woman she loved, then shook her head. "You and I are free to marry if we decided to do so. Just as you married your former husband."

Megan shook her head and they kept walking in silence for a short time. Then Megan said softly, "I like your time."

"And I like your time as well," Carol said. "So it seems once we get your heart fixed up, we can live in both."

"Together?" Megan asked, looking over at Carol.

"Together," Carol said, squeezing Megan's hand. "We'll just have to be more careful in your time."

"Much, much more careful," Megan said. They walked the rest of the way to the condo in silence.

Inside, Megan was impressed at the fantastic kitchen and huge fridge.

"Where is the ice?" Megan asked, opening the freezer door.

"It makes its own cold," Carol said.

She took a glass out of the cupboard. "If you want some ice for your drink, just put the glass here and push."

Megan stepped back slightly shocked as ice clattered into the glass.

"And if you want cold water, just put the glass here and push."

Water filled the glass on the ice.

"That is miraculous," Megan said, shaking her head. "And you don't have to stoke the stove either I would guess."

Carol turned on a burner on the flat-top stove and a moment later it showed orange and was generating heat.

Megan just shook her head again and moved out of the kitchen into the living room area.

"This is a beautiful place," Megan said.

Carol felt very, very proud that Megan liked it. She had hoped she would.

Then Megan went to the large orange and brown patchwork quilt tossed over the back of one couch. "This looks similar to mine."

"It is yours from another timeline," Carol said. "I brought it with me after you died the last time."

Megan looked at Carol, clear sadness in her eyes. "I hate that I put you through that."

"You had no choice, my love," Carol said, moving over and holding Megan.

They stood like that for a moment, then Carol said, "Let me show you my bathroom upstairs. You think the kitchen is miraculous, just wait. And then we can

get a cold drink and go sit on the patio and enjoy the evening."

"That sounds wonderful," Megan said.

Of course, they never made it to the patio. They ended up taking off each other's clothes and tumbling into Carol's huge bed.

And then two hours later, they scrubbed each other's backs and entire bodies under the wonderful shower.

A perfect evening as far as Carol was concerned.

Megan said the same.

CHAPTER TWENTY-SIX

March 7th, 2019
Boise, Idaho

AFTER A WONDERFUL night together with Carol, Megan had almost forgotten she was in the future. It wasn't until she got out of the huge, soft bed and wandered into the bathroom that she suddenly remembered.

And she remembered why Carol had brought her forward in time.

So when Megan went back to bed and cuddled with Carol, she asked simply, "Are we going to the hospital today?"

Carol nodded. "I don't think we dare wait any longer. But you don't need to worry, I will be there with you every step of the way."

"If it means I don't die suddenly on you," Megan said, trying to push down the fear, "then I am ready."

Carol kissed her and then smiled. "You are the most amazing and bravest woman I have ever met. Have I told you how much I love you?"

"Not in the last few minutes," Megan said, laughing and kissing Carol again.

After a time, it was hunger that drove them to get dressed.

Both of them took another shower, something that Megan knew she could come to really enjoy, especially the fact that she didn't have to heat the water to have it warm. It just came out of the tap that way like magic.

Carol gave Megan some clean underwear that felt wonderful, not at all like the ones she normally wore. And another sports bra, as Carol called it. After Megan was standing there in her underwear, Carol just stared.

"You get that look and we're never going to get something to eat," Megan said, laughing.

"Food is so underrated when it compares to sex," Carol said.

"True," Megan said, and stepped toward Carol, who retreated with a giggle.

Then the two of them went through Carol's closet to find Megan a nice blouse and some socks to wear with the tennis shoes she had gotten from the Institute the day before.

Finally, both dressed, they made it downstairs to make breakfast.

Carol showed Megan the modern choices of her kitchen. There was cereal with milk and juice, eggs with toast and juice, or a nearby restaurant.

"The lack of food choices comes from being too focused on my work far too much."

Megan decided she would rather spend the time alone with Carol and went for a flake-like cereal that was sweet, covered in milk and then some orange juice out of a container.

Surprisingly, it all tasted pretty good and she had two bowls.

Then they walked hand-in-hand along the river to the Institute, a walk Megan felt she could come to treasure.

On the second floor of the big building, they found Director Parks in his office and Carol introduced Megan to him. Director Parks smiled and asked how Megan was doing getting used to a strange new world.

"I have so much to learn," Megan said.

"Actually," Director Parks said, smiling, "any of us who travel into a different timeline and time have a lot to learn, no matter which way we are going. So you are very much at home here with us."

"Thank you," Megan had said.

Then Director Parks turned serious. "Are you ready for the hospital?"

"I think so," Megan said, her stomach twisting.

"You can't say anything about when you are from," Director Parks said.

Megan nodded and glanced at Carol, who was looking very serious. "Carol told me all about that."

"Good," Parks said and turned to Carol. "What's up first today, Doctor?"

Megan was shocked slightly that Carol was referred to as Doctor. Carol had told her she was, but Megan hadn't really thought about it.

"Bone marrow to get the growth of the new heart going in 2119," Carol said.

"Growth of a new heart?" Megan asked.

Carol nodded. "We are going to take some cells from your body today to grow you a brand new heart one hundred years from now. Then when it is ready in three months, we will go there and they will replace your damaged heart with a very healthy one."

"That is all possible?" Megan asked, stunned and scared to death of the idea.

"Very possible and very normal one hundred years from now," Carol said. "And after that you will be healthy and we can go where and when we please together."

Director Parks nodded, which Megan was glad to see. "I wish we could just take the bone marrow there to grow the heart and then jump forward in time three months until it is ready. But the crystals are on one-hundred-year limits jumping forward from here. So we have to wait."

"Can we jump another hundred years forward from there and then back ninety-nine years?" Carol asked.

Director Parks nodded. "We could, but then if the operation fails, Megan would end up a hundred years ahead still with a bad heart. Remember, when you jump back into another timeline, you are only gone for two minutes no matter what happens. We don't dare set Megan in a time until she is cured of this problem. Otherwise, she will always have a bad heart."

"Damn," Carol said.

Megan nodded, just trying to imagine all that and failing completely. But she was glad Carol understood.

"So today will be an easy day," Carol said, turning to her. "Then all we have to do is live here and enjoy life for three months."

"Oh," Megan said, feeling slightly relieved. "I thought the surgery was today."

"Not yet," Carol said, smiling. "First we have to grow you a healthy heart."

"Will it still love you?" Megan asked, smiling.

Director Parks snorted and Carol laughed.

"I'm having them build in even more love for me," Carol said.

Megan shook her head. "I don't think that's possible."

All three of them laughed and Carol kissed Megan

Then they all headed for the stables that held the big automobiles for a ride to the hospital.

Megan would have preferred to walk, but Carol said it was just too far.

CHAPTER TWENTY-SEVEN

April 17th, 2019
Boise, Idaho

THE FIRST MONTH after the bone marrow procedure went wonderfully as far as Carol was concerned. Megan and Carol had grown comfortable living together and they had explored many restaurants and a few of the bakeries around Boise.

At one point as Carol and Megan were sitting on the back deck watching the river, Carol had asked Megan if she ever thought of opening her own bakery. And not only supplying customers coming through the door, but other restaurants around town.

Around them the evening air was crisp, but not cold and the river was running strong and loud.

Megan had given Carol one of her not-understanding blank stares, then asked, "Would something like even be possible?"

"Very much so," Carol said, smiling.

"It would be so expensive," Megan said.

"Expense is not an issue," Carol said. She had told Megan that the Institute paid for her condo and all expenses, but she didn't remember telling Megan that before the Institute, Carol had been very comfortable when it came to money. Her parents were rich and they had set her up with enough money to do most anything she had wanted. She had even come out of medical school without an ounce of debt.

"Not an issue?" Megan asked.

"We will never worry about money no matter in what time we live," Carol said. "But I am sure with your art at baking, the bakery would be a success from the first moment forward."

Megan smiled and clearly seemed to be thinking.

After a moment she said, "I had never dreamed of such a thing before this very moment."

"Think about it and we can talk after you have a new and strong heart," Carol said.

"It sounds wonderful," Megan said, standing up and moving over to Carol's chair and kissing her.

After that the cool night air forced them back inside to the couches and Megan's new obsession with television and computers.

They were halfway through a new sitcom when Megan said softly, "Carol."

Carol glanced over to see Megan sweating and holding her chest.

Carol instantly grabbed her cell phone that she kept with her at all times and dialed 911. Then she went to Megan and had her stretch out on the couch.

"I'm sorry," Megan said, tears forming in her eyes.

"We'll get you through this one," Carol said. "You just relax. Help is on the way."

Megan nodded, then whispered. "I like the bakery idea."

"I do too, my love," Carol said.

Then as she held Megan's hand, she directed the ambulance to the right condo. Less than five minutes later, Carol sat beside Megan as they sped toward the hospital.

"Stay with me, Megan," Carol said softly as she and the ambulance attendant did everything in their power to keep Megan alive just a little longer.

CHAPTER TWENTY-EIGHT

April 17th, 2019
Boise, Idaho

MEGAN AWOKE TO the sounds of strange beeping. Her chest hurt worse than she could ever imagine, but at least she was still alive.

Or at least she hoped she was.

She opened her eyes slowly. They felt like they had been glued shut at one point, but she finally managed to stare at a very white ceiling that seemed to have a lot of tiny holes punched in it.

She blinked twice and the ceiling with the tiny holes did not go away.

This new world was a very strange world.

She was as thirsty as she could ever remember being. And there was a sour taste of almonds in her mouth.

Something was stuck up her nose, but she didn't have the energy to see what it was.

Beside her the beeping continued like nothing she had ever heard before.

She tried to turn to see what the infernal beeping was, but the pain made her moan.

She heard movement and Carol suddenly appeared in her line of sight. She was smiling and yet had that worried look on her face that Megan had come to love.

"Welcome back," Carol said. "We thought we lost you there."

A woman in a white uniform appeared to Megan's left and gave her an ice chip that she could suck on.

The ice chip felt like heaven. Wow.

"I'll tell Doctor James she is awake," the nurse said.

"Thank you," Carol said.

Then she turned to Megan and squeezed her hand.

"I love you, you know," Carol said.

Megan nodded.

At that moment a man came in. He had dark thick hair and wore black-rimmed glasses. He was thin and his white smock sort of hung on him.

"Glad you are awake, Miss Taber. You gave me and Doctor Kogan a scare there for awhile."

Megan said nothing as the man in the white coat shined a tiny light in her eyes, then listened to her heart for a moment through an instrument, then nodded and looked at Carol.

Megan could tell that wasn't a good look.

"We want you to just rest," the man said. "Doctor Kogan will take good care of you."

Megan nodded. Then through her cracked and dry throat she said, "Thank you."

He smiled, nodded, and then turned and left.

"What's happening?" Megan asked, turning her head to look at Carol.

"Your heart is giving out," Carol said. "We want to try to let you rest, keep you on drugs, and get you to the point where we can fix it."

Megan nodded. She could tell that Carol was about to cry and was just trying to be strong because that was what she did.

Megan needed to do something to help Carol. Death didn't scare Megan. She had known it was coming her entire life. But making Carol suffer again scared her more than she wanted to think about.

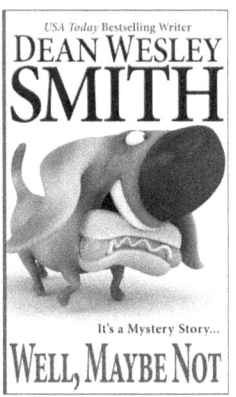

She indicated that Carol should come down close.

"Will my special heart in the future keep growing even if I die?"

Carol nodded. "But don't think that way. We'll get you through the next five weeks."

Megan said simply. "Just remember that part of me is there."

Carol smiled. "I could never forget. Just rest. Please?"

With that, Megan let the blackness take her.

CHAPTER TWENTY-NINE

April 17th, 2019
Boise, Idaho

CAROL LISTENED TO Megan's struggling heart for a moment and then made sure Megan was resting comfortably before leaving to find Doctor James. There was nothing good about this situation.

Nothing at all.

Dr. James was waiting for her in his office and indicated she close the door. He was one of the best, if not the best heart surgeon in the western part of the United States. And he was a very nice person as well, unlike many surgeons.

The office was fairly large, with a massive oak desk with three stacks of files on it. There was a couch, what looked like a small wet-bar, and a closet off of one side next to a bathroom. The entire place was decorated in brown tones and it felt comfortable.

"You know she's not going to make it," he said simply as Carol closed the door and sat down across from him.

"I know," Carol said, nodding. "I am just hoping to give her a few more weeks, maybe a month."

"Not going to happen," Dr. James said, shaking his head sadly. "Her heart is so damaged I am amazed she has lived this long. That should have been fixed when she was a teenager."

Considering that Megan grew up in a small cabin outside a small Montana town in the 1880s, that really wouldn't have been possible.

Carol knew the answer to her next question, but had to ask it just to be sure, to make sure she had missed nothing.

"A full bypass wouldn't help her, I assume?" Carol asked. "I'm grasping at straws here."

Doctor James shook his head. "It's the main body of her heart that is the most damaged, more than likely at birth. And everything around her heart has been damaged as well. She would never survive a bypass and it likely wouldn't work even if she did."

Now Available
from all your favorite booksellers
in trade paper and electronic editions.

Carol nodded. "I knew that. I studied the images of her heart as well. Just hoping against hope there was something I had missed."

"Sorry I couldn't toss you a straw on that one, Doctor. I doubt your friend will make it through the night no matter what any of us do."

"My diagnosis as well," Carol said, standing. "And as Megan said, thank you for helping her."

"Don't forget to take care of yourself through this as well, Doctor."

He stood as she stood and shook her hand across the desk.

"I will," Carol said.

She didn't know how, but she knew she would.

There was nothing more Dr. James could say as she left and headed back to the woman she loved.

The woman who she now had to watch die for the third time.

CHAPTER THIRTY

April 17th, 2019
Boise, Idaho

MEGAN AWOKE SLOWLY.

The pain in her chest still felt like something huge had kicked her. And the beeping kept going on and on and on.

She blinked her eyes a few times until she could focus.

The white ceiling with the holes was still above her and whatever was sticking out of her nose felt like a ham bone it was so large.

"That sound is very annoying," Megan said, her voice raspy.

Carol appeared above her, smiling. "Not to me, my love. That is the sound of your heart."

"I hope my new one won't be so annoying," Megan said.

With that, Carol actually smiled, which was wonderful to see.

Megan loved that smile, loved that woman looking down on her more than she could ever imagine loving anyone. At least if she was to die, she had had the chance to actually feel love.

Carol squeezed Megan's hand slightly and Megan squeezed back.

"What time is it?" Megan asked.

"Just before midnight," Carol said.

"I would be about to put my pies for the night into the oven. Then for the next hour I would stoke the oven just right and check the pies every five minutes."

Megan smiled at that memory, at how much she loved to bake.

Above her, Carol smiled as well. "Always great pies."

"You know I could bake us a wedding cake as well. Not back then, but in this time."

Megan imagined how wonderful that would be.

"Five layers. Very tall. White cake, fine decorations on it. I would promise it would be delicious. I can almost taste it right now."

Carol coughed and nodded, tears in her eyes. "You will bake that cake, my love. And it will be wonderful."

"Not this me," Megan said, "but another me will get that wonderful task."

"Don't say that," Carol said.

Megan looked up into the tear-filled eyes of the woman she loved more than anything. "Do me a favor?"

"Anything," Carol said.

"Don't give up on me. Give my new heart to the next me."

"I will never give up on you," Carol said.

"Good," Megan said, nodding and closing her eyes. "I really want to bake that wedding cake for us."

The annoying beeping changed.

And at that moment the pain in her chest felt like she had been stabbed.

Then blackness took her.

PART FOUR
A Fourth Chance

CHAPTER THIRTY-ONE

Four months earlier...

June 3rd, 1901
Boise, Idaho

MEGAN TOOK OFF her long blue apron after a long night's shift. She had just checked to make sure all her rolls were being stored correctly for the morning breakfast rush, and her pies and cakes were stored on racks cooling.

Around her the large kitchen of the Idanha Hotel was coming alive with breakfast orders and preparation for the day. The smells of sizzling ham and frying eggs were mixing with the sweetness of her pies and cakes.

At night she often had the kitchen all to herself. She liked it that way, but she never minded when the breakfast cooks arrived and the wait staff began to prepare the dining room.

She followed the same routine every morning before leaving for a breath of fresh air and then a bath and long sleep. Taking off her apron was the last detail in that routine.

The hotel had only been open for a short five months, and yet in just five months, Megan couldn't imagine being anywhere else. If she had her wish, she would just keep baking and die here.

She knew that outside the early summer air would be brisk, but not too cool. She loved that about Boise summers, how the evenings cooled off even though the days were hot. So even if she only stepped outside for a few seconds, the morning air helped her.

"Mrs. Taber," Chef Pickner said from behind her. "There are three early diners who would like a moment of your time."

She turned and looked into the smiling face of the man who had hired her. He was shorter than her by a good five inches and very round, seeming to play into the look that most thought chefs should be. His hair was balding and his eyebrows as bushy as she had ever seen. They often caught flour or bits of food in them and one of the other chefs was always giving him the sign to clean off his face.

She was about to object when he handed her a wicker basket full of her freshly-made bread covered in a white towel to keep them warm.

"Smothered in butter as you instruct," the chef said, smiling. "Just deliver these to the table near the fireplace. Two men and a woman."

She nodded and smoothed down her dress. "Am I presentable?"

The chef nodded. "As always."

He then turned away with a smile, leaving her standing there with the basket of breads in her hand.

She had no idea what this was about, but it seemed she had no choice.

The morning summer light through the big windows seemed almost orange in color, promising a beautiful sunrise over the mountains. The large stone fireplace sat dark and empty, a reminder of the colder winter days. The high-ceilinged room felt cooler than the kitchen had felt, but still comfortable. And the ceiling fans were not yet turned on, so the room felt quiet.

Later in the day she knew the windows on both sides would be opened allowing a light cross-breeze to keep the air as cool as possible and moving.

All the dining tables were made of polished oak and covered in fine tan tablecloths. Cloth napkins were folded perfectly at every place and the silverware gleamed in the morning light.

Only four tables of diners this early in the morning occupied the large room. In short order there would be many more. Summer breakfast was the restaurant's best time.

The three early diners she had been instructed to go talk to were sitting near the window facing Main Street. They all seemed to be in a good mood as they were laughing at something one of them must have said.

Dr. Stevens was one of the diners and she smiled at that. He had tried to save her husband all those years ago after her husband fell and hit his head. Then Dr. Stevens had helped her get a job in a kitchen, which had started her baking life.

She owed Dr. Stevens and loved talking with him when she could. Thankfully, in the six years since her husband had died, she hadn't needed to go see Dr. Stevens for any medical problems other than the lightheadedness. He had said simply and

bluntly that she had a bad heart and there was nothing that could be done. She had been told the same thing when she was younger and she just accepted it.

Except for being lightheaded at times, she felt wonderfully healthy, something she was grateful for every day.

The other two at the table she felt she knew from around town, but didn't know them by name.

As she approached, both men stood.

Dr. Stevens stuck out his hand and with a smile said, "Megan, you are looking wonderful as always."

"Thank you, Doctor," she said smiling back.

"This is Bonnie and Duster Kendal," Dr. Stevens said, introducing her. "This is Mrs. Megan Taber."

Duster Kendal bowed slightly and Bonnie said, "Wonderful meeting you."

"Can you join us for a few moments?" Duster asked, moving to hold a chair for her.

"Oh, I'm such a fright," Megan said. "I've been baking all night."

"Just for a moment," Bonnie said. "You look wonderful."

Megan smiled and sat down, enjoying the compliment from such an attractive woman.

Megan felt honored to be with Doctor Stevens and she knew of Bonnie and Duster by reputation around town as well.

"First off," Dr. Stevens said, opening the cloth covering the bread basket she had brought and pulling out a piece of warm bread glistening with melted butter. "I want to once again compliment you on this bread. I have no idea how you do it."

"It is wonderful," Bonnie said, smiling at Megan.

"Of that I can't argue in the slightest," Duster said and took the basket, helping himself to a piece as well.

"Thank you," Megan said, blushing. "Just having you all enjoy the bread makes my day."

"We enjoy it everyday," Dr. Stevens said, laughing.

Megan could feel herself blushing even more. Then for the next few minutes they talked about the weather and how warm the summer was promising to be and how they were all looking forward to the warmth after the cold weather.

And as the conversation went on, Duster and Bonnie finally got to the point of asking to see her. They wanted her to meet a woman writer interviewing strong women around the west.

Megan had no idea why the writer had picked her, but with a little push from Dr. Stevens, she agreed.

"Thank you," Bonnie said, smiling. "I think you will really like Carol."

"I'm sure I will," Megan said, worried that it might take too much time away from her new job. "I'm sure I will."

CHAPTER THIRTY-TWO

June 5th, 1901
Boise, Idaho

CAROL STOOD OUTSIDE the Institute, her horse saddled and ready to ride into town to meet Megan for dinner.

A new Megan.

But the same Megan.

A Megan who didn't know Carol and who hadn't fallen in love with Carol.

But this was basically the same Megan, just four months earlier in time.

Carol stood there, holding the reins of her horse, letting the warm evening breeze off the river blow around her, not yet willing to ride into town.

Carol wasn't certain she could go through with this again. Watching Megan die for the third time had just about torn her apart.

She had spent an entire month in her condo, doing nothing but reading and feeling sorry for herself and missing Megan.

And Carol figured she had a right to do just that. And she was thankful that no one tried to talk her out of it. They had just let her alone, as she had asked.

It wasn't until four weeks after Megan died for the third time that Director Parks called her.

"Megan's new heart will be ready in one week," he said simply.

She thanked the director and hung up.

Carol stood there by her fridge in her kitchen and remembered her last promise to Megan, to not give up on her. But over the last month Carol had given up on herself.

And that wasn't like her.

And Megan would be angry at her for doing that.

She needed to stand up and make a new plan. At least this time Megan had a new heart waiting.

She looked at the large trees around her, all showing the fresh green growth of a new start, a new season.

Carol nodded to herself. Then to the trees she said, "I'm not giving up on you, my love."

She climbed into the saddle and thirty minutes later she was sitting in the Idanha Hotel dining room, once again waiting for Megan, the love of Carol's life.

And a Megan that Carol had not yet met.

CHAPTER THIRTY-THREE

June 5th, 1901
Boise, Idaho

MEGAN FELT NERVOUS. She had on one of her best skirts and blouses, an outfit she saved for special occasions such as a staff party. The skirt was a pleated blue and the blouse a loose white with silk on the neck and sleeves. She wore a light matching blue jacket over her blouse and a small string of pearls from her mother.

Even though it was a warm evening outside, she felt she needed the jacket to look presentable.

She wasn't sure why she was nervous. This Carol Kogan sounded nice and impressive and wanted to just talk. Megan figured that was what was making her nervous, that someone actually valued beyond what they ate at their table what she did every night.

She brushed down her skirt one more time, then checked to make sure her hair was in place, even though as short as it was, there wasn't much she could do with it.

She nodded to the desk clerk as she moved across the stone-floors of the foyer and into the open restaurant doors beyond.

Stan, the evening host, greeted her with a smile. "You look wonderful this evening, Mrs. Taber."

"Thank you, Stan," she said, bowing slightly.

"Your guest is waiting at the table near the front window," Stan said, indicating that she should follow him.

The blinds on the west side of the room had been drawn to block out the direct evening sun and Megan was happy to see that the woman was sitting in a shaded area near an open window. The noise and smells from the streets might intrude at times, but even a slight breeze would be better than being stuffy.

As Megan approached, the woman she was meeting glanced around and seemed shocked.

Actually, it was Megan who felt shocked. The woman was stunningly beautiful and dressed in a similar style as Megan was.

The woman stood and extended her hand after a moment. "Mrs. Taber, I am Carol Kogan. The honor is all mine to meet you."

Megan took Miss Kogan's hand and was stunned at how soft and wonderful it felt. She didn't want to let it go.

And she didn't want to stop staring in Miss Kogan's eyes either. They were the most beautiful green Megan had ever seen.

And clearly Miss Kogan didn't want to break the grip either. Her face looked flushed and there was a slight look of panic in her eyes.

Stan moved around Megan and pulled out her chair, so Megan released Miss Kogan's hand and sat, allowing Miss Kogan to sit again as well.

"Would you enjoy a beverage to start?" Stan asked.

"Water would be wonderful," Megan said.

Stan nodded and turned away.

Megan looked at Carol, who was staring at her as well.

"Call me Megan," she said, deciding to break the ice a little, even though ice was a great distance away from this warm summer evening.

"I'm Carol. And I apologize for staring. I feel so like I know you and you are a very beautiful woman."

Megan could feel herself blush a little along her neck. She laughed. "No need to apologize at all, because I was thinking the same of you."

Now Carol blushed slightly and laughed what was clearly a relieved laugh.

From there over the evening they managed to talk about their pasts, about how Megan's husband had died, and then finally her baking.

It was a wonderful evening, especially when Carol called her baking an art. Megan thought of it as an art, but no one had ever said that to her before.

The evening ended with the two of them sitting and staring at each other for the longest and most wonderful time.

CHAPTER THIRTY-FOUR

June 5th, 1901
Boise, Idaho

CAROL HAD BEEN so nervous when Megan came into the dining room, she almost couldn't stand.

Carol had buried Megan three times, yet here she was again, walking across the warm, sunlit dining room like an angel.

There was no doubt it was the same Megan that Carol had fallen so completely in love with. And now seeing Megan like this again was like a dream.

All Carol wanted to do was hug her.

But she didn't.

This was going to be impossible, but to save Megan's life, Carol had to try to give Megan time to trust her.

But not take a lot of time.

That would be a very fine balance.

Thankfully, the dinner went well as it had in the last two timelines, and again they met the next morning for breakfast in Megan's apartment.

Carol touched Megan's beautiful patchwork quilt when she came in, knowing that it was also in her condo on her own couch in 2019. She had spent a lot of time wrapped in it this last month, not wanting to think about being in a world without Megan.

And now, she wasn't yet again.

The breakfast went almost identically as the first two times they had had breakfast together.

And from that moment forward they spent every dinner together and every breakfast, until the moment when Megan asked Carol to scrub her back.

And the romance turned physical from there, as it had the last time they had been together.

It was now time once again to take Megan to the future, to try to save her life with a brand new heart.

That evening at dinner, Carol asked Megan if she could get the following night off of work. She had a wonderful surprise to show her.

Megan nodded and smiled. "I would love to start to see some of the many surprises you hold."

"You saw a few of those this morning," Carol said, blushing.

Megan also blushed. "That's why I am interested in more."

Carol laughed.

As before, it had taken Carol one month to gain Megan's trust and love.

And for Carol, it had been once again one of the best months of her life.

Maybe the best.

Because after losing Megan three times, getting to spend a wonderful month with her again couldn't be anything more than the best.

CHAPTER THIRTY-FIVE

July 7, 2019
Boise, Idaho

MEGAN WAS VERY, very puzzled at the events of the last half hour and why Bonnie and Carol had taken her down into that tunnel under the Institute and then brought her back up here.

The day had started off wonderfully, with an easy and enjoyable ride to the Institute. Then Carol had taken them down underground to a large cavern and Bonnie Kendal had been there.

They had taken her even farther underground and then back up to the large cavern. None of it was making any sense to her, but Carol seemed to be smiling and as happy as Megan had seen her since they had met.

It wasn't until Megan really looked at the furniture in the large cavern room and the kitchen countertop and the things behind the counter that she started to get worried.

"Everything changed here since we went downstairs," Megan said.

Both Bonnie and Carol nodded.

"You are no longer in 1901," Bonnie said.

"That's my secret," Carol said, turning and staring into Megan's eyes. "I am from the year 2019."

Megan laughed, but Carol's expression didn't change.

After a moment, Megan said, slightly panicked, "You are serious, aren't you?"

Carol and Bonnie both nodded.

"Come on," Carol said, "Let me show you something."

"I'll stay here and make us a light snack before dinner," Bonnie said.

Megan let Carol take her hand and direct her to the elevator they had come down. Now it was sleek and had a full door instead of a cage. As they approached, the door slid open silently.

Carol stepped on and Megan reluctantly followed her.

"Trust me," Carol said, "this is a million times safer than that Otis in the hotel."

"Anything would be," Megan said, moving on and holding onto both of Carol's hands as the door closed.

She could feel a slight sense of movement and then the door slid back open.

A few moments later they were through the front room of the Institute and out onto the large porch.

Megan was stunned at what she saw.

In fact, she wasn't sure exactly what she was seeing.

"It's early June 2019," Carol said. "About twelve noon. Trees all now have their leaves and all those things going by are modern versions of the automobiles that were just getting started in 1901."

Megan just stood and stared, holding Carol's hand as if it were a lifeline to a sane time and place. Where before it had just been the three Victorian mansions sitting on a slight hill overlooking the river, now the entire area was full of homes and buildings of all types.

And the wagon road that had run past the mansion was now covered in some sort of pavement and strange-looking automobiles flashed past at impossible speeds.

Finally, after almost a minute of Megan looking around, she turned to Carol. "You really are from this time?"

"I am," Carol said. "I am a medical doctor and an historian. I traveled back to 1901 to learn about strong women and their medical conditions for a book I am writing."

"So I am a test subject," Megan said, feeling almost angry.

"No," Carol said, forcing Megan to look into her eyes. "You are the woman I fell in love with, the woman I want to spend lifetimes with. I had to get permission to share this with you."

Megan could see the worry and the love in Carol's eyes. She was telling the truth.

After a moment Megan nodded and kissed Carol who seemed to melt with relief in her arms.

Then she said simply, "I have a lot to learn it seems."

"If we want we can stay here for a while," Carol said. "But I would rather live in your time for now."

"We can go back?" Megan asked. She wasn't sure why she thought she couldn't go back, since Carol had gone back from here to meet her.

"Of course we can," Carol said. "We could spend months here and go back to within an hour of when we got off those horses to continue that wonderful day. And yet still remember the months here."

"Seriously?" Megan asked, actually starting to feel excited, even though what she was seeing around her scared her more than she wanted to admit.

"Seriously," Carol said. "Bonnie knows a lot more about all those sorts of things."

"So let's go back and get a bite to eat," Megan said, looking around at the amazing scene she never could have imagined. "And I'll start learning about your world since you know so much about mine."

Megan took Carol's hand and they went back inside. This all seemed impossible, yet Carol was very real and with her. So even the impossible might be all right as long as they were together.

CHAPTER THIRTY-SIX

June 7th, 2019
Boise, Idaho

CAROL WAS STUNNED at how level Megan seemed to be in the face of such insanity, although Carol shouldn't have been. How Megan was reacting this time was exactly how she had reacted last time. Almost down to the very same questions.

Megan was clearly an amazing woman, of that there was no doubt, in any timeline.

Carol and Megan and Bonnie all sat at the counter eating a light sandwich and salad.

So after some talk about living in the past and how little time was spent when a person went back into the past, Carol finally got around to telling Megan the problem.

"There is another reason we brought you here," Carol said. "It's your heart."

Megan smiled at Carol and nodded. "I had a hunch that was what this was all about."

Carol was stunned. Megan had said that the last time and Carol had tried to be more careful about talking about Megan's health this time around.

Megan smiled and reached over and squeezed Carol's hand. "Not a day goes by that you don't ask me a few times how I am feeling."

Bonnie laughed and Carol just shook her head. "I was trying to be careful and not do that too much."

"I didn't mind at all," Megan said. "You say you are a medical doctor from this time. So what is wrong with my heart?"

"Exactly what you have been told," Carol said, turning to face Megan directly. "You were basically born with a bad heart that will suddenly stop working. It is the cause of your feeling faint and the dizzy spells."

"Since you are from the future here, do you know when it finally gives up?"

"Every timeline is different," Bonnie said.

Carol took a deep breath and looked at Bonnie, who just nodded.

"I need to tell you a story, my love," Carol said. "And I promise every bit of it is true."

"This sounds very serious," Megan said, smiling.

"It is," Carol said, leaning forward and kissing Megan lightly. "And I have no idea how I would react if someone told me this story. Just remember I love you."

Megan nodded.

Carol took a deep breath and told the story of how she and Megan met the first time on the sidewalk. And what happened.

"Oh, I am so sorry," Megan said, squeezing Carol's hand.

"You had that fatal heart attack in May of 1902, so we assumed we had time," Carol said. "I went back six months earlier and we met on a cold early November day in the restaurant, similar to how we met this time."

"Oh, no," Megan said softly.

Carol nodded. "Meeting you and falling in love with you was wonderful, as it was this time."

"We have done all of the last month before?" Megan asked.

"I have," Carol said. "We had a wonderful couple of weeks of falling in love and then toward the end of the month, you had a heart attack that killed you, that time in your apartment."

"So you came back earlier," Megan said. "And now I am here and still alive."

"I did," Carol said. "But once again it didn't work out. That time you died in a hospital here before we could save you."

"I have died on you three times?" Megan said, her eyes round.

"You have, my love," Carol said.

"I am so, so sorry," Megan said. "How can you still want to be with me?"

"I want us to fix your heart this time," Carol said. "So that you and I can be together for a very long time."

Megan nodded, sitting there staring at Carol's hands in hers.

Carol let her just sit there. This was the turning point.

Finally, Megan looked up into Carol's eyes. "I hate that I put you through so much to get here."

Carol smiled at the wonderful woman sitting next to her. "Trust me, just the last month with you was worth it."

At that point, Director Parks came in and Carol introduced him to Megan and told her what he did.

"Are you ready to go?" Parks asked after a moment.

"Where are we going to next?" Megan asked.

"Another hundred years into the future," Carol said. "You have a new heart there waiting for you."

Megan just stared at Carol, then looked at Bonnie and Director Parks.

"You are all very serious," Megan said.

"We are trying to save your life," Carol said. "Just trust me a little bit more."

Megan finally nodded.

"I'll be waiting here for you three when you get back," Bonnie said.

Carol took Megan's hand and they followed Director Parks across the main living room cavern and into a tunnel.

"This is frightening," Megan said.

"For me as well," Carol said. "But we're together. That's all that matters."

And for Carol at this point, that was all that mattered.

CHAPTER THIRTY-SEVEN

June 7th, 2119
Boise, Idaho

TO MEGAN IT didn't feel any different moving forward a hundred years than it had moving to 2019 from 1901. She just held onto Carol as if they were in bed together and a moment later, without movement or anything, they seemed to be there.

Megan had always known she had a bad heart. She had been told that when she was eleven. And she had always known she could die at any moment. And when a person knew that sort of information, the only thing that person could do was just live normally and that's what Megan had been trying to do.

Until she fell in love with the beautiful Carol.

And then learned that death had visited three times in front of Carol.

Megan didn't want that again and was willing to follow Carol anywhere to keep that from happening once again to the woman she loved.

They moved from the caverns up and into where the horse stable used to be, but now held very fancy and strangely shaped automobiles that made no sounds when started.

Director Parks had let her and Carol sit in the back and he had taken the front seat. Then he had just stated a location and the car moved on its own.

"When we arrive at the hospital," Director Parks said, "I have modern identification for you. You are still Megan Taber, but the two of you are married."

"We can do that here?" Megan asked, looking at Carol.

Carol smiled. "We can do that in my time as well."

"This is really a place of wonder," Megan said, watching the sights go by outside and being amazed that Director Parks was not doing anything to control the automobile in any fashion. But yet somehow all of the machines missed each other.

"You can say nothing at all about being from the past," Director Parks said. "That is very, very important."

Megan nodded. "I understand. So what is going to happen to me?"

"A new, healthy heart has been grown for you here," Carol said, "and it will replace out your old heart."

"They can do that?"

Carol nodded and squeezed Megan's hand. "And from what I understand, it won't even leave much of a scar."

Megan could feel herself getting more and more tense.

"This is all very strange," Megan said.

"It will all be over soon," Carol said, "and then we can go forward with our lives together, either back in your time or in my time or both."

The car stopped in front of a gleaming, tall building that seemed to stretch up into the blue sky. From there, for Megan, everything went quickly.

They had her on what looked like a stretcher but was very comfortable and then Carol said she would be here when Megan woke up.

She kissed Megan firmly and then smiled. "Be nice to the handsome doctors."

"Only if they look as good as you look," Megan said, smiling.

A moment later there was a faint tap on Megan's shoulder from the cart and she relaxed and drifted off into a beautiful sleep, staring at Carol's wonderful face.

CHAPTER THIRTY-EIGHT

June 7th, 2119
Boise, Idaho

TO CAROL, THE next hour was like a torture, with time moving so slowly it seemed to almost stop.

Director Parks had gone back to the Institute to get some work done and said he would return when Megan came out of surgery. Carol had decided to stay. Even though the medicine of this time was far beyond what she knew, she felt she needed to be here anyway.

Carol waited in the room where Megan would be brought after surgery. It felt modern and comfortable, not like hospital rooms of a hundred years before, but more like a nice bedroom instead. Any equipment that was in here was well hidden.

Carol knew there was a problem when the surgeon appeared at one hour and thirty minutes into what had been scheduled to be a two-hour surgery. From what Carol had read about this surgery in this time, everything took exactly a set amount of time.

Carol stood.

The doctor had that look that Carol knew all doctors had when delivering bad news. She had used that look numbers of times herself. It was a look of attempted calm radiating extreme sadness and a little anger at failing.

"It didn't go well, did it?" Carol asked.

She could feel herself shutting down, going cold and numb.

The doctor shook his head. "Far too much damage to everything around the heart. We did our best to patch, but there was no possibility of holding pressure. We never got her new heart started. I am so sorry."

Carol nodded and sat down on the chair next to the bed.

Her world was just sort of drifting off into a distance.

"Again, I am so sorry."

"Thank you, doctor," Carol said. "You did your best. Megan and I both knew this was a risk going in, since she had so little time without the surgery."

The doctor nodded and turned as Director Parks showed up.

"What happened?" the Director asked, his voice a whisper as he watched the surgeon leave.

"There was too much damage around the heart for them to fix," Carol said softly.

"Oh, no," the director said, dropping into another chair.

The two of them sat there silently with the empty bed.

There wasn't a thing either of them could say.

PART FIVE
No More Chances

CHAPTER THIRTY-NINE

June 7th, 2119
Boise, Idaho

CAROL AND DIRECTOR PARKS made arrangements with the hospital to take care of Megan's body. As they were doing that, standing at what seemed to be a front desk of the hospital, Carol finally seemed to come out of her daze.

She couldn't believe that even a hundred years in the future from her time, this had still happened. She decided she needed just a bit more information.

She needed to have that information so she could go home and try to move past Megan. She had a hunch that was going to be the most difficult thing she had ever done in her life, but she had time.

Hundreds and hundreds of years of time.

She would do it, and having just a little more information would help her do that.

She would never forget Megan, but she would get past her.

"What was the doctor's name again that operated on Megan?" Carol asked Parks.

He seemed startled by the question, seeming to come out of a daze himself. He looked down at the screen in front of them. "Dr. LaBeck was the lead surgeon and the one that brought the news to us."

Carol nodded. "Think you could arrange for us to talk to him again. As a doctor, I just need a little bit more information to help me not dwell on this."

Parks nodded and turned to a nice man behind a desk nearby. After a few minutes, Dr. LaBeck agreed to meet them in his office on the fourteenth floor.

His office looked like a surgeon's office in a hospital might have looked a hundred years earlier. A couch, some chairs, and a large desk with a screen that seemed to come up from the desk. Three different electronic pads of some sort were stacked on one corner.

He greeted them and nodded to Director Parks.

Then he turned to Carol. "I am very sorry once again for your loss."

Carol was thinking enough now to know exactly how to take Dr. LaBeck off the hook.

"We know you did everything you could, Doctor," Carol said. "But for the sake of my curiosity and to settle a discussion Megan and I used to have, would there have been a time that a heart replacement operation would have worked for her?"

"Without a doubt," Dr. LaBeck said. "If she had had the same operation at about age eleven, the malfunctioning heart would have never had the time to destroy everything around it. I am amazed she made it to the age of twenty-five, honestly, considering the amount of damage around her heart."

That made sense to Carol. By age thirteen or fourteen, Megan was already doomed to die somewhere in the time frame that she had died.

"Why age eleven?" Director Parks asked.

Carol could have told him, but she let Dr. LaBeck do so.

"Because most of the growth of internal organs and the heart that is going to happen has happened at that point in a child's life," Dr. LaBeck said. "Earlier in age and the process of a heart replacement would be too dangerous. Later and the damage would have started to happen."

Carol nodded.

"In other words," Carol said, "there was nothing that could have been done to save Megan at her age."

Dr. LaBeck nodded. "I'm afraid that is correct."

Carol stood, which caused both Director Parks and Dr. LaBeck to stand.

Carol reached out her hand and shook the doctor's hand. "Thank you for giving Megan at least a small chance."

"I wish a miracle would have happened here," LaBeck said.

"We all did," Carol said.

With that, she turned and headed out the door on a path back to 2019 and a life without Megan in it.

CHAPTER FORTY

June 14th, 2019
Boise, Idaho

CAROL ALLOWED HERSELF just a week to mourn Megan. She had lost her four times and each time it had seemed to rip her heart out.

But the reality of the world was that Megan would never be a part of her life in any time. Carol couldn't go back and meet Megan again just to watch her die at any moment.

She loved Megan more than anything in the world, but she couldn't put herself through that again.

Then after a week, Carol took Megan's beautiful quilt and folded it carefully and put it in the top of a closet she never used and seldom opened.

Out of sight, out of mind.

Carol was under no illusion that would happen, but having the quilt in the living room to remind her of Megan every day wasn't a good plan either.

Maybe, down the road, Carol would bring the quilt out as a fond memory. But right now everything was just too raw and painful.

And it all felt so unfair.

She had been blessed with basically being immortal, being able to live entire lifetimes in other timelines and then only have two minutes pass.

Yet Megan, the woman Carol loved, got only a short twenty-five years in one lifetime.

As a doctor, Carol knew that life was basically unfair. But this just seemed to be over an edge.

So after one week, Carol went back to her office in the Institute library, put away all her notes on the Strong Women of the West book she had started writing, and opened up a new file.

It was time she tackled the women of ill-repute book in the West she had always hoped to write some day. She didn't have a title for it yet, but she knew she would, given time.

That would keep her mind busy for at least five years or more in real 2019 time and who knew how many decades of time back in the past. And when back in the past, she would make sure she stayed away from the Idanha Hotel.

And her plan worked.

Slowly, day after day, month after month, the pain of losing Megan dulled. It never really went away and almost everything reminded Carol of Megan.

But Carol knew she was getting better, slowly.

At one point Carol had gone into the cavern with the crystals from her trips back with Megan. For the longest time she sat and stared at the crystal with the timeline where she had first met Megan and Megan had died in front of the Institute.

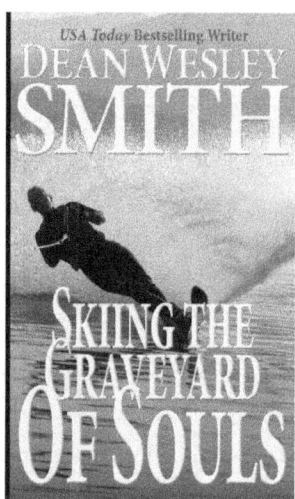

And beside that crystal was another crystal, another timeline, where Megan had died in her rooms.

And beside that one was another crystal where Megan had died here, in 2019. At some point, Carol needed to return to that timeline a day or so after they had left and tell the fine people at the Idanha Hotel that Megan had died suddenly.

Then there was the crystal where Megan had died in the future. Carol needed to go back yet again in that crystal and tell the fine people who were friends with Megan about her death.

But there was no hurry. Carol could do that at any point, since even ten years from now she could jump to just a day after they left.

She had all the time in all the timelines to do that. She could wait until the pain didn't feel so sharp and the memory wasn't so clear.

She would wait.

CHAPTER FORTY-ONE

September 6, 1898
Outside Missoula, Montana

FIVE YEARS LATER, measured by her alive time, but just over a month measured by 2019 time, on a trip into the past, Carol found herself in 1898 in Missoula, Montana.

The days were getting shorter and the nights colder. She planned on heading back south to Boise and back to 2019 in the next few weeks before the snow started to fly. She hated traveling in the fall alone in snow through the mountains. Just too dangerous, even though she felt she could take care of herself just fine. She didn't want to have to test that.

The small farming and mining towns around Missoula had some interesting battles with the brothels during those times and she had numbers of leads to talk with women in those small towns. She figured it might be a chapter in her book at least.

As she was sitting in her hotel room in Missoula, a map spread out on her bed, planning her next few weeks, she noticed the name of a small town thirty miles east of Missoula.

Placerville.

Megan's home town.

By September 1898, Megan would have been gone from there for four years already, widowed and living in Boise. But a number of times Megan had mentioned that she missed her mother. Her father was dead, but her mother and two sisters still ran the family farm, as much as it was.

Carol decided she wanted to see where Megan grew up. Just curiosity, more than anything else. The five years had dulled the ache enough that Carol thought she could manage the visit.

So two days later, she rode up to the small log and wood home tucked off in some trees near a creek. It was a far more beautiful place than Megan had described.

Carol had decided to tell them she had met Megan in Boise and since she was riding by, working on her new book, she said she would stop in and say hello.

She reverted back to working on the Strong Women in the West book for her story and gave her name as Ann, her middle name. She didn't want word getting back to Megan and making her wonder who this strange woman was visiting her family.

Turns out Megan's mother was a strong woman in her own right.

Her name was Marie and she was short compared to Megan, but had Megan's dark, intense eyes. If Carol ever got back to working on that book, she would have to include a chapter on Marie, of that there was no doubt.

Marie invited Carol inside to the comfortable-feeling living area and kitchen. A wooden table that showed decades of use filled one area beside the kitchen.

Marie offered Carol some tea and a shortbread cookie as she sat and Carol gladly accepted. There was no sign of the other two daughters being close by, but it seemed clear they were living here.

Marie had raised four daughters alone in this small cabin after her husband was killed by another man in a fight. Megan had been the second to the youngest, but still had pitched in and worked to help.

Carol enjoyed talking with Marie as they sipped their tea. Carol now understood where Megan got her calm and sense of humor about the tough things in life.

At one point, the conversation came around to Megan and her mother beamed and asked how she was doing. "Her last letter said she was baking at the Thunderbird."

"Seems fine," Carol said. "She is still baking at the Thunderbird Hotel and her breads are making her a strong reputation."

Carol knew Megan's history by heart and so wanted to go to Boise to meet her again, but just didn't dare. Nothing but pain would come from it.

"She always could cook," Marie said, smiling. "We miss her pies around here."

"She mentioned something about having a bad heart," Carol said. "Sure doesn't seem like it slows her down any."

"Never did," Megan's mother said, "even before it was fixed."

"Fixed?" Carol asked, almost leaning forward too quickly for the old wooden chair she was on. It cracked in complaint, but Marie didn't seem to notice at all.

"Sure thing. Doc said we might lose her at any point because of her bad heart, but then Doc found her some help. I couldn't get away to take her to Missoula, so that Marshal and beautiful Bonnie the nurse came and picked her up and took her to the fancy doctors in Missoula."

"What happened?" Carol asked, not believing at all what she was hearing. Megan had never said a word about going to Missoula for her heart.

"Two weeks later she was back, all good as new. And it was all free as well. Marshal said the nice people at the hospital paid for everything because Megan was so special."

Carol just sat there, her mouth open like a fish out of water. She didn't know what to think.

"Did Megan say anything about the operation and who did it?"

Marie shook her head. "Megan said she was out cold most of the time and only remembered small flashes of faces and things until she completely woke up headed back here. She did say everything was real white and smelled funny, not bad, just funny."

Carol again just sort of sat there, staring at Marie.

"A Marshal came and picked her up. You remember his name?"

"Oh, sure, everyone around here knows Marshal Duster Kendal. He marshaled over in the mining camps north of Missoula for a time and cleaned things up there real proper like."

Carol had nothing more to say.

Nothing.

CHAPTER FORTY-TWO

July 12th, 2019
Boise, Idaho

AFTER THANKING MARIE for the fine tea and company and promising to say hello to Megan when she saw her, Carol headed at a fast ride to Boise.

The ride took her three long days of thinking and wondering and being alternately angry and excited about what she had discovered.

And she kept wondering why Duster and Bonnie would do something like that without including her, although as she had learned more and more about jumping to different timelines, they might not have done anything yet in the 2019 main timeline she had left.

In fact, her going back to 2019 and telling them might be what triggered the action. If that was the case, she was going to have to ask how that could even be possible.

So as she rode into the Institute, took care of her horse, and then got herself back into the caverns, she made herself calm down. She was in desperate need of a shower and some decent food, since she had only eaten jerky for most of the ride.

But she also needed answers.

When she unplugged the wire from the crystal, she carefully made a note on the pad below it that it was the timeline where Megan had had an operation. And noted her time in the past carefully so that she didn't make a mistake and start a new timeline by crossing over at any point.

Then she headed upstairs.

There was no one in the large living room area, as there hadn't been when she left this time about ten minutes earlier. She had spent almost a year in the past, but only a few minutes had gone by here. She loved that about jumping into new timelines.

So she got herself a snack of cheese and a sports drink and headed for the showers.

Thirty minutes later, refreshed, dressed in jeans and a white blouse, and feeling clean for the first time in days, she headed upstairs carrying the sports drink in her hand.

She found Director Parks in his office. It was a former bedroom of the large mansion and had wide windows looking out toward the river. He had furnished the office in period pieces, an ornate oak desk from the 1800s and a modern comfortable couch and chairs. Somehow it all fit together.

Especially for the director of an institute that specialized in history.

He smiled up at her and offered her a seat. "Just get back?"

"I did," she said, nodding as she dropped into one of the director's soft chairs facing his desk.

"How are you feeling?" Parks asked. In this time it had only been a month or so since Megan died the last time. So he would be worried.

"It's been five years for me since we lost Megan the last time," Carol said. "So up until three days ago I was doing fine."

"What happened three days ago?" Parks asked, closing his computer screen and focusing on her, clearly concerned.

"In the fall of 1898 I was investigating some brothels outside of Missoula for my new book."

Parks nodded.

"I noticed that Megan's small hometown was close by, so I stopped and visited with her mother, knowing at that point that Megan had been in Boise for years already."

"Why would you do that?"

"Same reason I think I needed to talk with the doctor in the future," Carol said. "I just needed more closure and I am slowly getting to that point. Or at least I was."

Parks looked puzzled.

And worried.

"I learned from Megan's mother, a wonderful and strong woman in her own right, that Megan had had a surgery when she was eleven to fix her heart. And it had been successful."

"What?" Parks asked, halfway coming out of his chair.

Carol smiled at that. "I had the same reaction. Damn near broke one of Megan's mother's chairs."

Parks sat back, shaking his head.

"It seems," Carol said, "that a wonderful Marshal and his nurse Bonnie came to pick up Megan and take her to a hospital in Missoula since Megan's mother didn't dare leave her other children alone at their farm."

"Son of a bitch," Parks said, shaking his head.

"Got any idea where Bonnie and Duster might be?" Carol asked.

"They flew up to Monumental Lodge today. They don't plan on returning until next week."

Carol felt disappointment with that. She really, really wanted some answers.

And it seems Director Parks did as well.

"Let's head for the airport," he said. "Seems we are having dinner at the lodge tonight."

Carol smiled and stood. "Good. I could use a really good meal. Should we tell them we are coming?"

"I'll call and tell Dawn when we get to the airport," Parks said. "That way she can save us a few trout."

"Wonderful," Carol said. "I really need to know what happened. Or what is going to happen as the case might be."

"As do I," Parks said, heading out the door ahead of Carol and turning for the stairs. "As do I."

CHAPTER FORTY-THREE

July 12th, 2019
Monumental Lodge, Idaho

CAROL LOVED THE Monumental Lodge. It sat on a saddle looking down thousands of feet in both directions over the wonderful Central Idaho Mountains.

The first time Carol had stayed there, she had simply sat for hours, having drinks and eating dinner on the wide deck that looked out over Monumental Creek and in the distance the River of No Return.

Stunning didn't begin to describe the views from the massive log lodge.

And the lodge itself was stunning, with massive polished logs and stone fireplaces, it felt comfortable.

And it should. Bonnie and Duster and Dawn and Madison had built it in the past. In fact, in any timeline they visited where the lodge wasn't built, they all spent the two years building it again exactly as all the others.

Carol had helped one year in the building and enjoyed it more than she wanted to admit. So she never grew tired of going back to the lodge in any timeline.

The Institute helicopter dropped them off on the pad about two hundred yards down a valley from the lodge and Parks and Connie started up the stone trail. It was that helicopter pad that allowed this lodge to be used year around. No road was passable into here except in the late spring through the early fall. And Carol had been up that road once before with Duster driving and decided riding a horse in was much, much better.

Or flying in. This was the first time she had gotten to do that and had been stunned at the fantastic beauty and ruggedness of central Idaho. Most of it had been designated a wilderness area so no new roads could be built.

It was very much like most of the West that Carol had been traveling in back in the late 1890s. But somehow, this massive part of an entire state had kept its wilderness feel and look.

Carol loved that.

The walk up the trail was wonderful, with the smell of hot pine filling the air. The air was dry and starting to cool down. Clearly it had been a perfect summer day here at the lodge.

As they reached the lodge, they could see that most of the few people lucky enough to book one of the ten rooms available to the public were sitting on the massive deck.

And the parking lot had about thirty cars in it that had managed to come up that twisted, winding road. More than likely many of them would just stay for dinner, sit and enjoy the view for a while, and then go back down into civilization, if you call Yellow Pine, Idaho, civilization.

As Carol and Director Parks stepped inside the lodge, Dawn looked up from behind the large, wooden front desk and smiled. "Wonderful to see you both."

Dawn and her husband Madison had been the first two travelers into other timelines besides Bonnie and Duster. Both of them were major historical writers and Dawn specialized on the old mining town that was five miles below this lodge in the valley.

Carol loved them both and trusted both of them as much as she trusted Bonnie and Duster. They felt like family to Carol.

Dawn came around the desk and hugged Director Parks, then Carol. Dawn and her husband, Madison, were half-owners of the lodge with Bonnie and Duster and they worked it. In fact, in different timelines, they had raised many families here in the past.

Dawn looked at Carol. "Very sorry to hear about Megan. That was horrible."

"Thank you," Carol said, smiling.

Dawn hugged her again.

"It's Megan that is why we are here to talk with Bonnie and Duster," Director Parks said.

Dawn looked puzzled. "I thought what Megan had was inoperable in any time?"

"It was," Carol said. "But it seems we have another wrinkle in the equation."

"Okay…" Dawn said, looking puzzled. Then she shook her head and turned for the dining room area that was mostly empty.

Carol and Director Parks followed.

"Got the back room set up for all of us," Dawn said. "Bonnie and Duster are already back there waiting for you when they heard you had arrived. And I have you both a fresh-caught trout reserved."

"Where's Madison?" Parks asked.

He took a run for supplies into McCall with the truck. He'll be back tomorrow."

"Sorry I'm going to miss him," Carol said. "But dinner sounds wonderful. After a seven-day horse ride and a helicopter flight, I could eat an entire stream of trout."

"We have that," Dawn said, laughing.

CHAPTER FORTY-FOUR

July 12th, 2019
Monumental Lodge, Idaho

BONNIE STOOD AND gave Carol a hug before they sat at the table.

The back dining room at the lodge could hold twenty people easily and like everything else here was made of log walls and log beams and polished wood floors. The large table was of light pine and the chairs were wood with padding on the seats.

A stone fireplace was dark in the back corner. The lighting was fake lanterns around the walls that looked antique and gave the place a feeling of age and a large wood and copper chandelier hung over the center of the table.

The room felt comfortable to Carol and she loved it every time she got to eat in here.

"How many years have you spent since we lost Megan?" Duster asked.

"Going on five," Carol said, sitting down and taking a sip of the ice water in front of her plate. "I'm doing better."

"I hate to be pushy," Bonnie said, "but the two of you showing up here unexpectedly together has us all really puzzled."

"We needed to ask you and Duster some questions about Megan," Director Parks said. "And neither of us could wait until you got back, so here we are."

Carol laughed at their surprised looks. It wasn't often you could surprise Bonnie and Duster or even worry them.

Dawn sat beside Bonnie, smiling. "This I got to hear."

Parks indicated Carol should tell her story and she did and why she had gone to see Megan's mother.

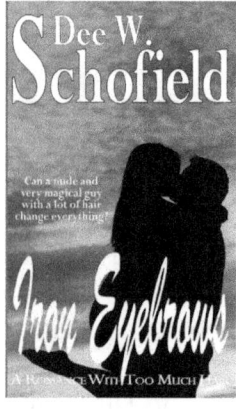   

Both Bonnie and Duster nodded to that.

"At one point I asked how Megan had done as a child with a bad heart," Carol said. "Megan's mother said she had done fine, especially after she got it fixed at eleven."

Bonnie, Duster, and Dawn all three sat forward, clearly shocked.

Carol held up her hand so that she could keep going.

"Megan's mother said a nice Marshal Kendal and a nurse named Bonnie came and picked Megan up and took her to Missoula to some fancy doctors. Seems Megan doesn't remember any of it except a white room that smelled funny."

Duster was just shaking his head.

Bonnie looked at Carol, then at her husband. "How the hell did we pull that off?"

"Or are you going to pull that off?" Dawn asked.

"That's what Carol and I were wondering exactly," Director Parks said.

Carol looked at Bonnie and Duster. "So I'm guessing you have not done that?"

"Can't imagine how it would be even possible," Duster said, "to get an eleven-year-old girl from the middle of 1880s Montana to Boise and then a couple hundred years into the future."

"And then back," Bonnie said.

"Back is the problem," Dawn said. "Wouldn't this mean that Megan is set at some point in the future as an eleven-year-old girl? So when she dies, even of old age, she will end up back in the future and eleven years old?"

"And with the memories of all her years as an adult," Bonnie said, softly.

"Oh, shit," Director Parks said.

"Is there a way around that problem?" Carol asked.

She stared at Bonnie and Duster, the two greatest math minds on the planet, the two that had discovered how to step into other timelines, the two that had lived for hundreds of thousands of years.

Both just sat there shaking their heads.

And that scared Carol more than she wanted to admit. Not for her, but for Megan.

CHAPTER FORTY-FIVE

August 22nd, 2019
Boise, Idaho

BONNIE AND DUSTER had spent over a month working on the problem, with help from other mathematicians who knew about the Institute and who worked for them in the past.

While they were doing that, with Director Parks help, Carol had gone forward two hundred years to study the transplant technique.

When they first got there, Director Parks had insisted that he take Carol yet another hundred years into the future. "That way, if you accidently get killed here in 2219, you will just go back to 2319."

She thanked him for that. But what he had done was just make her even more immortal. The life she was living right now in 2019 was only two minutes of time in 2119 and only two minutes of time in 2219 and now would also be only two minutes of time in 2319.

She so wanted Bonnie and Duster to figure out a way to give Megan that same gift of being basically immortal.

Carol studied the technique of full heart transplant and the more she learned, the more she realized that it really would save Megan's life. She even watched three other eleven-year-olds go through the same surgery. They ended up being fine within a few days. And by all indications from research on them from the future, the three kids had perfectly healthy and long lives. In fact, a hundred years farther along, two of them were still alive.

Carol knew she shouldn't, but as time went along she let a little hope creep back into her heart. She tried to stop it, but she just couldn't seem to.

So for eight months, Carol worked two hundred years in the future, learning everything she could about complete heart transplants and the surgery it required.

And learning medical procedures she could have only dreamed about when she went through med school.

Then she went back to 2019 only four weeks after she had left.

She liked the future, but she liked the free spirit of 2019 more, and she loved even more the complete roughness of life in 1902. It seemed she was an Old West girl at heart.

Finally, on August 22nd, sitting in Director Parks' office, Bonnie and Duster gave her what Carol had been fearing.

"It can't be done," Bonnie said.

The bluntness and finality of the statement shocked Carol.

"Even if Megan was knocked out and one of us was carrying her," Duster said, "it would reset her at the age of eleven two hundred years from now."

"And a hundred years from now as well," Director Parks said.

"We would never allow that to happen for any reason," Bonnie said. "I'm sorry, Carol."

"I agree," Carol said, her stomach twisting and feeling as if she might have just lost Megan one more time. "That can never happen. But thank you for doing the work."

"This pushed us into an area of math and timelines that we had never looked at before," Duster said. "So we need to thank you."

"But that still begs the problem," Director Parks said. "Why did the two of you pick up young Megan and return her with the surgery?"

Bonnie laughed. "Oh, we had that figured out in the first week."

Carol sat forward and said simply "What?"

"I must admit I am not following you either," Parks said.

Duster nodded. "We all assumed we had taken her for a full heart transplant into the future. But since that is not possible to do without setting a person in the new timeline when we bring them back, it is clear to me what we did."

Carol just stared at Duster until finally Bonnie said.

"She was operated on in 1888," Bonnie said.

Carol opened her mouth, then shut it.

"Of course," Director Parks said. "Of course, of course, of course."

All Carol could do was sit there and try to force the images of Megan dying in her arms from her mind.

There was no way she was going to risk an eleven-year-old Megan dying under her hands in an operation.

Carol knew, without a doubt, that if that happened, it would kill them both.

No matter what timeline they were in.

PART SIX
The Last Chance

CHAPTER FORTY-SIX

August 25th, 2019
Boise, Idaho

CAROL TOOK THREE days back in her condo to think about what Bonnie and Duster had suggested.

And clearly, in one timeline, she had done this and been successful. But as Duster had said, just because it worked in that timeline doesn't mean it actually worked in unlimited numbers of others.

Finally, Carol took out Megan's quilt and wrapped it around her, even though it was still almost seventy outside. Carol knew that Megan would take the chance. She knew that without a doubt.

In fact, the women Carol had been studying in the Old West took far more chances than this every day, just by getting out of bed.

Megan's mother had raised four kids on her own in the late 1880s Montana wilderness. To Megan, to her mother, the decision Carol was facing just seemed obvious.

Did Carol love Megan?

The answer was yes.

Did Carol now have a real chance of saving Megan's life?

The answer was yes.

Carol knew at that moment she had to try, no matter what.

She arrived the next morning in Director Parks' office and he was smiling.

He said she should come with him and they went to the living room cavern and then off to one side, to an area that Carol had paid little attention to.

Director Parks reached a door and pushed it open.

The room was empty, carved out of stone, with a moderately high, flat ceiling.

The only light coming in was from the door they stood in.

From what Carol could tell looking into the shadows, it was large, very large. Maybe the size of a three-bedroom home. Hard to tell in the darkness.

"Three thousand square feet," Director Parks said. "I'm going to take a crew from the future and we are going back to 1880 when we built this place and wire in electricity and water to this room and then build walls and insulate it completely."

Carol looked up at Director Parks, who was beaming.

"This area closest to the door will be sort of a waiting room and serve as an airlock to keep the rest of the area completely sterile."

"You are going to make this into a medical area?" Carol asked, now understanding why the director was excited about showing it to her.

"Exactly," Parks said. "I've been thinking we needed this from the beginning, but it just never came to the top of my list. Now, no matter what you decide to do with Megan, this has spurred me to put in a state-of-the-art medical center."

"Wow," Carol said, staring at the big empty space.

"One area of the room will be set up for each time period," Parks said. "In jumps of one hundred years, to accommodate medical knowledge of each time."

Carol understood that. Even though she was a trained doctor, she had seen things nurses were doing two hundred years from now that made no sense at all to her.

"And it will be available to any researcher who knows about it in any timeline," the director said. "And as we did with the Institute, we are going to install this far enough back that it will just ride with the Institute through all time-lines and always be available."

"How long will this take to build and install?" Carol asked.

"About one month in this time," Director Parks said. "So before Thanksgiving at the latest. After that it will always be available."

"Will I have to go to 2319 to train on the equipment to do the heart replacement on Megan?" Carol said.

"No," Director Parks said, smiling at her. "If you decide to take a chance with Megan, which I hope you do, I'm bringing back one of our researchers from 2319 who is also a medical doctor and has done a lot of heart transplants. He will do the operation and you will assist him."

Carol could feel the weight lifting from her shoulders.

"But I will still want you to go to 2219 for six months or more and assist on the surgeries there, since you are now established there in the hospital. Get used to the modern equipment and methods of that time. From what I have been told, if you do that, it won't take you very long to get up to speed on the differences."

"I would think the differences would be huge," Carol said, surprised at that.

"On many things, yes," Parks said. "But from what I have been told, on this kind of heart-replacement surgery, only the level of expertise went up and the

number of fatalities, if done at the right age, went down. They just don't have Star Trek ability to beam a heart into a body yet, even two hundred years from now."

"Bummer," Carol said, laughing.

"It is, isn't it," Parks said, closing the door on the big empty room with a thud that echoed through the cavern.

CHAPTER FORTY-SEVEN

September 30th, 2019
Boise, Idaho

CAROL DID AS Director Parks had told her to do and spent six months basi-cally learning everything she could learn about the medical practices of 2219.

It felt like she was in medical school all over again. Only without all the boring lectures.

She found it interesting that doctors and nurses and the support staff in hos-pitals hadn't really changed in their basic structure over the two hundred years. Surgeons were still surgeons, hospital regulators were still just that, and the nurses pulled the bulk of the work.

What had changed was the level of protections for everyone involved. Every inch of every floor of the hospital was being swept of all unwanted bacteria and germs. Hospitals had gone from being a dangerous place to being the cleanest and safest places on the planet.

Body scanning and body regulating equipment wasn't even recognizable to Carol, but thankfully a researcher from the Institute was also on staff at the hospital and stayed right with Carol every moment.

And drugs were seldom used for pain or to treat most anything, actually. The understanding of the human body had come a long ways and blocking pain and fixing most any problem quickly and without pain had become common.

In fact, a broken leg could be mended and a person back walking within a few hours because a way had been discovered to fuse bones back together, basically accelerating growth.

A logical advancement as far as Carol was concerned.

Cancers were mostly curable, but most people still got them at one point or another in their lives. And the disease of aging had been slowed so that people could remain healthy and active far past one hundred years of age.

All the advancements were wonderful to see for Carol and to learn about, but she was also disappointed that medicine hadn't advanced further. She wasn't sure what she had expected.

But, of course, a complete heart transplant was just being talked about in her time. Having it be just a regular surgery was a major advancement, of that there was no doubt.

And being able to grow replacement hearts and other organs from stem cells also was a clear advancement. And both of those things just might be able to save a young Megan's life.

Carol returned to 2019 on September 30th, just a week after she had left. She had wanted a little time to pass just to make sure she felt like she had been gone and to give Director Parks more time to move forward on the plan to install the major medical facility.

He was making headway, gathering the equipment and the researchers to help with the construction.

"Do you want me to help at all?" Carol asked.

"No, I think we have it," Parks said. "Thanks. But there is one thing you might consider doing."

Carol nodded and Parks took a deep breath.

"You have the timeline marked where Megan was given the operation, correct?"

Carol nodded.

"Jump twenty years after you will meet Megan to see if she is still alive, to see if the operation worked," Parks said. "But don't let her see you."

Carol felt stunned.

She wasn't sure if she wanted to see a Megan in a future time. But she knew Parks was right. There was no point in going through all this if the operation didn't work.

They all needed to know.

"Good idea," Carol said. "I'll go tomorrow."

That evening she walked back to her condo, taking her time in the crisp fall evening air.

Then she took Megan's quilt and wrapped herself in it and went out on her patio to just stare at the river.

CHAPTER FORTY-EIGHT

June 10th, 1912
Boise, Idaho

CAROL HAD DECIDED to follow Director Craig's instructions, but not exactly. Instead of jumping twenty years ahead in the timeline where she met Megan, she jumped only ten.

She figured it would be easier to trace Megan after just ten years. And if Megan's heart wasn't fixed, she never would have lived those ten years.

Besides, twenty years put her into a different time in Boise where the old poker room in the basement of the Idanha Hotel had been converted to a secret speakeasy. Carol wasn't sure if Megan would have stayed at the hotel through those times.

She had first asked Duster why going back to check on Megan was even possible. She had told Duster that if the surgery worked and Megan lived, then Carol would want to go back to the same point in 1902 and meet Megan one more time. And then the events that Megan lived past that time would be changed.

"Alternate timelines from that moment in 1902," Duster had said. "In one timeline you go back and decide to meet her and the other you don't. Or as in this case, you haven't yet. Every decision point starts an infinite number of timelines."

That had helped.

Sort of.

So Carol jumped back to June 10th, 1912.

It was about six in the morning, and the sun had come up promising a warm day, even though the air still felt cool and smelled of fresh growth.

Boise was a booming city, more so than even the ten years before. Warm Springs Avenue in front of the Institute was now a fairly smooth two-lane road and other mansions had been built along the river's edge on both sides of the Institute homes.

She had dressed in slacks and a nice blouse and a sweater over the blouse as was the riding fashion of the women of means of the time.

Carol had decided to still ride into town, even though many of the roads were now crowded with the new automobiles. She doubted she could drive one of those things, anyway.

The stable that had been behind the hotel had moved six blocks farther toward the edge of town, which was fine with her. She could use the walk anyway to get a sense of the time and the growing city.

The Idanha Hotel still towered above the other buildings along Main Street. The brick and stone looked inviting to her, like something solid moving through time.

Carol glanced at the time and made sure she was across the street from the entrance to the hotel on the side, pacing slowly up and down. That side door was where Megan always stepped out for a breath of fresh air after a night shift of baking.

Carol waited there, slowly pacing, for almost an hour without luck. She didn't want to feel panicked. But she did.

Just a little.

She wouldn't let herself believe that Megan had died after the surgery.

Carol headed toward the front door and went into the large hotel lobby. Nothing had changed other than the wooden benches looked a little worn and the tile on the floor also showed major traffic wear. But the old Otis elevator still dominated one side of the room next to the grand staircase.

Carol turned to the right to go into the dining room.

The dining room hadn't changed in the slightest either. Same tables, same large windows, and same stone fireplace dominating one corner of the room. Ten years of time had not made any inroads into this restaurant that Carol could see.

And the smells were as wonderful as Carol had remembered.

A man in a formal suit greeted her and showed her to a table near the window looking out at Main Street.

The room might not have changed much, but the view through the window sure had. Instead of horses and wagons and a dirt road, the wide street had been paved and both sides were lined with automobiles parked facing inward. A few horses were still tied up in places along the road, but very few.

And the noise from the street was much louder. The world of the noisy car had started and wouldn't quiet down for almost two hundred years when electric cars completely took over everything.

After Carol had ordered poached eggs, two pieces of toast, and fresh berry juice, she asked the waitress if Mrs. Megan Taber still worked at the hotel.

The woman laughed lightly. "She runs our kitchen. And helps with the baking."

"Thank you," Carol said, trying to contain the smile.

That was the best news that Carol could have ever imagined.

"Would you like me to mention you are here?" the waitress asked.

"Oh, no bother," Carol said. "I am just a fan of her wonderful cooking. But thank you."

Carol ate a leisurely breakfast, taking her time and savoring the wonderful flavor of the bread.

She knew that Megan was just on the other side of that closed kitchen door, doing what she loved, and living a healthy life. That thought made Carol as happy as she had felt since her last day with Megan at her Condo.

After almost an hour, and with only a glimpse at the closed kitchen door as she left, Carol walked through the cool morning air to get her horse and go back to the Institute and 2019.

It was time they saved Megan from her own heart.

And healed Carol's heart in the process.

CHAPTER FORTY-NINE

June 7th, 1888
Montana Territory

MEGAN HAD BEEN twenty-five when Carol met her in 1902. So fourteen years earlier, in 1888 Megan would have been eleven. Montana was still one year away from statehood and was a very rugged place.

Megan's home was on a small farm near Placerville, thirty miles east of the growing mining town of Missoula. Placerville wasn't more than a few general stores and a couple of saloons and was a distance off the main road into Missoula.

Carol and Bonnie and Duster had gone back to 1888 the last week of May and had spent almost two weeks working their way to Missoula from Boise, taking their time and planning every step of what they were going to do.

And planning every bit of the journey back to Boise with Megan, which they were going to need to do as quickly as possible. Duster bought and had new horses standing by at three different places along the trail.

In essence, when it boiled right down to it, they were going to take an eleven-year-old girl with permission from her mother and her local family doctor to have an operation. That was the surface plan.

They decided it would be best to not tell the mother and local doctor that they were going to take young Megan all the way to Boise for the operation instead of just Missoula.

They told the local doctor and Megan's mother that Megan would be gone just over two weeks, and not to worry if it was a day or two beyond that.

Megan's mother had said simply to Duster, "As long as my daughter comes back healthy and with a strong heart, that's what matters."

Carol was amazed that Megan's mother had allowed her daughter to go like that, but it seemed that Duster had a strong reputation in the area. And the local family doctor knew enough to know that Megan wasn't going to live very long without some help.

The local doctor must have made that clear to Megan's mother.

The plan was as simple as they could make it. Bonnie and Duster would go pick up Megan, then Bonnie would give her a shot on the way back to Missoula to knock her out.

Carol would join them at a point outside of Missoula and ride in the wagon with Megan to make sure she stayed comfortable and out cold.

So on the bright morning of June 7th, 1888, ten miles outside of Missoula, Carol joined them. Megan was already out cold in the back of the wagon.

Carol tied her horse to the back of the wagon and climbed in on the thick padding with the young Megan.

Bonnie got on her horse and went ahead of the wagon and they headed around Missoula and south for Boise as fast as they could go.

Carol was stunned at how much the young Megan looked like the beautiful woman she would grow into being.

Carol just sat there staring at Megan.

This had to work.

Just had to.

Carol kept Megan as comfortable and cleaned up as she could as they drove the horses and wagon as hard as they dared.

She gave her fluids and nutrition intravenously every time they stopped.

They changed out the horses as planned three times in the four days it took them to get to Boise.

Once they got there and had Megan downstairs, they cleaned her up completely and got her ready, putting her in a warm bed and keeping her sedated.

One hour later, the doctor from 2319 arrived.

His name was Teel. Dr. S.T. Teel, but he liked to be called just Teel.

Carol liked him at once. He seemed charming, calm, and very assured. He was about six feet tall, had deep brown eyes, and a smile that Carol bet many women and men liked.

And since the same operating room was in his Institute in his time, he knew exactly where to go and what was needed.

He did a quick check of Megan, ran some scans and got images of her heart and the area around it, and then turned to Carol. "First things, first, we have to grow her a new heart."

"Doesn't that take months?" Carol asked, shocked. They couldn't keep Megan for months. For some reason she thought they would be using the stem cells from the Megan who had died in the hospital a hundred years in the future.

"It will take two days," Teel said, smiling, indicating a large machine sitting against a back wall of the medical center. "And we will grow it to match exactly her size now so that it will continue to grow with her over the next few years."

Carol nodded and made herself take a deep breath. It made sense that the organ replacement growth would have sped up in a century. Complete sense.

They did the stem cell extraction from Megan easily, then Teel showed Carol how to keep Megan asleep without using any drugs at all.

"You will have to revert to drugs on the way back to Montana," Teel said, "but for the next few days and while she is recovering, this is a much better way."

Carol could only agree to that.

After the young Megan was settled in and resting comfortably, Dr. Teel turned to Bonnie and Duster and Director Parks. "I would love to see this fair city during this time in history. And I am dying of hunger. Pizza any good here?"

Duster laughed and reminded Teel, "This is 1888. But in 2019 we have pizza and Italian food to die for."

"To 2019 it is then," Teel said, shaking his head.

They invited Carol to go along, but she declined, saying she wanted to keep an eye on Megan.

Carol made herself a sandwich and got a sports drink and went into the area near where Megan slept, staying outside the glass that kept the medical area germ and bacteria free.

There was a couch in the outside room and a coffee table, so Carol put her feet up and ate her dinner, sitting alone with a young girl who would hopefully, given luck with this surgery, grow into the woman of Carol's dreams.

Twenty minutes later Carol dozed off from the stress of the long ride. Bonnie woke her when she and Dr. Teel came back to check on Megan, who was still doing fine and resting comfortably.

Bonnie convinced Carol to go home and get a real night's sleep. Dr. Teel would be staying upstairs in the Institute and the machines would alert him if anything changed with Megan.

Carol did as Bonnie suggested, jumping back to 2019 and walking along the river trail to her condo, then taking off her clothes, taking a shower, and curling up in Megan's quilt on the bed.

She didn't dare dream about having the adult Megan with her here. That dream had been dashed too many times already.

CHAPTER FIFTY

June 14th, 1888
Boise, Idaho

CAROL WAS SCARED to death.

Today Megan's new heart would be ready and they would be doing the surgery.

Even though Carol had assisted in a dozen of these two hundred years in the future, and Dr. Teel was from a hundred years farther forward, Carol still felt scared.

She couldn't eat any breakfast, but did manage to get down a little juice.

And she made herself walk slowly along the river path to the Institute, just to get herself in some form of calm before jumping back to 1888.

As a doctor and surgeon, she had done her share of operations. And today she was only assisting.

But she had lost Megan four times, a thought Carol just couldn't allow to surface very often. Losing her again, especially at the age of eleven, would be just too much to bear.

As it turned out, Carol didn't have much to do at all except monitor equipment that surrounded Megan. It was a necessary job, but not a difficult one.

Carol had to make sure of the levels of unconsciousness, the levels of pain blockers, and the levels of Megan's breathing and blood flow. As they started the operation, everything was at normal for an eleven year old girl with a damaged heart.

Dr. Teel had Megan opened up and on life support in less than fifteen minutes. Megan's blood now flowed through a very small machine that sat silently beside Megan.

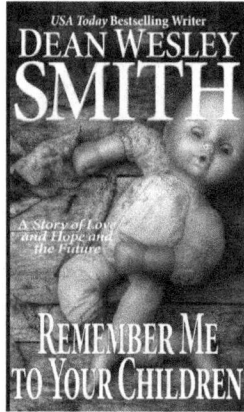  

The change-over hadn't even hardly been noticed on the monitoring machines. Carol was impressed at that.

Dr. Teel, using a form of laser, removed Megan's damaged heart and a few minor areas around her heart, then placed the new heart into Megan.

Working quickly, yet without seeming to be in a hurry, he sealed up each blood vessel with an instrument that seemed to just blend and heal the tissue together instantly. After a moment, Carol couldn't even see the line where the seam had been before.

That took him only thirty minutes, his hands working so fast they seemed like a blur.

Then he spent another twenty minutes carefully checking every detail, sometimes sealing a small area again, but mostly just nodding and saying nothing.

Carol liked the fact that when he was out in public, Dr. Teel was a nice, friendly person. And she really liked the fact that he didn't bring anything but business into the operating room.

No chattering, nothing. He did his job and he expected her to do hers.

Then Dr. Teel started Megan's new heart and let it beat in time with the pulses from the machine for a few minutes before removing the connections of the machine and sealing up those areas as well.

The complexity of the operation was staggering to Carol, yet Teel did it smoothly and carefully, never hesitating with anything.

Megan's new heart was beating fine and to Carol the heart looked completely healthy and strong.

And all the instruments Carol was monitoring said the same thing.

Megan had gone from a young girl with a bad heart to a young girl with a very, very strong heart.

Dr. Teel carefully sealed back up Megan's chest, one layer at a time, making sure he had missed nothing with each step.

Carol loved how completely meticulous and careful he was even with the closing procedure.

Finally, he sealed the skin he had opened on Megan's chest, leaving a faint white scar running vertically.

He smiled and nodded as he ran a healing light over it. "She won't hardly be able to see that scar in two years."

That was the first thing he had said all operation.

And all the machines monitoring Megan gave perfect, healthy readings.

Carol just stared at Dr. Teel as he ran more scans of Megan, continuing to nod to himself as he did.

Finally, he nodded and stepped back, clearly finished.

"It will be safe to move her in that wagon in two days," he said. "Better if you wait three."

"After all this," Carol said, "I think we can wait four to be really safe."

Teel nodded and smiled. "I will stay around and watch over her for the next day and then check in a few times per day after that until you are ready to take her home."

Carol nodded. She felt numb.

It was over.

Megan had survived.

Then as Carol and Dr. Teel left the operating room to let Megan rest, Carol hugged him.

"Thank you," she said. "Thank you. Thank you. Thank you."

He seemed as embarrassed as any doctor would be.

Carol didn't care. The relief she was feeling was just too strong to not hug someone.

Megan was alive and had a new, strong heart. And that was all that mattered.

And outside the operating room, Duster, Bonnie, and Dr. Parks were smiling huge smiles and applauding.

CHAPTER FIFTY-ONE

June 18th, 1888
Boise, Idaho

CAROL SAID GOODBYE and thank you to Dr. Teel outside of the Institute on a crisp June morning. The sun wasn't even close to being up yet and only a lantern held by Bonnie on her horse lit the area.

"Please come forward and visit me," Dr. Teel said to Carol. "And if things work out with Megan, bring her along as well."

"I hope to do just that," Carol said.

Duster nodded to Teel and Bonnie waved and then they headed down the mansion drive and out to the wagon road leading back toward Boise.

Megan rested comfortably on the thick pads in the back of the wagon.

Dr. Teel had given Carol a more future version of a sedative and a quick lesson in how much to administer.

So the journey to take Megan home had started.

One more step.

They again went straight through, taking turns napping on the bed beside Megan as they traveled.

Four days later, again very early in the morning to the east of Missoula, just two weeks and one day from when they had picked up Megan, Carol said goodbye to the sleeping girl.

"She should wake up in about an hour," Carol said to Bonnie as Bonnie gave the reins of her horse to Carol and climbed into the back of the wagon. "Dr. Teel tells me she will be hungry and thirsty. Water is fine, a little bread would also be fine until she reaches home."

Bonnie nodded and smiled. "Don't worry, we have her from here."

Carol knew that they had three hours of travel left to get Megan back home.

And Carol knew she didn't dare go the last little bit with them. Megan could never see her if there was any hope the two of them could have a relationship in the future.

Carol turned away as the wagon started off and went to build a camp along a stream where she could wait for Bonnie and Duster to return.

Megan was alive.

Only eleven years old and very much alive.

But leaving Megan again had hurt.

Stupidly. Carol knew that.

It was amazing how much she was willing to go through for Megan's future love.

Nine hours later, in the heat of the late afternoon, Bonnie and Duster rode back into Carol's camp without the wagon.

"We waited for the local doctor to come and check out Megan," Bonnie said as they both climbed down from their horses. The local doctor pronounced Megan fine."

"How was she feeling?"

"Tired and level and glad to be home," Bonnie said, smiling. "Megan is a very amazing girl."

"An even more amazing woman," Carol said.

"So what happened to the wagon?"

"My butt is what happened," Duster said. "It's going to be a few centuries of time before I'll ride in a wagon again."

"We gave it to Megan's family to use," Bonnie said, winking at Carol and then laughing.

And for the first time in a long time, Carol laughed as well.

And wow did that feel good.

PART SEVEN
Once More for Love

CHAPTER FIFTY-TWO

June 6th, 1901
Boise, Idaho

MEGAN FELT NERVOUS. She had on one of her best skirts and blouses, an outfit she saved for special occasions such as a staff party. The skirt was a pleated blue and the blouse a loose white with silk on the neck and sleeves. She wore a light matching blue jacket over her blouse and a small string of pearls that her mother had given her when she got married and moved to Boise.

Even though it was a warm evening outside, Megan felt she needed the jacket to look presentable.

She wasn't sure why she was nervous. This Carol Kogan sounded nice and impressive and wanted to just talk. Megan figured that was what was making her nervous, that someone actually valued beyond what they ate at their table what she did every night.

Dr. Stevens had really played this Carol up as a major writer and a really nice person. And that Megan deserved to be in her research for the Powerful Women of the West book.

Megan brushed down her skirt one more time, then checked to make sure her hair was in place, even though as short as it was, there wasn't much she could do with it.

She nodded to the desk clerk as she moved across the stone-floors of the foyer and into the open restaurant doors beyond.

Stan, the evening host, greeted her with a smile. "You look wonderful this evening, Mrs. Taber."

"Thank you, Stan," she said, bowing slightly.

"Your guest is waiting at the table near the front window," Stan said, indicating that she should follow him.

The blinds on the west side of the room had been drawn to block out the direct evening sun and Megan was happy to see that the woman was sitting in a shaded area near an open window. The noise and smells from the streets might intrude at times, but even a slight breeze would be better than being stuffy.

As Megan approached, the woman she was meeting glanced around and seemed shocked.

Actually, it was Megan who felt shocked. The woman was stunningly beautiful and dressed in a similar style as Megan was.

After a moment, the woman seemed to take a deep breath and then stood and extended her hand. "Mrs. Taber, I am Carol Kogan. The honor is all mine to be talking with you."

Megan took Miss Kogan's hand and was stunned at how soft and wonderful it felt. She didn't want to let it go.

And she didn't want to stop staring in Miss Kogan's eyes either. They were the most beautiful green Megan had ever seen.

Deep green, caring green.

And clearly Miss Kogan didn't want to break the grip either. Her face looked flushed and there was a slight look of panic on her face.

Megan thought that odd, since she was the one who should be panicked, not the famous writer.

Stan moved around Megan and pulled out her chair, so Megan released Miss Kogan's hand and sat, allowing Miss Kogan to sit again as well.

"Would you enjoy a beverage to start?" Stan asked Megan.

Miss Kogan already had a glass of water in front of her.

"Water would be wonderful," Megan said.

Stan nodded and turned away.

Megan looked across the table at Carol, who was staring at her.

"Call me Megan," she said, deciding to break the ice a little, even though ice was a great distance away from this warm summer evening.

"I'm Carol. And I apologize for staring. I feel so like I know you and you are a very beautiful woman."

Megan could feel herself blush a little along her neck. She laughed. "No need to apologize at all, because I was thinking the same of you."

Now Carol blushed slightly and laughed what was clearly a relieved laugh. At that point, Carol seemed to relax.

And that helped Megan relax.

From there over the evening they managed to talk about their pasts, about how Megan's husband had died, and then finally her baking.

It was a wonderful evening, especially when Carol called her baking an art. Megan thought of it as an art, but no one had ever said that to her before.

The evening ended with the two of them sitting and staring at each other for the longest and most wonderful time.

Megan knew she should have felt uncomfortable, but she didn't. Not in the slightest.

It just felt right.

CHAPTER FIFTY-THREE

June 6th, 1901
Boise, Idaho

CAROL HAD BEEN so nervous when Megan came into the dining room, she almost couldn't stand. Her stomach was twisted into a tight knot and she was sweating even more than the warm summer evening caused.

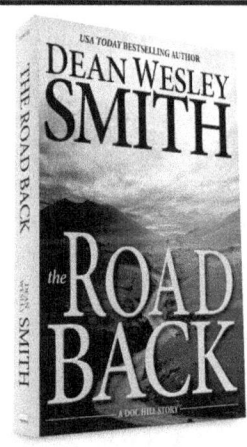

Carol had buried Megan four times, yet here she was again, walking across the warm, sunlit dining room like an angel.

And this time, with a healthy heart.

There was no doubt it was the same Megan that Carol had fallen so completely in love with. And now seeing Megan like this again was like a dream.

All Carol wanted to do was hug her.

And never let Megan go.

But Carol didn't.

She knew she had a script to follow and she didn't dare mess it up for fear of losing Megan, not to death, but to stupidity.

This was going to be impossible.

This would be a very fine balance.

She had to do it.

Dr. Stevens had arranged this meeting this time without Bonnie and Duster, since there was a chance Megan would remember them. And Dr. Stevens had managed it, but Carol didn't know what the fine doctor had said about her. She was going to have to play that by ear.

Thankfully, the dinner went well and as it had in the last three timelines, they met the next morning for breakfast in Megan's apartment.

Carol touched Megan's beautiful patchwork quilt on the couch when she came in, knowing that it was also in her condo on her own couch in 2019. Carol had spent a lot of time wrapped in that quilt over time, not wanting to think about there being a world without Megan.

And now, that was possible.

If Carol stayed on script.

The breakfast went almost identically as the first breakfast that they had three times together.

And from that moment forward they spent every dinner together and every breakfast, until the moment when Megan asked Carol to scrub her back.

Carol had agreed, then as Megan lowered her beautiful body into the tub, Carol could see the very faint white scar.

Very faint and as far as Carol was concerned, the most beautiful scar she had ever seen.

Period.

As Carol took the washcloth and soap and got it ready, she asked, "Did you scratch your chest?"

Megan laughed. "That is from an operation I had as a child. My mother said it fixed my heart."

Carol wanted to say it fixed far more than that, but she said nothing.

After a moment, Carol said, "Would you mind if I joined you in the bath? Better than getting my blouse and skirt soaked.

Megan blushed slightly and said, "I would love that."

And the romance turned wonderfully physical from there, as it had the last time they had been together.

Carol knew what Megan liked and made sure Megan enjoyed every second.

It was the most wonderful time Carol had ever had.

That evening at dinner, before Megan went to her baking, Carol asked Megan if she could get the following night off of work. She had a wonderful surprise to show her.

Megan nodded and smiled. "I would love to start to see some of the many surprises and secrets you hold."

"You saw a few of those this morning," Carol said, blushing.

Megan also blushed. "That's why I am interested in more. That was wonderful."

Carol laughed. "I thought so as well."

As before, it had taken Carol one month to gain Megan's trust and love.

And for Carol, it had been once again one of the best months of her life.

Maybe the best because this time she wasn't worried about Megan dying at any moment.

Because after losing Megan four times, getting to spend a wonderful month with her again couldn't be anything more than the best.

CHAPTER FIFTY-FOUR

July 8th, 1901
Boise, Idaho

MEGAN COULDN'T BELIEVE how much and how quickly she had fallen completely in love with the mysterious Carol Kogan.

And clearly Carol had fallen for her as well. In fact, it felt as if Carol was in love from the first moment they met.

Megan had never actually had an affair with a woman, but with Carol everything just felt right and wonderful and each moment precious.

Megan had no doubt that she would love to just touch Carol's skin for the rest of her life. And it surprised Megan that she wanted to spend the rest of her life with Carol. Not a thought she ever would have thought possible just a month before.

And every day that feeling got deeper and deeper.

And since Carol was now willing to start opening up about some of her secrets, Megan felt encouraged. Megan had never pushed or asked, but she could tell that Carol kept a lot hidden.

Megan got up a little earlier than normal in the afternoon and got dressed in her riding clothes. She hadn't been riding in a very long time and was very pleased to discover her riding clothes still fit perfectly. Considering she was a baker and didn't mind sampling her own work, that was saying something.

"We are going to need some early dinner," Megan said as they left the hotel and turned toward the stables.

Both of them were wearing big cloth hats with wide brims as well to shade their skin from the sun. Megan hadn't worn her riding hat since the last time she wore her riding clothes. It actually felt odd on her head, but Carol's hat made her look even more alluring.

"I have dinner planned for us at the Institute," Carol said. "It will be like nothing you have ever tasted, I promise."

Megan couldn't get even a hint more from Carol, so they got saddled and headed slowly out of town. Carol said that the horse Megan was riding was an Institute horse. A brown mare that seemed very gentle and Megan took a liking to her at once.

It was a beautiful summer day. The leaves still all green and the day didn't seem like it was going to end up too warm.

Megan had brought along a jacket just in case they were late coming back in the evening, but she wasn't wearing it at the moment.

Carol rode like an expert, which didn't surprise Megan at all. She had a hunch that nothing would surprise her about Carol.

As they neared the Institute, Megan could see the three large Victorian homes standing on the rise above the river among a large stand of oak and cottonwood trees. The homes were beautiful and majestic.

"Two friends of mine I want you to meet will greet us at the Institute," Carol said. "They are going to help with the surprise. And actually be one of the surprises as well."

"Should I be worried about this surprise?" Megan asked as they got closer to the three large homes.

"Not in the slightest," Carol said. "I am very much in love with you. And I want you to know everything about me."

Megan was very pleased to hear Carol say that.

Very pleased.

As they dismounted in the stable behind the center mansion and gave their horses to a stable hand, Carol looked at Megan with an intense look. "Remember as you learn more about me, I love you."

"I will," Megan said, smiling.

Carol beamed at that and then the two of them started toward the back entrance to the mansion, taking off their hats as they went.

"Then it sounds like you are ready for some secrets," Carol said.

"As much as I'll ever be, I suppose."

CHAPTER FIFTY-FIVE

July 8th, 1901
Boise, Idaho

CAROL LED MEGAN through the back door of the large Institute mansion, then instead of taking Megan on a tour, Carol touched a secret panel that slid back and stepped through.

"The Institute is so much more than the three buildings on the surface," Carol said. "Let me show you."

She held out her hand and took Megan's hand.

"Secret panels in a mansion," Megan said, smiling. "Like a story right out of *All Story Magazine.*"

"It is, isn't it?" Carol said, happy that Megan didn't seem afraid in the slightest. Carol remembered the first time she saw what was under the Institute. It had scared her more than she wanted to admit.

They went through the wide hallway lit by electrical bulbs and to an elevator.

"Much safer than the Otis at the hotel," Carol said. "I promise."

"You telling me that thing in the hotel isn't safe?" Megan asked, laughing and stepping on beside Carol.

"I'd never ride it," Carol said, laughing in return.

"I knew you were smart," Megan said.

The elevator took them down two floors and opened up into the big cavern.

"Wow," Megan said as Carol led her through the arrangements of living room furniture and toward a kitchen counter where Bonnie and Duster sat. "This is really some place."

"No one really knows about it," Carol said. "Only about thirty people total. One of my many secrets I promised to show you."

Bonnie and Duster were sitting at the kitchen counter against one wall of the large cavern. Carol had no idea if Megan would remember them or not. It had been fourteen years earlier.

As Carol and Megan approached, Bonnie and Duster turned around, large smiles on their faces.

"Megan, you look wonderful," Bonnie said, standing and coming forward.

Megan was holding Carol's hand and after two steps Megan stopped suddenly.

Carol glanced at the shocked look on Megan's face. Clearly Megan recognized Bonnie and Duster.

"I'm Bonnie," Bonnie said, standing and moving toward Megan with her hand extended. "This is Duster."

"You took me to my surgery," Megan said. "Didn't you?"

"We did," Bonnie said. "And we can explain why we are here after Carol shows you a few more secrets."

"This is a pretty good one," Megan said.

"Now we want to show you something and a kitchen you can only dream about," Bonnie said. "Follow me."

Carol took Megan's hand and they went through a big door in the far wall and then down two flights of stairs and into a large room full of clothes and supplies. Duster followed along not talking.

"I'll explain all this shortly," Carol said, squeezing Megan's hand.

"Good," Megan said, "Because this is the biggest and strangest store I have ever seen."

Carol watched Megan carefully as they went into the long, narrow crystal room.

Bonnie and Carol had decided to just go quickly through the process as they had before, get her established a few hundred years ahead, and then go back and show Megan what it looked like in 2019.

"Those are very beautiful crystals," Megan said, pointing to the glowing crystals in the stone wall.

"They are, aren't they," Bonnie said.

Carol looked at Megan and then said, "Right now I need you to do something I love a lot."

Megan looked puzzled, then asked what that might be.

"I need you to put your arms around me and hold me very tightly."

Megan blushed and then with a glance at Bonnie, who was smiling, stepped closer to Carol and hugged her.

"A little harder," Carol said, noting that Bonnie was about to pull the wire from the box that would send her to 2019.

Megan squeezed Carol harder in a hug Carol wished would never end.

Bonnie pulled the wire and vanished.

Megan was still holding her.

Both of them were in 2019.

Carol kissed Megan. "We made it. Together."

"Made what?" Megan asked, staring into Carol's eyes and wide smile.

"We made it to the place where I can show you my secrets."

Megan laughed. "We could have stayed in my rooms at the hotel if a hug would get you to show your secrets."

"That was just a wonderful benefit for me is all," Carol said, laughing.

"I enjoyed it as well," Megan said, then kissed Carol again.

"Sorry to interrupt, ladies, let's go back upstairs and do that a few more times, then have some dinner," Bonnie said as she and Duster appeared just behind Megan. "We've got a lot to talk about."

Both Carol and Megan blushed and then as if they were two teenagers, they went hand-in-hand back up two flights of stairs to the big cavern living room.

And then then back down again into a different cavern and repeated the hugging in the crystal cavern process twice more.

CHAPTER FIFTY-SIX

November 14th, 2019
Boise, Idaho

MEGAN WAS VERY, very puzzled at the events of the last half hour and why Bonnie and Duster and Carol had taken her down into that tunnel and then brought her back up here and then down into different tunnels twice more.

It wasn't until she really looked at the furniture in the large cavern room as they got settled in around the kitchen counter and the things behind the counter that Megan started to get worried.

"Everything changed here since we went downstairs," Megan said.

Both Bonnie and Carol nodded.

Duster excused himself and said, "I'll let you two explain it all." Then he headed for the elevator.

"You are no longer in 1901," Bonnie said.

"That's my secret," Carol said, turning and staring into the eyes of the woman she loved. "I am from the year 2019."

Megan laughed, but Carol's expression didn't change.

After a moment, Megan said, "You are serious, aren't you?"

Carol and Bonnie both nodded.

"Come on," Carol said, "Let me show you something."

"I'll stay here and make us a snack before dinner," Bonnie said.

Megan let Carol take her hand and direct her to the elevator they had come down. Now it was sleek and had a full door instead of a cage. As they approached, the door slid open silently.

Carol stepped on and Megan reluctantly followed her.

"Trust me," Carol said, "this is a million times safer than that Otis in the hotel."

"Anything would be," Megan said, moving on and holding onto both of Carol's hands as the door closed.

She could feel a slight sense of movement and then the door slid back open.

They stepped into an empty room and Carol went to a place on the wall.

"Checking to make sure no one is in the Institute's front room that shouldn't be."

There wasn't, so she pushed a button and a panel slid back and Megan let herself be led into the front parlor of the mansion.

Megan was surprised that it actually looked dated.

"The Institute keeps this front entrance room looking exactly as it looked in the 1880s when the Institute was founded."

Megan nodded as Carol led her to the large wooden front door and pulled it open.

As Megan stepped out, she was stunned at what she saw.

In fact, she wasn't sure exactly what she was seeing.

"It's November 2019," Carol said. "About twelve noon. Trees are really losing their leaves and all those things going by are modern versions of the automobiles that were just getting started in 1901."

Megan just stood and stared, holding Carol's hand as if it were a lifeline to a sane time and place. Where before it had just been the three Victorian mansions sitting on a slight hill overlooking the river, now the entire area was full of homes and buildings of all types.

And the wagon road that had run past the mansion was now covered in some sort of pavement and strange-looking automobiles flashed past at impossible speeds.

Finally, after almost a minute of Megan looking around, she turned to Carol. "You really are from this time?"

"I am," Carol said. "I am a medical doctor and an historian. I traveled back to 1901 to learn about strong women and their medical conditions for a book I am writing."

"So I am a test subject," Megan said, feeling almost angry.

"No," Carol said, forcing Megan to look into her eyes. "You are the woman I fell in love with, the woman I want to spend lifetimes with. I had to get permission to share this with you."

Megan could see the worry and the love in Carol's eyes. She was telling the truth.

After a moment Megan nodded and kissed Carol who seemed to melt with relief in her arms.

Then she said simply, "I have a lot to learn it seems."

"If we want we can stay here for a while," Carol said. "But I would rather live in your time for now."

"We can go back?" Megan asked. She wasn't sure why she thought she couldn't go back, since Carol had gone back from here to meet her.

"Of course we can," Carol said. "We could spend months here and go back to within an hour of when we got off those horses in July 1901 to continue that wonderful day. And yet still remember the months here."

"You are not joking?" Megan asked, actually starting to feel excited, even though what she was seeing around her scared her more than she wanted to admit.

"I am not," Carol said. "Bonnie knows a lot more about all those sorts of things and can explain all the details, I promise."

"So let's go back and get a bite to eat," Megan said, looking around at the amazing scene she never could have imagined. "And I'll start learning about your world since you know so much about mine."

Megan took Carol's hand and they went back inside.

This all seemed impossible, yet Carol was very real and with her. So even the impossible might be all right as long as they were together.

CHAPTER FIFTY-SEVEN

November 14th, 2019
Boise, Idaho

CAROL WAS STUNNED at how level Megan seemed to be in the face of such insanity. Seeing over a hundred years into the future had bothered Carol when she had jumped forward the first time to 2119. She could only imagine what Megan was going to think, yet Megan had seemed to take it almost in stride.

Megan was an amazing woman, of that there was no doubt.

Carol and Megan and Bonnie all sat at the counter eating a light sandwich and salad. Carol and Bonnie had planned to take Megan to their favorite Italian restaurant as they had done the last time Megan had come here.

So after some talk about living in the past and how little time was spent when a person went back into the past, Carol finally got around to telling Megan what had happened.

Carol looked into Megan's eyes and said simply, "I have a story I need to tell you before we go anywhere."

Megan smiled. "I was wondering why the snack before dinner."

Carol laughed, then said, "You have sat here at this counter before. In fact, you have been in this cavern three times before."

"How is that possible and I not remember it?" Megan asked, looking shocked. "This cavern would be very difficult to forget."

Carol nodded. "Let me start at the beginning. Otherwise I will make no sense and get myself confused."

Megan nodded.

"I first met you on the sidewalk outside the Idanha Hotel in May of 1902."

Megan looked puzzled. "We just met a month ago and I remember it was summer of 1901."

"I was back in your time doing research on my book," Carol said. "Remember the crystals downstairs? I was in a different crystal."

Megan nodded, so Carol went on.

"I was staying here at the Institute, but I loved going into the Idanha and eating breakfast and having your wonderful breads. So when you went out onto the sidewalk after your baking shift, I happened to be coming by and that's how we first met."

"I wish I remembered that," Megan said.

"It was you in a different timeline," Carol said. "And you would not want to have remembered it because while we were talking you had a heart attack."

"Oh, no," Megan said.

"Dr. Stevens and I got you to the hospital and then we tried to bring you here to the future for an operation, but you died before we got you to the Institute."

Megan nodded and said nothing.

"So I went back earlier, in the fall of 1901, and we met in the dining room after Bonnie and Duster and Dr. Stevens convinced you to meet with me."

Megan again said nothing.

"We were falling in love, had spent two wonderful weeks together, when I left you to rest and when I came back to your apartment, you had had a heart attack and died."

Megan shook her head and looked white.

"So I went back in the summer of 1901 the next time, we spent a wonderful month together, fell in love, and I brought you here for an operation to fix your heart."

"I assume something went wrong," Megan said.

"Before we could grow you a new heart to replace your bad heart, you died, this time in the hospital here."

Megan nodded. "You said I had been here three times before? What happened the next time?"

"I went back even earlier and we met and fell in love again," Carol said. "And the next time, since we already had a heart grown for you, we took you a hundred years into the future to have the surgery."

"I did not survive the surgery, did I?" Megan asked.

Carol shook her head. "The damage to your heart and everything around it was too much for even the doctors of one hundred years in the future to fix. You were basically born with a bad heart that got worse and worse until it suddenly stopped working."

"And even though you were from the future, you did not know when it would finally give up?"

"Every timeline is different," Bonnie said.

"So why did you pick me for a surgery?" Megan asked Bonnie.

"Because the doctors from the future said that if you had the surgery at eleven,

you would be fine for a very long time," Bonnie said.

"Is that true?" Megan asked.

"We went and got permission from your mother and your local doctor to take you into Missoula and fix your heart," Carol said. "But then we brought you here, to this cavern, and a surgeon from three hundred years after your time came and did the surgery."

"So my heart is now fine?" Megan asked.

"Completely," Carol said. "We have as much future ahead of us as we want to live."

"Are you sure?" Megan asked. "Completely sure?"

"As much as anyone can be sure about a person's health," Carol said. "I can show you later where you had the surgery when you were eleven and we can run some tests then."

"A big white space," Megan said. "That's all I remember."

"I'm glad that's all you remember," Carol said, smiling. "Because that long wagon ride we took from your home to here and back was rough on all of us."

Bonnie laughed. "I think it will be a few thousand years before Duster ever drives a wagon again."

Megan looked puzzled at that.

"Don't worry," Carol said, "I'll explain it all."

Megan nodded. "I'm completely sure I don't understand everything, or much of anything, actually, that you just told me. But I do hate that I put you through so much to get me here. I am so, so sorry."

Carol smiled at the wonderful woman sitting next to her. "Trust me, it was worth it, my love."

And with that she leaned over and just kissed Megan.

And Megan kissed her back, and that felt wonderful as well.

Three hours later, after a wonderful Italian dinner that was as Carol promised, nothing like Megan had ever tasted before, they went back to Carol's condo.

And started their new life together.

EPILOGUE

May 29th, 2023
Boise, Idaho

THE DAY WAS as beautiful as could be imagined. The wonderful garden behind the Institute had been converted to a gathering place with a small stage and about fifty chairs, all filled with people talking and laughing and waiting for the event to start.

A wide aisle led through the chairs and up two stairs to where a woman stood in a suit, smiling.

Behind the people was a long table full of food and drink and a massive cake, especially made by the city's newest sensational bakery.

As the music changed and the bridal march started, Bonnie and Duster came out of the back door of the Institute, both dressed in their finest, with Bonnie in a long gown reminiscent of the early 1900s and Duster in a suit, with his standard cowboy hat and long duster coat over the top of it.

They stopped at the bottom of the stairs and waited as Carol and Megan came out, both dressed in beautiful flowing bridal gowns.

Everyone in the audience applauded.

Carol and Megan moved down to where Bonnie and Duster stood and as they approached, Bonnie took Carol's outside arm and Duster took Megan's outside arm.

Then all four of them moved slowly toward the woman ready to do the ceremony.

As they neared the steps in front of the stage, they stopped. Bonnie kissed Carol lightly, then Megan, then moved to sit down.

Duster did the same and moved over to join Bonnie.

Then Carol and Megan stepped up in front of the woman.

"Are you sure?" Megan asked, smiling at her beautiful partner.

"I lost you four times," Carol said. "You're stuck with me now."

Megan laughed and turned to the woman in front of them. "Then let's do this. There's cake to eat."

Carol laughed. "Why do you think all these people are here?"

Everyone behind them laughed as the woman in front of them smiled and said simply, but loudly for everyone to hear, "We are gathered here not only for wondrous cake, but to watch these fine two women join their lives together for all eternity."

The audience laughed again and Megan glanced at Carol. "Think that will be long enough?"

"We'll make it long enough," Carol said. "Of that, I promise."

Megan squeezed Carol's hand and said simply, "I know you do. You have proven that. Over and over and over again."

Coming Next Issue in *Smith's Monthly*

THE IDANHA HOTEL

A Thunder Mountain Novel

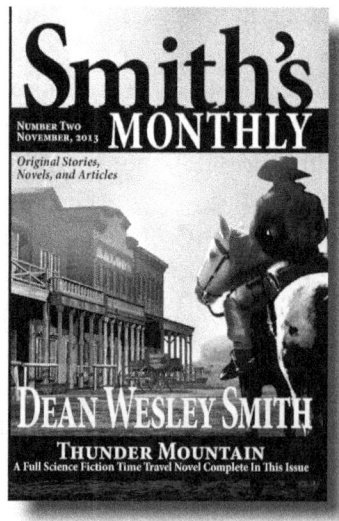

#4...January 2014

#5...February 2014

#6...March 2014

#7...April 2014

#8...May 2014

#9...June 2014

#10...July 2014

#11...August 2014

#12...September 2014

#13...October 2014

#14...November 2014

#15...December 2014

#16...January 2015

#17...February 2015

#18...March 2015

#19...April 2015

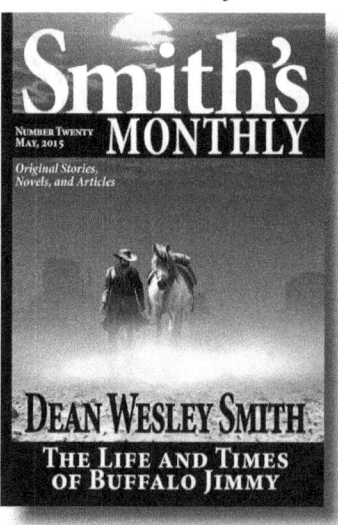

#20...May 2015

#21...June 2015

#22...July 2015

#23...August 2015

#24...September 2015

#25...October 2015

#26...November 2015

#27...December 2015

#28...January 2016

#29...February 2016

#23...March 2016

Thank You!!

I would like to thank the following wonderful people who support my blog and my work through Patreon. Your support is very important to me. Thanks!

Betsy Wilcox	Erick Lindman
Irette Y. Patterson	Christopher Ridge
Kathryn Rooney	Terry Mixon
Wendy Lee Maddox	James Husun
Jamie Curierre	Sherman Cox
Chris Cousino	Chong Go
Jane Lawson	Maria Grace
Shantnu Tiwari	Grondpom
Miguel Angel Alonso Pulido	Fen
Nancy Hendrickson	Robin Brande
Ryan M. Williams	J.R. Murdock
Jacob Proffitt	Kathleen McClure
Marian Goldeen	Gunnar Gunderson
Gary Speer	F.I. Goldhaber
Megan Bryce	Mary Jo Rabe
Michelle Tatam	John Kilgallon
Ann Tucker	Dave Hendrickson
Kari Wolfe	Jabberwocky
Albert Lemke	Eric Goebelbecker
Stacey Larson	Marsha Kessler
Diane Darcy	Scott Gordon
Krystle Jones	Martyn Folkes
Kari Gallagher	John
T. Thorn Coyle	Cj Lehi
Tasha Turner Lennhoff	Brenda Smith

www.ingramcontent.com/pod-product-compliance
Lightning Source LLC
Chambersburg PA
CBHW081150170626
46813CB00009B/3138